NO G[illegible]

for the

ORCHIDS

JC Linden

First published in paperback by
Michael Terence Publishing in 2017
www.mtp.agency

www.jclinden.com

ISBN 978-1-521-11664-7

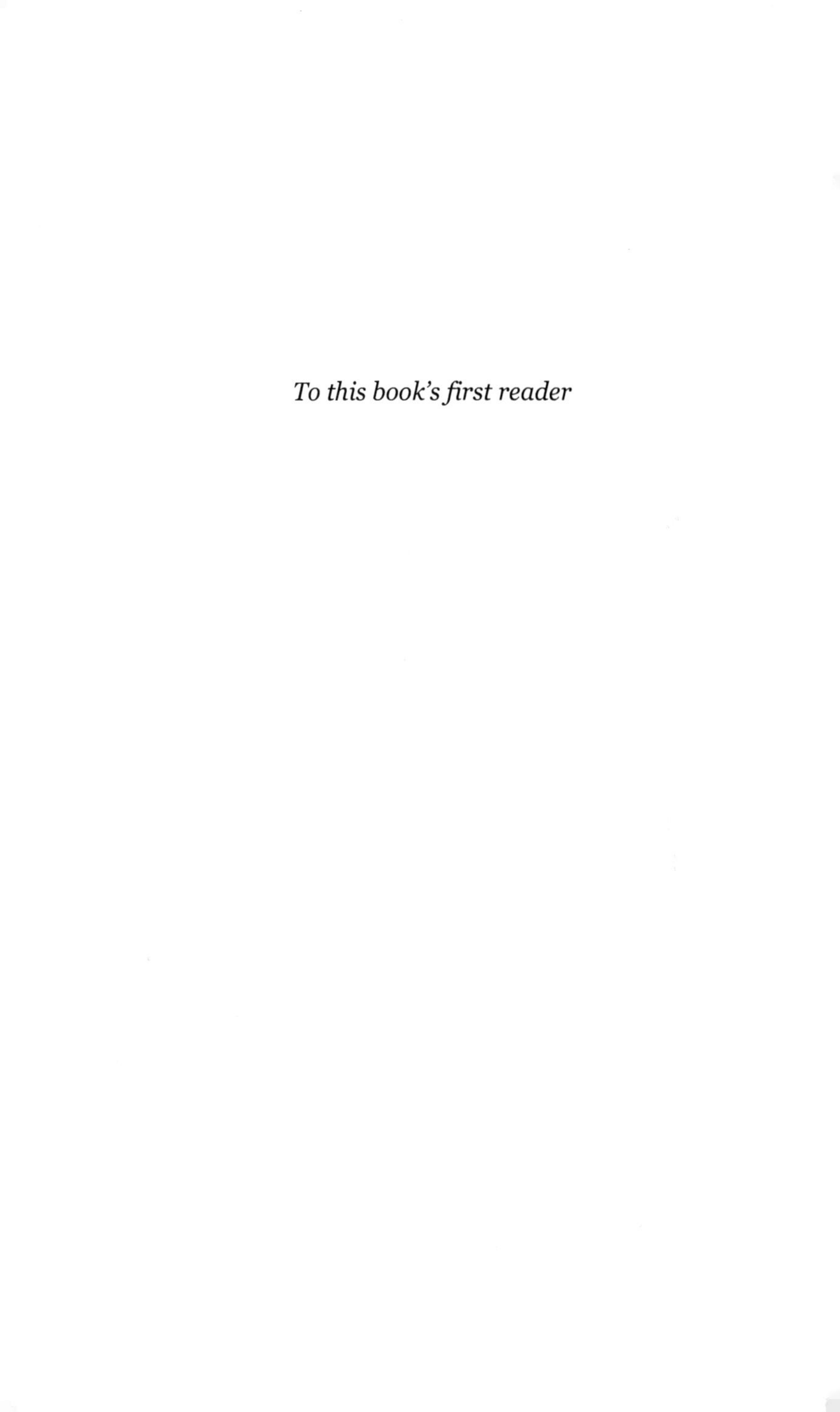

To this book's first reader

Acknowledgement

With grateful thanks to my family
for their loving support

NO GRAVE

for the

ORCHIDS

JC Linden

Kasimir

In a ruined world there is only survival. No one knows this more than my mother. And now there is not only herself to protect. There is me, her unborn child.

Aiden

The door slammed behind Aiden. He hadn't intended to use such force but he needed to be out of the house. His jaw tightened and he sagged against the yard's wooden fence, as the pain in his stomach became unbearable. It was a regular occurrence and his sister had her own ideas about the cause, linking it to premonitions and suchlike. It drove him mad and he would tell her to shut up with her theories for they had a habit of making the pain worse. She offered him medicines but they did little to help. Sometimes he pretended they worked, but usually the pain passed within a day with or without her remedies. He rubbed his face dry on his shirt sleeve, puffed out some shallow breaths to ease the tension in his gut and pulled away from the fence.

He should be with his parents on their latest expedition but they had refused to listen and promptly denied him any opportunity, as their last journey hadn't ended well. He knew they worried for his safety, but safety be damned. He was a man now. Why couldn't they see that?

The sun rising higher in the sky shone fiercely and he wanted none of it. He headed to his favourite spot in the woods, the old fallen ash tree. Sheltering in the shade he hunkered down on the trunk and chipped into the bark with his hand axe. The mindless repetition calmed him, allowing his thoughts to wander, but the memories that surfaced were fierce. His father forcing him to smash the head of a trapped fox with a flint hand axe. Not the one he had now but a smaller one. Twelve years old and Aiden had cried like a baby. He felt shame now thinking on it, but his father had given no word of reproach.

'I'm proud of you. You've learned something important today, son.'

Warm blood had spurted over Aiden's hands, sticky with a metallic smell. 'Why did you make me do it? You could have used your gun.'

'What will you do when there are no more bullets? When I'm no longer around? You must learn to kill. I will teach you.'

Aiden had buried his face in his father's shoulder. His chest heaved until he thought he would be sick and all the while his father just held him.

Restless once more, Aiden stopped his chipping and wandered along a familiar track, which opened into a small clearing where Cuckoo Zara lived. None of them were allowed near Cuckoo Zara's house, but sometimes in secret Aiden crept close, more because it was forbidden than wanting to spy on the woman. Cuckoo Zara owned a few cows and a couple of goats. She would barter her precious cheese for all kinds of goods brought back from excursions.

Aiden checked the clearing. No sign of Cuckoo Zara. The door to her cottage hung open, perhaps she'd gone into town. Crows pecked and fought over some kind of fetid mess and Aiden nudged them with his boot to get to the doorway. He held his breath, bit his lips to stop himself puking, and peered into the dimly lit room. At the entrance to the kitchen, a gaunt cow stood in her own manure, staring at him. Aiden stared back before prodding her with his hand axe. The kitchen smelled sour, cluttered with part used pans of milk on the turn. He moved along the dingy hall. The living area held no sign of its owner, no mementoes, no knick-knacks, just a pile of dirty plates stacked by a chair which looked as if the stuffing had been kicked out of it.

A shuffling sound sent Aiden searching for an exit. He tried the window but it was stuck shut, so he hid behind the door as Cuckoo Zara made her shambling entrance into the room, mumbling to herself, her shirt undone and spilling from her waistband. Aiden's breath caught as he stared at her blackened, round nipples. No matter they were grimy from years of sleeping in the barn with the farm animals, she stirred something in him and he felt his face flush.

A crow bobbed through the doorway, its beady eye on the pile of plates and Cuckoo Zara chased it away with a shout. Aiden watched her leave with some relief and breathed out a sigh before realising he'd been holding his breath. The breeze wafting along the hallway held no hint of freshness as Aiden followed her cautiously. By the time he reached outside, Cuckoo Zara had stripped completely. She clambered onto the roof and stood facing away from Aiden, howling like a jackal. Naked and soiled she looked truly mad. Aiden was backing into the bushes, his gaze fixed on the woman, when a hand grabbed him.

'What do you think you're doing?' Sophia asked in a furious whisper. She shook his arm like she wanted to shake every bone from his body.

A rage swelled through him. It came from nowhere. 'Are you spying on me?'

'Spying on you? Are you joking?'

Cuckoo Zara must have heard them. She hopped from the roof onto the outhouse and looked straight at Aiden. Placing her hand on her groin, she said invitingly,

'Come inside. I'll be good to you.'

Sophia pulled him away, pointing her finger in his face. 'You stay away from her.' She hissed the words like a snake.

Aiden pushed her hand away. 'Back off, Sophia.'

'Back off? That woman's nuts. You shouldn't be here.'

Feeling guilty at the compromising position Sophia had found him in, he followed her. 'So what are you doing here?'

'We've packed lunch to eat by the river.' For the first time he noticed the basket in her hand, the contents covered in a cloth. 'I thought I might find you here.'

Aiden felt unsure what to make of her comment and pretended he hadn't heard.

Further along the path, Grayson waited, stomping a pine cone into the ground. 'What were you doing?'

Sophia strode past them both.

'Just messing,' Aiden said. He didn't like being at odds with his sister. 'I was being dumb,' he told Grayson, loud enough for Sophia to hear. Her pace slowed.

'Dumb is right,' she said, but at least her face had lost the frown. 'What the hell were you thinking?'

Nothing, he thought. I was thinking nothing. His stomach hurt again, shapeless pain that made him breathless. A sour taste flooded his mouth. He swallowed and immediately regretted it. He spat to clear his mouth, wiping the saliva from his lips with the back of his hand.

'Can we talk about this later?'

Sophia caught his arm and draped it over her shoulder, her face puckered with worry. 'Okay, come on.'

Grayson reached for his hand. 'Your tummy?'

'I just need to catch my breath.'

'We can always go to the river tomorrow.'

'I'm no cripple, Sophia.' He wished she'd stop looking so anxious. No one had died. 'Besides, I don't want to go home yet.' Home without his parents there just accentuated his own sense of worthlessness.

'All right, then the river it is.'

The path to the river changed with the seasons and now with autumn here the air held the somnolent weight of a summer passing. Aiden's senses heightened as his stomach ache receded. Dappled light lanced through the trees. Aiden focused on the glinting light as he trod down the grasses still damp from the morning mist, releasing their fragrance. Sweetness filled each breath.

Grayson lagged behind, plucking fruit from the blackberry bushes, placing some in Sophia's basket but mostly stuffing his mouth. Aiden smiled. Sometimes just watching his brother was enough to make him feel better.

They descended a trail of dry mud, ambling to the river's edge, the point where it pooled into stillness sheltered by the rocks. The perfect place to swim. The brothers stripped and Aiden hopped on one leg in his effort to be first, feeling no shame at trying to beat his younger brother. They threw their clothes onto the rocks, snagging them on the lichen, and ran into the shaded water that reeked of mud and algae, shattering the quiet of the surroundings with their shrieks as the cold water bit into them. Aiden swam to the other side of the river. He leaned back lazily kicking his legs, staring at the birds' free-wheeling on the air currents. Aiden wished he was up there with them. If only his parents hadn't objected so fiercely he would have already left town. Whenever he talked of going, his father would make wild claims. 'Life is dangerous out there. People would kill you for the boots on your feet.' But it wasn't his father's words that stopped him. It was the anguish his mother tried to hide.

Sophia undressed neatly piling her clothes onto the bank, and carefully unhooked her necklace and tucked it into the pocket of her jacket. She waded in breast-deep before swimming over to Grayson and when close enough grabbed his waist, pulling him underwater. They broke the surface spluttering and laughing, and screeching like wild things. Sophia chased Grayson into the shallows where she pinned him against a rock jutting from the water. He wriggled like a worm, begging her to stop.

'Enough. Stop, I'm starving.' Hunger was always Grayson's get-out clause and it made Aiden chuckle.

They dressed and then sat on the moss, eating berries and nuts and sharing a lump of goat cheese. Soon Sophia and Grayson dozed head to head in the shade of a weeping willow. Struggling to avoid sleep, Aiden gave his face a hard rub to shed some of the lethargy.

His gaze lingered on the sandstone slope of the mountain to the north. The mountain moved something within him and he pictured himself making a journey there. The furthest he'd ever gone was to a seashore in the south. He had swum in the warm, saffron waves much to his mother's dismay. The water wasn't always like that, she told him. The colours had once been blue and grey, sometimes red in the twilight. They had spear-fished and gotten a fire going on the shore to roast their catch. Aiden ate and listened to his father speak about how the water had once teemed with fish. Later, he found a coat half-buried in the sand, torn and rank, but better than anything he owned. He had washed it in the sea and given it to Grayson. His brother had been so proud of his new acquisition that for several weeks he wore it all the time, even on the hottest days.

A tanned, weathered man in a flat cap wandered out of the woods, his careful movements sending a prickle of unease running across Aiden's scalp. His chest tightened when a second figure trudged through the muddied grass. A boy about his age.

Aiden nudged his sister. 'Wake up.'

Sophia stifled a yawn. 'What?'

'People.'

She rose slowly, looking over at them. 'Do you know them?'

'No.'

Now what the hell could they do, trapped with the river at their rear? Grayson lay sprawled deep in sleep. Aiden shook him awake. He jumped up, while Sophia reached for the knife tucked in her waistband. Her fist tightened around the hilt but she didn't draw it. Aiden mirrored her movements clutching at his own knife.

The older man wore his scrawny toughness like a badge. He tilted his cap back as he called, 'Hello to you boys. And to you, lovely girl.'

'We're just about to leave,' Aiden said.

'No, no. I don't think so. Not before we've completed some business.'

Keep calm, keep calm, Aiden told himself. They

couldn't escape, not with Grayson. He wouldn't be able to outrun them. Red blotches appeared like a rash on Grayson's face as he struggled not to cry.

'We're going,' said Sophia.

The younger man hung back, considering her, while the elder moved close enough for Aiden to see the veins in his eyes. Aiden stood his ground and shoved him. The man nearly lost his footing but still managed to whip a blade from his boot and move forward. 'We're not going empty handed.' The blade gleamed in his fleshy hand. 'One of you is coming with us. But I'll have the good grace to let you pick who that's going to be.'

'Aw, let's take the girl, she's so pretty.'

'Nah, Jake, I like to see them choose.'

Aiden felt his breath hitch and had to remind himself to breathe. Sophia's eyes glittered feverishly. 'Just go, get out of here,' she said.

The man leered at her but spoke to Aiden. 'Boy, you ought to tell your girl to keep her trap shut. Can't abide a woman's backchat.'

From the corner of his eye, Aiden saw Sophia pull the knife from her waistband and before he could stop her she lunged towards the man. He swatted the knife from her hand with his own, slashing a gash across her palm. Blood seeped through her fingers.

'Stupid bitch, only good for laying on your back,' the man sneered.

Panic built to a pressure, hurting Aiden's chest as it tightened even more. A red haze of rage swept over him, filling every crevice of his body. He roared and plunged his knife into the man's scraggy neck. He felt the resistance of tissue and bone. The man groaned an inhuman sound and when Aiden withdrew the knife a gush of blood spurted across his face.

Jake rushed toward his companion to catch the man mid-fall. He held him until the blood eased its pumping and the twitching stopped. Then he let go of the body and stood. The body lay sprawled face down at his feet where it had spilled from Jake's arms, blood pooling in claggy puddles beneath him.

Barely glancing at him, Jake shifted the knife from hand to hand. He pounced forward and grabbed Grayson. The blade nicked his throat. Grayson yelped, and thrown off balance sagged against the man.

'Leave my brother alone.' Aiden's voice sounded broken.

'He's coming with me or I slit his throat right now.'

Grayson's eyes widened, his pupils surrounded by a perfect white rim that held Aiden's gaze with an expression that begged for help.

Aiden reached out his arms. 'I said leave him.'

'Stay away. You'd do well to listen.' Jake walked backward toward the woods, holding the blade to Grayson's throat. Grayson's legs grappled to find a purchase on something as he was pulled away.

Sophia staggered toward him, clutching her bleeding hand. 'I'll come with you like you wanted, just let my brother go.'

'Don't come any fucking closer. I swear I'll finish him if you do.' Jake dragged Grayson with him, his eyes flitting between Aiden and Sophia, giving neither of them a chance to get near.

'Take me.' Sophia said. 'He's just a kid. He's no good to you.'

'Sophia, stay where you are,' Aiden told her as they watched the youth haul Grayson through the mud. As soon as his brother disappeared into the forest all he wanted was to sprint after him.

'I'll follow them. Go back to town.' Why the hell did this have to happen now, just when his parents had gone? 'Find Oliver. Tell him to get his pistol and come find me in the woods.'

'I'm not going back to town. I'm coming with you.'

'No, you're not.' He tore a strip from the picnic cloth and jammed it into her hand to stem the bleeding. *Bloody hell, why hadn't they just stayed at home.* This felt like his doing. 'You need to get this cleaned.'

'But what if he has friends over there?'

Friends or no friends, he'd have to risk it.

Kasimir

I came into being on the crest of my mother's first orgasm. My father, long spent, thrust at her determined she would scream his name from the pillow. He misread her. She didn't cry out at all. She shuddered and clamped her lips together, hugging her joy to herself. Maybe she knew even then our journey would be a lonely one.

Sophia

Sophia clutched her throbbing hand and hurried to Oliver's lumber mill on the outskirts of town. She should have paid attention to the signs. They were all wrong from the moment she had got up this morning. Everything had pointed to disaster but she thought it was channelled towards her parent's journey, not herself. Or Grayson. A sob caught in her throat. Oh, Grayson, his face was so frightened.

She found Oliver chopping timber. Agitated, she shook his shoulders, her gasping lungs pressing into her rib cage, making her speak faster than she breathed.

'Two men came from the woods. One's dead.'

Oliver held up a calming hand. 'Slow down. What happened?'

She took a deep breath and made sure she articulated every word distinctly. 'A man took Grayson. He had... a... a knife.' Her voice trembled, the son of a pig had a knife at her little brother's throat. Her teeth chattered and the healer in her knew she was going into shock.

Oliver, partially deaf, had a fixed absorbed look that came with studying people's faces for clues to their language and Sophia sometimes found it difficult to maintain eye contact with him, but now his stare was like a sharp ray piercing through her head with its intensity. 'Where?'

Shivering, she answered as best she could. 'Down by the river. Just now. He's run south back into the woods. Aiden's gone after him.'

'I'll get my gun,' he said. One of the things she liked

best about Oliver was how she could depend on him. She nodded her thanks and he added. 'And I'll round up some help. Miranda will want to know.' He stared pointedly at her hand where the wound leaked through the makeshift bandage and her pressed hand was doing a poor job of staunching the blood. 'Will you manage to get to Hannah?' He covered her hands with his own. 'Want me to come with you?'

Such a tender gesture nearly pulled her apart but she pushed him away. 'I'll be fine. Just go.'

Hannah the healer lived on the edge of barren farmland and Sophia ran across the field, stumbling on the soil's rutted surface. The sap-coloured earth smelled like ripened barley, the phantom aroma unmistakable. It led straight to Hannah's place. Her cottage had the mark of a crudely painted pentacle on the front door. The five pointed star, enclosed in a circle and drawn in black tar, served as a protective sigil against all evils. Pinned around the frame were the dried, scaly cases of locust and other insects strung together, a necklace to fend off a host of plagues that might attack the town's small holding. They rattled crustily when Sophia pushed her way inside.

A mephitic vapour hung in the air, emanating from numerous opened jars along the window ledge. The odd assortment contained the organs, scales, and ground bones of mice and frogs and other small creatures. Hannah would boil them to a liquid and keep them for their healing properties.

'Hannah?' Sophia called out.

The healer, a thin husk of a woman with striking red hair she hennaed fortnightly, sat at a huge wooden table, which dwarfed her diminutive frame. Her cheeks, the texture of a shrivelled peach, had been daubed with streaks of red, a mix of berries used to deter vindictive spirits, giving her the appearance of a cooked beetroot. She was bent over a bowl brimming with water, a tool she used for scrying and meditation. Even as she watched, Sophia saw the fluid darken as Hannah trailed her gnarled fingers through the glossy liquid. 'Speak to me, Spirits of the Earth,' Hannah muttered. 'Clear the waters, scatter the shadows.'

With some hesitation, Sophia shook Hannah's shoulder, reluctant to bring her from her trance too quickly. 'Hannah, I really need you to wake up,' she said.

Hannah's eyes opened, her pupils so dilated Sophia thought she was staring into two black holes. Frightened, she shook Hannah's shoulder again, more violently this time. 'Please, wake up, Hannah. I need your help.' But her words had no effect for the healer was having a desperate internal discussion with some unseen presence, begging for answers.

'But what can we do? No, not that. There must be another way. So many deaths...'

Sophia felt her gut twist. 'Come out of it, will you?' Hannah's eyes closed and then fluttered open, the pupils constricted to reveal their natural periwinkle blue. A giddiness gushed through Sophia, forcing her to sit.

'Your hand. You should have come straightaway,' Hannah said.

'I couldn't... A man from the woods took Grayson. Aiden's gone, too. Oliver's getting help and going after them.'

Hannah patted Sophia's arm then rose, picked up

the bowl from the table and threw the dark water out the window. 'We need to talk,' she said, and grabbed Sophia's arm and undid the improvised bandage. 'Hmm, knife wound?' With prying fingers she probed the already swollen cut, and Sophia howled unable to stop herself. Hannah extracted her finger, crimson with blood, and placed it in her mouth. 'Your blood is tainted, dear,' she said. 'The blade was oiled with some cankerous concoction. The taste is unmistakable.'

Sophia's mouth went dry. She didn't like the way this conversation was going. Hannah probed the wound again, testing the area around it. An untidy purple line ran under Sophia's skin from the cut, past her wrist, and almost to the crook of her arm.

'See this?' Hannah said. 'The infection is travelling.' She used any opportunity to teach Sophia. 'If it gets to here...' she poked Sophia in the breast. 'Nothing will save you.'

'You could.' Even if her hand had been severed in two, Sophia believed Hannah would know how to mend it.

The healer pursed her lips, pushing them forward into a slight pout, the nearest she ever got to smiling. She reached for one of the jars which contained a brownish serous fluid, put it on the table, and dipped her finger into it. 'The pancreatic secretion of a bat brewed with a mix of sorrel and yarrow crushed to a pulp.' Hannah traced her dripping finger over the wound. 'All right, that should sort it.'

Sophia leapt from her chair, flicking her hand to and fro to ease the pain, as the stinging tonic penetrated the cut. Her sweat-drenched shirt clung to her back. Hannah waited calmly until Sophia sat again and then wrapped a clean strip of rag around the wound and tucked a cushion under Sophia's arm to raise it. 'The blood should clot soon,' she said. 'I'll just brew some tea for the pain.'

A pan of hot water simmered constantly on the stove, ready for seeping herbs, boiling innards, cleaning wounds, and making medicinal teas. Hannah handed Sophia a cup of foul smelling, yellowish liquid. She threw a sprig of fennel across the top and Sophia sipped reluctantly, the heat of the strange brew numbing her mouth.

Taking flowers from the pile of dried plants heaped in a basket ready for sorting, Hannah busied herself with splitting stems from petals. All would be bagged and stored. Some Sophia recognised, chamomile, feverfew, lavender... Her shivers receded and an ease spread through her, just watching Hannah brought comfort.

Only now Hannah appeared somewhat disturbed, though she was good at disguising it. 'My visions have no clarity,' she told Sophia. 'I suspect the abduction of Grayson is only the start. You saw the water turn foul?'

'Yes.'

'Blackened water bodes ill. That much is sure.'

'But what does it mean?'

'More invaders on their way. They won't stop with Grayson. They need young men to train as soldiers, and girls... for other needs.'

The vision must have spooked Hannah for Sophia had never seen her teacher so uncertain. 'We have fought raiders before and managed to defend our community. We'll fight them again.'

'Hmm, this time there may be too many.'

A sense of urgency compelled Sophia to rise. 'I must catch up with Oliver. Thanks for your help.' She staggered towards the door, her legs buckling, but all Hannah did was sit back in her old chintz chair. The long-faded pattern of various leaves intertwining kept blurring. Sophia focused on the small curling leaf on the arm rest, blinking to clear her vision, but her eyelids became heavier and soon she struggled to keep them open. 'What's happening to me?' she asked, her words slurring. 'I have to help Aiden.'

'Oliver will do the helping. You won't be going anywhere, anytime soon. The valerian oils will give you rest.'

Hannah's voice sounded indistinct and far away as though coming from a tunnel. Fighting the blackness that threatened to enfold her, Sophia struggled to concentrate on what was being said, but in the end proved powerless against the drug coursing through her blood. A few moments more and the creeping shadow stole her consciousness.

Kasimir

My mother senses me before her monthly bleed begins. Her breasts ache, and I create nauseous waves as I burrow into her, digging my foundations. I am relentless in my quest for life and she pays the price, even before she understands what this means. Poor mother. She thought she had troubles enough.

Grayson

Grayson gave up scrambling to stand upright and his feet dangled awkwardly. His heels caught on hard tufts of grass and pain jolted through his legs, jarring both knee joints. The man dragged him over scrubland with arms wrapped across Grayson's chest, clamping his breath so he could hardly take air. The knife was no longer held tight against his throat, though he still felt a sting where it had nicked his skin. The wet, warm patch on the front of his trousers cooled and shame nearly scorched a hole through him. What a baby he was, but stuffed under an arm like a parcel it was difficult to behave like a man, even more so when he was thrown down like a sack of turnips by the clump of tents they just arrived at. 'Stay put,' the man growled.

A girl about his sister's age wandered over to him, inspecting him the same way he would look at an ugly insect, and though she seemed slight in her oversized coat, he didn't think she would hesitate to squash him underfoot.

'Get up,' she said. He struggled to obey her, rolling onto his knees before standing, his hands shielding her view of the damp stain on his trousers to avoid further shame. She gripped his hands and spread them apart, staring pointedly at the wet patch. 'Don't reckon you want to stay in soiled pants,' she said. 'Come with me and we'll see if anything fits you. But I'm warning you, you run off, and I'll set the dogs on you. Understand?'

He nodded, conscious of his sticky hands between her cool fingers. They walked towards a group of tents set apart in a densely wooded area where rags of leaves rotted into the soil. He shifted his gaze to his feet at seeing more armed men and women, and nearly peed himself again. The girl told him to step into one of the tents and followed.

Grayson had never seen so many clothes piled in one place. The girl pulled out a thick corded pair of trousers and measured them against his waist. 'These should do.' She thrust them at him. The fabric, worn thin, was soft to touch. He searched for somewhere to hide for privacy but the girl gave him no opportunity. 'Well, get on with it. You don't have anything I haven't seen before, little boy.'

He hurried to do as she ordered and was rewarded with a nod of approval. 'You do as you're told and no one will harm you,' she said. He didn't know if he believed her, though he really wanted to, wondering if *no one* included the man who had put a knife to his throat. Grayson suspected he might want to harm him, especially after Aiden had stabbed his friend.

A young man came into the tent, glancing first at Grayson, then the girl. 'Cassandra,' he began, then whispered something, half looking at her and half at the ground. Grayson figured he was telling her what had happened at the riverbank and braced himself for the fallout. As soon as the man had gone the girl turned to face Grayson. 'Seems like your brother's been busy.' She grabbed hold of his hair and shook his head, pulling a few strands from the roots.

'Let go,' he screamed. His flailing hands clawed at her as he fought, scratching her throat in a vicious swipe that extended to the top of her breast. He then shoved her with such force they both tumbled onto the hessian matting.

Grayson lay whimpering, staring at the long red

mark his fingernails had gouged into her skin, and positive the next step would be his death, for surely she would kill him now.

Instead she just lay there staring at him. She was too well padded with bulky layers of clothing to have taken a serious fall but the scratch looked fierce and he was sorry for it. He had never knowingly hurt anyone before. 'I'm sorry,' he said, hoping to soften any anger.

She drew her finger along the red ridge, then pulled in close to him, so close he felt her breath hit his face, and she jabbed her finger in his chest. 'Lucky for you I never did like that bastard your brother killed.' Slowly she got to her feet and adjusted her coat, dark coloured, like that of a military man, and a couple of sizes too big. She brushed the nap, although he could not see any mark on it, and then held out her hand to pull him up. 'What's your name, boy?'

'Grayson.'

'Well, Grayson, a word of advice. Next time you're tempted to retaliate, stuff your hands in your pockets and put up with the beating. Understand? Or you won't make it to the end of the week.'

Grayson nodded, although he wondered what retaliate meant.

'Come on.' She led him in a different direction to the way they had come. The path was littered with potholes, each filled with a slurry of rainwater that had an oily slick covering the surface, creating a dreary rainbow of muted pinks and purples. It was difficult to avoid them and he darted about trying not to splash the trousers. He didn't think the girl would be too pleased at having to offer him another change of clothing.

'What are you going to do with me?'

'I don't know. Who would want a scrawny, snivelling boy? Maybe exchange you for some food and livestock.'

That sounded promising until he remembered his people had rarely anything to trade. Fish didn't always come to their streams and most of the apple trees didn't grow apples anymore. And Cuckoo Zara, well, he didn't think Cuckoo Zara would give up her cows for anything in the world, least of all for him.

They came to three tents set close together. The middle one was the largest and from it came a clatter of pans and the aroma of cooking, and he hoped that was where they were heading. The bouquet of scents triggered his hunger and he suddenly felt weak, but the girl bypassed that tent and went into the smaller one alongside it.

Inside he saw she had made this space her own. It was swept clean and the bedding was rolled and covered in a ground sheet against the penetrating damp. Her clothes hung from overhead struts to keep them as dry as possible. Grayson decided she must think like a man because everything was structured in much the same way his father would have arranged things. It made him feel strange, glimpsing into her private world, for he knew what kind of people she came from and what they did.

She watched him and as though reading his thoughts said, 'We're just people, you know, like you.' He stared back at her but said nothing, refusing to believe they were anything like him. 'You call us plunderers and raiders. Ring any bells?' She paused but when he didn't answer, gave a sad smile. 'The only difference between you and us is *no one* takes what we have. We Seafarers are a free people.'

'Seafarers? Why are you here then? So far from the sea?'

'That's like asking why an owl would hunt mice.' She sighed, perhaps sensing his resistance to what she was telling him, and produced a small brown bag from one of the sacks in the corner of the tent. She opened it and tipped the contents onto the matting, letting a number of glass marbles roll out. Pretty little things in reds, blues, and blacks. Taking a piece of string she made a circle on the ground.

'For one hour forget about everything outside this tent,' she said. 'We'll play a game I loved playing with my mother. You take one of the bigger marbles, such as this one, and flick it, like so, towards the other marbles. The aim is to knock the smaller ones from the circle but keep the big marble within.'

Was this a trick? It felt like one, whiling the afternoon away, playing this peculiar game with this strange girl. The marbles clinked and he tried to concentrate and ignore the rumbling pains of hunger.

The girl played to win. She made no allowance for the abnormal setup, shouting at him to focus. Perhaps this wasn't so much a trick as a test. If he beat her would that mean release for him, or death? Or was it just like she said, a game she loved to play? The last throw was hers. Taking careful aim she rolled the large marble and hit the last remaining small one, a beautiful pearlescent stone that held the potential of many colours. It shot from the circle, bouncing over the string. The large one looked like the victor but that, too, kept rolling, until they were left staring at an empty circle.

The girl shrugged. 'Sometimes there are no winners.'

He wondered if she meant more than just the game.

The tent flap was pulled and held open. A man stood at the entrance, his braided hair hung like thick hemp rope and his goatee beard, sharp and pointed, elongated his already tapered chin. He stared at Grayson as if he wanted nothing more than to wring his neck, eyes shining with the same luminosity as Cuckoo Zara's. Narrowing them he switched his gaze to Cassandra and placed a possessive hand on her belly. 'Everything all right?'

'Everything's fine, Ray,' she said in a low voice, not at all like the girl who had been playing a moment ago.

'Go eat something. I'll stay.'

Cassandra glanced at Grayson before saying, 'Why don't you bring me whatever you had?'

'Don't you want some time off?'

'I'm all right, Ray. Really.'

'Fine, I'll send something over,' he said and kissed her, his hand placed in the small of her back drawing her close, and when he went Grayson was relieved not to be left alone with him.

A couple of minutes later a boy brought in a bowl of soup, sweet with the scents of herbs and lemons. Cassandra drank half the bowl in a gulp then handed it to him. 'Go ahead. They won't give you anything to eat before we go home and even then you can only expect scanty rations.'

Grayson drank the rest of the soup before asking, 'Where's your home?'

'Up north, over the mountains, and down by the

coast. You ever seen the sea?'

'Once. In the south.' Other than that he had never been farther than the neighbouring town and that was only a couple of times when the weather had promised an easy journey and a quick return. He tried hard not to think of her coast beyond the mountains but his imagination had a will of its own, and a picture of the place came to mind, a stark, lonely image that couldn't be diluted by the girl's kindness and generosity. A landscape in colours of snow and shale made it incomparable to home. His stomach heaved and he vomited the remnants of his lunch onto the matting.

'Oh shit.' Cassandra grabbed the empty soup bowl and thrust it under his chin and he refilled it, spluttering lumps. He spat and spat to clear his mouth, continuing to retch until he was only spewing bile, and then when his stomach could give no more, he started to cry.

The girl squatted down next to him and cuffed his face with her sleeve.

'I want to go home,' he sobbed.

'I know you do, but that's impossible.'

Frustration getting the better of him, he punched out, accidentally hitting her.

Cassandra gasped and gave him a shove. 'Oi. Don't do that!'

Grayson kicked out, each foot catching her somewhere. A shin, a knee, the base of her stomach. 'You can't keep me here,' he shouted.

She caught hold of his thrashing legs and slapped him hard on the face. 'Calm down, you little brat. This is not my doing.'

'Yes it is,' he said, although he no longer knew if it

was or not and felt the fight in him die away. He slumped against her, spent, his cheek stinging.

Cassandra smoothed his tangled hair, combing it with her fingers. 'Don't cry,' she said, rocking him gently, resting her head on top of his. 'I didn't mean to smack you so hard.' He believed her. She kept him close until he calmed down. 'Come. I'll take you to where you're going to sleep tonight.'

'But I want to stay with you.'

'You can't.'

'But I want to.'

'Now listen. You do as I say because the others will not be as nice to you, you understand me?'

He did understand, but didn't like what she was saying and reluctantly followed her outside.

On a rise against the setting sun silhouettes of men armed with rifles looked like an army to him. Were they coming home after a day's plundering, to drink soup and tell jokes and laugh around the open fire? He moved closer to Cassandra. If he couldn't go home she was the nearest thing he felt to being safe.

Tents straggled so many pathways. Gently Cassandra pushed him into one that was stark and unfriendly, made even more so by the presence of the man she had called Ray. Grayson hoped she wouldn't leave him, but said nothing, his tongue compressed to the roof of his mouth.

Ray held a coil of rope and used it to tie Grayson's hands behind his back. Then he forced Grayson down, binding his legs together. The rope sawed into his wrists, rough and bristly every time Grayson moved. He felt his lip tremble and knew he would cry. Finally Ray gagged him. The rag tasted bitter, cutting across his mouth, and dried his mouth like a sponge. Grayson cast a pleading look at Cassandra.

'Is that necessary?' she asked Ray.

Ray finished the task before raising himself to face her. 'Cassie, Cassie, Cassie,' he murmured. 'Don't you think I know what I'm doing?' He tweaked under her chin gently. 'When are you going to trust me?'

'I do, Ray.'

'Good.'

'But he's only a boy.'

'Enough. Don't waste affection on him.' He leaned into her and kissed her mouth. 'You know I like your thoughts to be of me.'

'Of course,' she said.

They left together and Grayson sat still, trying to keep his breath even around the wodge of rank material in his mouth and his hands from not moving so they wouldn't be shredded with the coarse rope.

He slept fitfully and half woke when Cassandra crept back in. She prised some of the gag loose and dribbled water over the remainder which gave some relief to his throat. She did nothing to loosen the binding on his hands and feet. 'Be brave, little Grayson,' she whispered and was gone so quickly that alone in the dark he wondered if she had ever been there.

Kasimir

I bludgeon through my mother's mind, mess with her feelings, and burden her thoughts so they weigh infinitely heavier than the bulk I make of her belly.

What's wrong, she wonders. Favourite foods taste strange, they make her sick. She pees a lot. It's inconvenient.

My father laughs and says she's blooming. He wants a son. She wants none of it.

But in the dark, when he sleeps, she touches her stomach and says *hello*.

Aiden

The meadowsweet-scented wind rushed against Aiden's face as he ran across fields and scrambled wooded slopes until his lungs hurt with the effort. The evening sun bled through the treetops, red shafts of light that drowned in the marshy mud, and he shivered in his thin jacket. He tried to still his mind from its constant replay of events but his concentration skittered away from him like a nervous colt.

Once again he felt the force of the blade going through flesh, the rubbery tearing of artery. His whole body trembled and he clenched his fists so tight his nails dug into his palms. The belief that someday he would kill someone had always lurked at the back of his mind, such was the way of things, but he never thought the day would come so soon.

In the woods Aiden moved stealthily, the way he hunted. Jake and Grayson were nowhere in sight but he saw their footprints. He could tell Jake had tried to cover their tracks, poorly at best, yet luck must have been on his side for they disappeared at the brink of a stream. Aiden stood at the water's edge, staring at the last sighting of his brother's footsteps. Using protruding rocks as stepping stones he negotiated the fast flowing water carefully, but once on the other side he could only guess the way to go.

A sound of rustling and a thread of music danced on the air. Already uneasy he paused, feeling as though a hundred eyes were latched on to him. Did the animals he hunted feel this way just before he lobbed a rock at them, or skewered them with a spear, or smashed their brains with his hand axe? He walked in the direction of the sound, telling himself that sometimes the animals he hunted escaped, and so a violent end was not inevitable.

Soon he saw a telltale sign warning of a nearby camp. A thin plume of smoke corkscrewed into the air. Whoever had lit the fire hadn't worried about hiding and Aiden felt his confidence start a steady descent into despair at these strangers' lack of concern. Every heartbeat told him to turn and flee but he kept creeping closer to where the smoke billowed.

Crouching behind a tree trunk he saw the flickering flames of the campfire. A man sat beside it playing the harmonica. He was good. Aiden recognised the melody, a song his mother used to sing. He remembered some of the lyrics.

'Don't you cry when you say goodbye, sweet boy of mine,

Because I know we'll meet again another day...'

The man put down his harmonica before he finished the song and drank from a bottle, swigging the contents in three big gulps before throwing the bottle aside. He wiped his glistening chin and then lay back against a tree and shut his eyes.

A man and woman emerged from the woods, rifles slung over their shoulders, then disappeared behind one of the many tents pitched in a clearing. From the size of their camp Aiden was sure they wouldn't be satisfied with one small boy. These people meant to raid a town. He couldn't tell how many raiders there were. He thought he counted nine, but he may have doubled up as they moved from place to place. A spurt of red heat surged through his body at the thought of his brother being dragged here, the murderous rage engulfed him, surprising him at its intensity, and he knew he would kill again without hesitation.

But he needed to be careful. No one knew he was here and that played in his favour. He had his knife, not much against their rifles, but Aiden trusted it more than any gun. He peered through the gloom, hoping for a sighting of Grayson. Nothing. Still he could wait until only the moon and the fire gave light. The dusk lingered and night was slow coming now he wanted it in a hurry. The waning moon creeping into the sky cast its shadowy light. When it was as dark as he could hope for he crept nearer to the fire. Golden hues gutted the threadbare moonshine and ribbons of smoke wove childlike effigies into the cold air around a girl standing in the firelight. She spoke to someone Aiden couldn't see, all the while her hands outstretched toward the fire, making fists, opening and then closing them again.

'Tomorrow is Edward's birthday.'

'So?'

'What do you think he'd want for present?'

'The dead don't care for such things, Cassandra.'

'I know, but I thought I'd give him this.' She pulled something from the pocket of her coat to show the man. 'Jake gave it to me.'

Her face held a wistful expression and the man spoke gently. 'You keep it, Cassandra, wear it in Edward's memory. Here, I have a leather lace you can use.'

Aiden gazed silently at the girl, as she tied the leather strip around her throat. Hard to believe she was a raider. She had the look of someone who wouldn't hurt another.

A hand settled on his shoulder, another around his

mouth, and he felt his bowels turn to water. Oliver gave him a nod before letting his hands fall back to his side. Aiden fought the urge to punch him, bloody idiot scared him half to death. Creeping up beside him was Josiah, the town's priest, who was good with a gun. Behind him was Miranda, the town's natural leader whenever conflict threatened. Aiden forgave Oliver for the earlier fright seeing the backup he brought, especially when he drew a pistol from his belt and put it in Aiden's hand.

'Aiden?' Even in a whisper Miranda's deep guttural voice commanded attention. Aiden respected her, she had taught him a lot when she had taken him hunting. She rotated her finger. 'How many?' He realised she expected him to have surveyed the scene.

'I counted nine.' Aiden tried to sound definite and erred on the larger side of his calculations.

'Okay.' She tapped him. 'You, with us. We'll search the tents.'

A man stoked the campfire with fresh logs. He poked at the wood until it caught, then sat down and stared into the flames with the relaxed demeanour of a man not expecting an attack.

Away from the fire the light of the moon edged the trees in stony white. It was not enough to see clearly but they had to make do. They crept towards the middle of the camp when a snore emitted from the flap of the first tent caused Aiden to gasp. Miranda frowned and put her forefinger to her lips and he nodded an apology, while waiting a few moments to check no one had been alerted.

Moving on to the next tent Miranda almost tripped over a man sprawled across the entrance. He leapt up and backed away in blind confusion. This allowed enough time for the others to storm inside.

Oliver grabbed the man, crushing him around the waist. He scrabbled to break free but Oliver head butted him. The man gave a low groan and Aiden looked more closely at him.

'That's him, Jake, the one who took Grayson.' He pulled his head up, as he slumped over Oliver's arm. 'Where's my brother you piece of shit?' Aiden wanted to kill him and Oliver too, for knocking him unconscious, but Miranda shoved him aside.

'Come on, we'll look elsewhere.' She looked at Oliver. 'Badly done, son, you're too quick with the head butts and fists. Josiah, help truss the boy. Maybe use him for cover.'

Aiden pushed open the flap of the next tent, allowing moonlight to trickle through but not enough to reveal much. He noticed a shadowy figure huddled on the far side of the canvas. Grayson. Bound around the feet, his hands tied behind his back, he was going nowhere. Startled by the sudden shaft of light Grayson started, his eyes round as an owl. He might have cried out but for the gag stuffed in his mouth. Aiden went over to him and tugged it away. He cut through the rope with his knife, freeing Grayson's hands, then set to work on the ties binding his legs, gently paring and fraying the rope apart.

'Can you stand?'

Grayson nodded but Aiden wasn't so sure. In his desperation to leave, his brother would have said yes to anything. Aiden helped him to his feet. He wobbled.

'Give his legs a rub to restore circulation,' Miranda

said.

Aiden did as he was told. 'Better?'

'Better.'

For a moment Aiden didn't know what else to say. Then he hugged Grayson, pulling him close and closer still. His brother smiled, the wateriest grin, so unlike Grayson's usual beam it caught at Aiden's heart. 'Come on,' he whispered. 'We're going home.'

They were just beyond the entrance when someone lifted the flap from another tent. It was the girl Aiden had seen at the fire.

'Cassandra.' Grayson let out an anguished whisper and she stopped dead. She showed no recognition for Grayson and Aiden wondered if his brother was mistaken or more shook up than he had first supposed. Aiden couldn't afford to take a risk and pointed his gun at her.

The moon shone brighter, shedding its cloudy overcoat and the necklace at her throat gleamed in the light. It held a gold coin, no... a button. It was exactly the same pattern as Emmet's, the old soldier who had gone on the expedition with Aiden's parents that morning. Aiden could have drawn it blindfolded he had seen it so many times. Sophia loved the damned thing. As a youngster she had sat for hours with Emmet as he diligently polished his jacket's shiny buttons, their burnished gold gleaming rich against the shabbiness of the material, listening as he told of things past, a time bright with hope...

Aiden stepped nearer to the girl and hooked his gun under the leather strip to lift the button closer to him.

'Jake gave you this?' he asked, remembering her conversation by the fire. The girl stared boldly into his face but said nothing, her silence a defiance and a challenge. Aiden pushed her away, wanting to strike her.

Oliver and Josiah joined them, dragging Jake between them. He groaned, regaining consciousness. A flicker of concern flashed across the girl's features, so fleeting Aiden wondered if he had imagined it. The wind stirred her clothing and for the first time Aiden noticed the protrusion of her belly and realised she was pregnant. She must have seen something change in his face for she spoke harshly, contempt flavouring every word. 'Don't pity me.'

But he did. Sorrow swept over him and the girl must have seen something of that in his face because she waved him away. 'Just go,' she said. Aiden kept pointing his gun at her but his hand wavered. Not because of the cold and not because he was afraid. But because of the strength he saw in her eyes and he knew he couldn't fire at her. He may have killed a man today but he wasn't a murderer after all. Random killing was not in his nature. Speaking in a low undertone he barely heard her say, 'Stay or leave, it won't matter. You'll die all the same.'

'You keep quiet, little girl, and go back into your tent or we'll hurt your friend here,' said Josiah, indicating Jake by a jerk of the head. The girl glared savagely, her gaze sweeping over them all, before she raised the tent flap and went inside murmuring, 'Goodbye, Jake.'

Aiden nodded his head towards Jake. 'We need to bring him with us,' he said to Miranda. 'He knows something about my parents, and this morning's expedition.'

'All right,' said Miranda.

The group cleared the camp and they ran for a

couple of miles with Grayson stopping often to catch his breath. Aiden wished he didn't appear so delicate.

'You okay?'

'Yeah. Just hungry.'

'They hurt you?'

'No.'

'You'd tell me if they did?'

'Yeah.'

They stepped into a cloud of mist that poured down a steep hillside and hung between the trees, blanketing their vision. Aiden held Grayson's hand and told him not to let go.

The group walked in silence, only broken intermittently when Josiah cleared his throat of phlegm. 'We can't afford any slowing down so pick up the pace,' he said.

'You're right,' said Miranda. 'That girl has probably woken everyone by now.'

'You think they'll risk coming after us tonight?'

'Why not? We did, didn't we?' said Miranda.

They made haste even though the mist had thickened. It poured coldly into their clothes. Grayson's teeth chattered as the dampness bit and Aiden could feel him shivering.

'Come on. Faster. It'll warm you,' he said. Grayson looked at him with miserable eyes but stepped up his pace all the same.

Kasimir

Fearless, that's how my father first saw my mother. He would have said so to anyone who asked, although to himself he was brutally honest. Once he realised she had no idea of his standing in society he wondered if ignorance was a mark of true courage and decided it wasn't. Yet in a city of culture, ignorance brings its own mystique.

Sophia

Slowly the room shifted into focus, with every part of Sophia hurting. The throbbing ache behind her eyes had her wincing, and she clumsily rubbed her temples before attempting to sit up, her body still influenced by the remnants of Hannah's soporific tea. Her hand, now covered in clean bandage, pounded too. Loud chirping of crickets through the window sounded like a volley of shots through her head and she moved to pull it shut, stifling a juicy curse. 'Hannah, what have you done to me?'

She sat down to ease the dizziness, tendrils of her hair clung to the moistness on the back of her neck and she lifted the bulk of it away from her skin with her good hand. When the fog in her mind dispersed, she poured herself a tumbler of water from a jug by the sink and guzzled it down, then poured another and drank that, too. Wiping her mouth with the back of her bandaged hand, Sophia sighed. Enough of her time had been wasted. Now she had to find her brothers.

Lunar brilliance diffused by a mist of dew steeped the dead farmlands in silver. The fringes of the fields climbed to mounds where yew trees swayed. Last autumn, when Sophia had been taken ill and coughed blood, Hannah said dreaming under the yews would cure ailments related to the blood. Night after night Sophia had gone there to sleep on the soil, for Hannah had forbidden her to take a sheet or a bedroll.

On the first night Sophia, reluctant to sleep alone, persuaded her mother to stay as well. When Hannah found out the next day, she chided Sophia, telling her she shouldn't have let her mother join her under the yews, or anyone else for that matter. Dreams were purest when she was alone. On the second night, Sophia lay by herself. Smelling the soil, facing the heavens, she endeavoured to count the stars and must have continued counting them in her dreams for when she awoke, Sophia felt she had done nothing but count the whole night. She slept under the yews for a fortnight and within a month ceased to cough blood.

Once more she breathed in the cool healing air, scents of wet dirt, and ferns and yew sank into her lungs, clearing the last of Hannah's drug from her system. Standing undecided at the foot of the knoll, the shifting haziness a reflection of her confusion, she wondered whether to go back to town, or search the woods. Sophia tried to link to Aiden's mind, certain that the bonds to her twin were strong enough to support this. Sometimes she believed she succeeded, though he always denied she did, but this time her thoughts came back as hollow as an empty promise. Drowning under a deluge of despair Sophia sank to her knees, suddenly crippled by the knowledge she had lost everything, the bare landscape echoing her own bleakness. Where could she go from here? All her life she searched for signs to give herself hope. What a fool.

Time stalled and she had no idea if one hour, or many, had passed, before she saw figures looming through the swirl of the mist, a weary gaggle of bodies. The first two made her heart give a skip. They were her brothers. Aiden had done as he promised. She ran towards them, arms outstretched to embrace them both. How thin Grayson felt in her arms, her fingers thrumming his bony ribs. Now that she had almost lost him he was so much more precious to her. His body smelled of earth and moss and she kissed his grubby face, light pecks over his forehead and cheeks, his lips and his nose, until he squirmed away from her.

'Sophia!'

'Are you all right?'

He rubbed his eyes. 'Yeah,' he said. To Sophia he didn't sound that certain.

'Are you sure? You're not hurt?'

Grayson cast a look behind and Sophia followed his gaze, and saw Jake.

'You brought *him* back with you?' She directed the question at Aiden.

'We did.' Aiden looked fierce, his face and hands dirty with caked blood. 'We need him.'

'Why? I'd like to skin him alive,' she said.

Aiden gave her a long, steady look. 'I said... *we need him.*'

'What the hell for?'

'I'll tell you in town. Not here.'

'We best get moving,' said Miranda. 'His friends might be coming after us and we need to prepare.'

They quickly spread the word through town to expect a night-time raid and the townspeople armed themselves with rifles and pistols, as drilled by Miranda. Then they positioned themselves at the four-foot stone wall that encircled the northern and western parts of town. Those further afield were told to barricade themselves in their homes.

Sophia regretted having to leave Grayson after his ordeal and he protested loudly at having to stay with Hannah, but Sophia wanted him safe and the healer was the only one she trusted with the responsibility. Cold and wet through, his objections soon died away when Hannah wrapped a thick blanket over his shoulders as he said his goodbyes.

Then Sophia and Aiden went to the barn where Jake was held. In the doorway Aiden paused. He pulled Sophia toward him and spoke in low tones. 'Something happened to mum and dad.'

'What do you mean something happened to mum and dad?'

'I saw one of the girls in their camp wearing a button. One from Emmet's war jacket.'

'Are you sure?'

'It looked exactly the same. There's no mistake. It was one of his.'

Sophia leaned against the barn door. A cold sensation stole over her, like a glacier moving forward, freezing all it touched, taking all the colour from the landscape and replacing it with the stonewash neutrals of winter's frost. Her mother and father gone, just like that, on the whim of someone like that raggedy tramp, Jake.

'What are we going to do with him?'

'Find out what we can.'

Sophia moved forward into the barn, trying to summon enough energy for the ordeal ahead. Inside Josiah pushed Jake hard against the wall. 'I wouldn't mind killing you, you bastard.'

'Then do it. You fucking savages. Kill me like you killed my friend.'

Josiah shook Jake and threw him onto a heap of sawdust. Brushing the dusty particles from his mouth, Jake slowly gathered himself together and sat watching warily, as Josiah and Aiden stood either side of him. Sophia kicked the sawdust at him.

'We're not the savages. You came to us. Took our brother. Ambushed our truck...'

'I don't know what you're talking about.'

Sophia moved in closer. 'Just tell us about the ambush.'

'Look, I'm nobody. Don't ask me. We Seafarers have leaders who make decisions, I just do as I'm told. I didn't even want to come here.'

For all his protests, something insincere about him struck Sophia. It was there in his eyes, the cunning, beady expression of a rodent. He would say whatever he thought she wanted to hear. How she wanted to hurt him, see dread on his face, hear fear in his voice, but even now he looked at her as though she was no threat. Oh, he was *a nobody* all right, and soon he would *really* believe it.

She extended her hand to Josiah and he looked her in the eyes for a moment, then put his gun in her uninjured hand. This hand was weaker and she felt it quiver as she tightened her grasp, feeling the gun's weightiness. Her sore hand throbbed and she took that as a warning and rubbed the bandage with the butt of the gun.

'Let's talk about the ambush. You killed them?'

'I told you, I don't know any more than—' Before he said another word, Sophia rapped his hand with the gun. He gasped in pain, propelled spit at her feet. 'You fucking cunt!'

'Oh sorry, I'm such a girl. That's not how to use a gun.' She narrowed her eyes. 'Hey Jake,' she said quietly. 'I know you and your dead friend think I'm only good for laying on my back, so I'd better make sure there's enough bullets, just to be sure I get one hit in.'

Expertly she swung open the cylinder and tipped the bullets from the chamber. They formed a tidy heap in her bandaged hand. 'Oh, a couple short,' she said, and Josiah handed her two more bullets. She made an elaborate show returning them to the chamber, taking her time before clicking the cylinder back. 'Bound to miss a few times,' she said, and then she cocked the gun. Jake flinched, raising his arms to protect his face. Good, at last he was starting to believe she meant it.

'Okay, Jake, last chances.' Sophia returned the safety catch and with her bandaged hand pulled him close by his hair, her exposed fingers entwining around his lank locks. She placed the gun at his head. Jake pulled away but she shook him hard enough to tear a few hairs free. She threw them aside. He squeezed his eyes shut and made no other movement bar tensing his shoulders a little higher and catching his breath on an inward gulp. A pulse beat strongly in his temple. One tear of sweat trickled across Sophia's forehead. 'Look at me,' she said. Slowly Jake opened his eyes as she curled her finger around the trigger. 'I don't want to do this, really I don't, but I will, because if you don't talk you are of no use.'

His shirt tightened as his back tensed. 'We hadn't planned it. We'd been raiding town after town as we travelled south to gather food and supplies for winter. Then the men said it was enough and we should turn and go back home before it snowed. But others said we should wait a day or two and see if anything turned up. That's when we saw the truck with your people, it just fell into our hands. There was some resistance but nothing we couldn't handle.'

'Where did you take them?'

'To our city.'

'For what purpose?'

'To work in our fields and workshops, or send them overseas to trade for supplies.'

'So either way, if they survive, they live as slaves,' said Josiah.

Sophia pushed her face close to Jake's. 'Were they alive when you took them? You must tell me this.'

'I wasn't in the group that attacked the truck. I just heard the stories. If anyone survived, they have already been taken away, so I don't know.'

Somewhere in the proceedings, Miranda had entered the barn. She moved forward, away from the door. 'Where is your place? This city?'

'North. By the coast. None of this is useful to you. You don't honestly believe you can go there and free anyone.'

Miranda spread a map before him. 'Can you read this?'

'Yes.'

'We're this dot over here. Where's your place? And don't think I'd hesitate to put a bullet through your brains if I find you lied.'

Jake ran his finger all the way to the top of the map. 'Here. We live here.' Now he was talking he held nothing back, Sophia could read the truth he was telling. Her lip quivered and she covered it quickly with her hand, realising she could cry quite easily. She handed the gun to Aiden, then left the barn. The need to see Grayson, hug him close, swelled within. But that would have to wait.

Outside she took position at the sparsely guarded section of the wall and peered down the bank of the stream. The raiders would likely look elsewhere to attack the town, anyone mad enough to ford the stream in an attempt to storm the wall would be shot a dozen times before they could become a threat. Still, Sophia reckoned every spot had to be guarded.

'Mum... dad...' She grabbed a fistful of dirt and crumbled it, the same way some unseen hand squeezed all humanity from her heart. A spirit of mischief whispered through her mind saying her parents were dead.

'It's going to be a long night,' Aiden said, as he put a jacket around her shoulders. The glow of the lantern in his hand accentuated the concavity of his gaunt cheeks.

She looked up at him. 'What did you do with Jake?'

'We tied him down. Josiah's with him. He'll have to be dealt with.'

Sophia rose and they sat on the wall. Aiden leaned against her shoulder, his hair dusting her neck, the worn fabric of her jacket soaking his tears that spilled freely in the dark. 'What do we do now?'

Sophia held his hand tightly. 'I don't know.' She searched inside herself for a spark of hope to hold on to. 'We live. For ourselves. For Grayson.'

Somewhere to the north someone lit a fire and before long the night air smelled of rum, woodsmoke, and cigarettes. In one of the cottages a baby was crying and someone lisped a lullaby until the crying stopped. All through the night they stood watch. 'I should have gone with them,' Aiden said.

'You would have been killed, too.'

'You don't know they are dead,' Aiden said sharply. 'You don't know mum and dad are dead.'

'I don't. But I'm better off assuming they are.'

'How can you say that?'

'We'll never see mum and dad again. You understand? They are gone for good, like all those other people who left to forage or barter with other communities and never came back.' Aiden stared at her as though she had gone mad. Sophia leaned into him. 'It's you, me and Grayson now,' she whispered, her words sounded strange, as if someone else said them. 'Just us.'

The long night ended and the raid did not happen but still Aiden and Sophia stood watch until dawn, when someone else came to take their place at the wall. Then they went to Hannah's to get Grayson, only to find the healer distracted and Grayson gone.

Kasimir

Family ties on my father's side are complicated. That's why he loves my mother. Her straightforwardness excites him, annoys and reassures him that not all in this world have hidden agendas. Or so he believes. But then women aren't his line of expertise.

Grayson

Grayson had slept fitfully through the night expecting trouble, but it seemed the raiders, or Seafarers as he now knew them to be, had decided against storming the town. Now standing on Hannah's doorstep in the cold dawn light all he wanted was to get home and for things to revert to normal.

He crossed the farmland where nothing ever grew and headed towards the cool gloominess of the trees, which suited his mood exactly. His anger at being left had abated somewhat. There wasn't any doubt he loved his brother and sister, he knew for certain he did. It was just sometimes the twins considered themselves a separate unit, especially Sophia, and somewhere in the mix Grayson got discounted, though he knew she never meant it that way. Still, Hannah had dried his wet clothes, fed him some supper and, best of all, made no attempt to discuss his recent kidnapping experience that even he couldn't look at too deeply yet.

The sun started a slow climb to daylight, a haze of gold on the horizon. Grayson took the longer paths towards home, the quieter trails where he was less likely to have encounters with other townsfolk. Or so he thought, for just ahead of him, Helen Leedham stood in a clump of rhododendrons holding a rabbit trap. The grass around her silvery, the dew agleam with splintered light.

She picked a couple of late blooms with her free hand and set them in her hair. Lemon flowers crisp on their edges with a shrivelled, bedraggled appearance were strangely complementary against her white blonde hair. Retrieving a doll perched on a tree stump, Helen tucked it under her arm before sauntering into the woods. Grayson lingered momentarily behind a rock before continuing to trail her, dodging behind shrubbery every time there was a chance of being seen, his gaze fixed on Helen. The lovely, *silent* Helen, who was now *singing* in a rusty unused kind of way.

'Sweet fragrant flowers and rocks. Tender loam and heartfelt prickles.' Her voice dropped to a whisper. 'Can you hear me? Are you there?' She stooped and placed the rabbit trap in a bush.

Helen was creating enough of a mystery to wipe yesterday's bad experience from the forefront of his mind for now two things filled his thoughts. Firstly, how could Helen possibly sing? In all his life he had never heard her speak, let alone hum a melody, and secondly she used some truly fancy words for a mute.

With a rustle of leaves he clambered from the bush to confront her. 'Who are you talking to?' he demanded.

Startled, Helen rose and turned to face him, her song petering into silence, and for the longest time she remained quiet, before finally saying, 'I didn't speak to anyone.'

'But I just heard you,' said Grayson.

Helen tramped towards him, only stopping when their boots touched. Their eyes, now inches apart, fixed closely, warily, on each other. Gone was the timid creature he had known and in her place stood this angry girl, her face flushed with indignation. 'Have you been following me, Grayson? What a wicked thing to do!'

Grayson did what he'd always do when faced with unpleasantness. He apologised and then lied. Eight times out of nine it worked a treat and he trusted he was good enough at spying for her not to have seen him before.

'Sorry. Didn't mean to snoop. Just saw you with that rabbit trap and thought you might need help.' Grayson wondered if she believed him, recognising in her a similar furtiveness he, too, possessed.

Helen scowled. 'Don't stare. Why are you looking at me like that?'

'Because... I thought you were mute,' Grayson said. He shrugged. 'Everyone does.'

'Now you know, please don't tell anyone.' Taking his arm she prised open his fingers with the force of a boy, noisily swished the spittle in her mouth, then, confidently and accurately, spat in his palm and shook his hand. 'Promise me, Grayson. Promise you will never talk about this to anyone.'

'Okay, I promise. But you did it wrong, silly goose. I'm supposed to spit in my hand, you in yours, and then we shake.' She looked at him as though he was telling her some exciting, well-guarded secret.

'All right, we do it like that.' So they spat and shook hands and perhaps because of Helen's fascination with his way of making a promise she didn't let go of his hand, not right away anyhow.

'Then why don't you ever speak?' said Grayson. 'You have a sweet voice.' A distraught look came over Helen's face and he immediately regretted asking her. His parents often reprimanded him for being nosy.

'I can't tell you,' she sighed, her ribs heaving agitation. 'I'm not supposed to speak.'

'But you just did. So who were you talking to?'

Helen kicked the dirt at her feet. 'Why should I tell you?' Her face flushed again but this time with embarrassment not anger. 'Anyhow, you wouldn't believe me if I did.'

'I promise I will.' He tapped his forehead. 'Tell you what, if I don't, you get to punish me whichever way you pick. I'll eat mud if you want.'

Helen smiled. He had no doubt she'd have him eating all kinds of foulness if he reneged on the deal and he knew all about broken pacts. Sophia was always accusing Aiden of reneging on deals. Grayson thought it kind of cool the way his older brother paid no mind to Sophia, no matter how much she needled.

Helen took a deep breath. 'I speak to... *spirits*.'

'Spirits? You mean dead people?'

'No, not really. Mum called them *spectral forest children.'* Helen stopped abruptly.

'What are they?'

'Oh, nothing, forget it.'

She had piqued his curiosity with her talk of spirits and now her mother. He knew her mother had disappeared a couple of years back in mysterious circumstances. That's how Sophia had described it to Hannah. *Mysterious circumstances*. Even now the words had the power to thrill, sending a tingle of excitement chasing through him. He had overheard the conversation by accident, having been given one of Hannah's foul medicines to prevent brain fever after cutting himself diving in the shallows of the river. He remembered the occasion perfectly, leaning against Hannah's outside wall, snivelling under the open window, though now he would say *incident* instead of *occasion,* because that's how spies talked. This would always be a crystal glass memory for it was the moment he decided to become a sleuth. Some suspected Helen knew her mother's whereabouts even back then and now it appeared she did.

'Tell me,' he demanded.

Helen frowned. 'How can I trust you with two secrets when I don't know you can keep one?'

'I promise I won't tell a soul. Really, I won't.'

Whispering to her doll momentarily, Helen reached a decision. 'Mum has gone to live with the spectral children for a while. She told me they need her more than I do.' Helen kissed the doll. 'But she left me Marigold. She said Marigold will watch out for me and tell me when mum is ready to come home.'

Grayson didn't think the doll was capable of such responsibility, threadbare with one of its button eyes missing it definitely didn't look capable of speaking, but he didn't like to mention that.

'Where do the children live?'

'Here in the forest.'

'They are here?' He looked at the trees crowding around them, trunks so gnarled and twisted, he wondered they didn't reach out and snag him. Then he looked beyond them in case the children were hiding in the shadows.

'William said they don't exist. He says I'm...' Helen wound her index finger around and around by her temple and went boss-eyed, indicating madness, but didn't follow up with exactly what William did say.

She looked funny and cute and not at all crazy. 'Huh, what does he know?' Grayson knew he'd said the right thing for Helen's eyes lit up like someone had placed a candle behind them. Then unexpectedly she leaned forward to kiss him, a light brushing of breath, before skipping away. Undecided whether he liked this wet intrusion, he checked she wasn't looking and then wiped his mouth surreptitiously. He'd been kissed before but this was different. This would need thinking about.

'Come on, Grayson. Don't just stand there.' Helen called without looking back, as if she didn't have to see him to know what he was doing.

Surprised at how fearless Helen moved through the densest tracks he followed, taking paths he hadn't known existed. Paths where dead trees had keeled over and fallen midst the living branches of others, creating such a tangle that the sun's rays didn't penetrate. Clambering over the debris he felt a stab of envy at Helen's daring, for the girl appeared unconcerned by the shady, untrodden trails.

'So, what do they look like these *spectral forest children*?' he asked, stumbling with the strange words, as he tripped on loose twigs underfoot, this whole experience making him feel clumsy.

Helen gave him such an impish look he suspected she was enjoying his awkwardness. 'They glow. A dark violet.'

'What?'

She giggled. 'They call the misty light that surrounds them *radiation*.'

'Radiation?' he spoke warily. That was nothing to giggle about. His parents were forever going on about its dangers. There was nothing to protect from radiation. You could bundle up to the ears in a big wool coat, even wear two pairs of pants, and still it would do no good if radiation happened to drift your way.

But Helen didn't have a mum and dad, she only had William, her brother. And William had a troubling oddness about him. Grayson wouldn't trust him to explain anything. William's blank stare made Grayson feel invisible whenever he passed their house.

'What do they look like?'

'Some wear hats, which they wrap around their heads using rubber straps. They have snout things attached, covering their noses. Have you ever seen such a funny thing?' Helen gave a look that told Grayson no way would she wear one.

'Sound like gas masks to me,' Grayson pondered. He stopped under an overhang of brambles to untangle his hair caught on the prickly spikes.

'*Gas masks.*' Helen appeared to marvel at the words.

She clutched him by his sleeve and they walked deeper into the woods, their feet tearing holes in the mass of wet leaves littering the soil. Pausing in a clearing, she waited. 'This is the best place to spot them.'

At the far side of the clearing a lake pooled. Grayson could just make out the glint of water. Colours rose and hovered over the surface, like a rainbow had fallen from the sky. 'What is that?'

'It's their home. We can't go any further, or their glow will engulf you and make it hard to breathe.'

Grayson backed away. Much as he wanted to see them he didn't like the risk. 'We should go,' he said, hoping Helen wouldn't think him a coward and was relieved when she nodded her agreement willingly enough.

Helen Leedham's house was more decrepit than any of the other cottages. Hammer and nails were left strewn on the ground, a pair of rusty shears were stabbed, point down, by a tree, and sheets of mud smeared the front step. Grayson's dad would have been madder than a hare if Aiden had not carefully maintained his tools and their mum would have had a fit if they constantly dragged mud through the house.

William was busy shooing three scraggly chickens into a dilapidated coop. He had a face that called attention to itself. Pale complexion broken by a livid scar that ran across his right cheek, a beard so thin it looked like yellow string hanging from his chin and all framed by short cropped hair that stuck out at different angles. But for all that he had a look of Helen about him. He wore shorts and long horizontal striped socks that did nothing to make his skinny legs look any fatter and reminded Grayson of a spider.

'You best leave before he sees you,' Helen whispered.

'Where you been?' William's gruff voice made Grayson flinch and he sank back into the shadows of the woods not wanting to get Helen into trouble. He saw her face tighten as she stepped clear of him and went towards her brother.

She shook her head. 'Nowhere.'

'I thought I told you to keep near the house, dummy,' William said. 'You went into the woods, didn't you? To speak with your ghostly friends, no doubt?'

'Yes.'

'I warned you what happens to crazy people, didn't

I? What happens to little girls communing with devils?' Helen looked sulky. 'Well, what happens, devil worshipper?' She took a long time answering. 'Well?' William prompted.

Helen heaved a sigh. 'They get chased away or burned at the stake.'

'Yeah, and that will be your fate if anyone hears your stupid wittering.'

'But I'm telling the truth, William.'

'Bloody hell, Helen, you're hell bent to cause us troubles. Honestly, I wish mum had never gone and left me with you, or better yet never given birth to you in the first place, devil worshipper.'

Helen stomped her foot. 'I'm not a devil worshipper, and they are not devils, they are just like me.'

'What? Idiots? Oh get inside. And put that bloody doll out of my sight.'

Grayson wanted to shout at William to stop being horrid. How dare he threaten her? Getting chased away would be bad enough, but burned? Still he'd never heard of either happening in their town, so maybe her brother was just trying to frighten her. It must have worked because Helen scampered indoors and looked like she was crying.

Kasimir

Either things go well or they do not. No half measures for my father, until my mother. She shows him the beautiful complexity that lives within a *maybe*.

She boils the water and fills the bathtub from a pail while the two little girls undress one another and step inside. The younger sits between the legs of the other, facing away, both are timid and shivery. My mother cannot bear to see them so and sloughs the dirt from their skin, the snot from their noses. The larger child smiles at her and following my mother's example scrubs the back of the younger.

'See,' my mother says to my father. 'They are only children, people, like us. How easy they are to teach.'

'Maybe,' he replies, and for the first time she sees a chance of a better life. She makes a pledge. When our child can walk, we'll be gone. There will be no more of this.

Sophia

After a night of escalating emotions, knowing Grayson had deliberately put himself at risk when there had been a chance of a raid, stumped Sophia the most. He was only nine years old. How dare he disappear like that? And now all they could do was go home and wait.

'Grayson's been through a lot,' Aiden began and for a few moments they were silent, before he added, 'and we still have to tell him about mum and dad. I don't really know how to do it.'

'Yeah, I know.' Sophia sighed, feeling the burden of duty press down on her.

The back door creaked open and they heard the thump of his feet as Grayson came inside. 'They didn't come, did they? The Seafarers?' he said as soon as he saw them. 'I didn't hear any shooting.'

'No. Nobody came,' said Aiden, putting his arm on Sophia's, effectively silencing her. 'You stayed awake the whole night?'

'I did sleep a bit,' Grayson said.

'Where have you been?' Sophia asked tightly.

'Just talking to Helen.'

Sophia returned Aiden's puzzled look with one of her own. 'I thought Helen was mute.'

'Yeah, well I guess I did most of the talking.'

Sophia thought Grayson was reluctant to say more and she just patted the sofa for him to come and sit down. Neither she nor Aiden knew where to begin, so they each took one of his hands in their own. The set up was so artificial, Grayson started to cry before they said a word, and in the end Sophia just blurted the news. 'The truck was ambushed. Mum and dad have been taken.'

'Were they hurt?' said Grayson through his tears.

'No, they weren't,' said Aiden.

'They will take them to the sea,' Grayson told them, and Sophia felt an unseen hand clutch at her heart, as the realisation of what Grayson had been through struck her anew. 'Why do they do it? Steal people?'

'I don't know,' said Sophia. 'There are bad folks out there.'

Grayson swallowed his sobs. 'It's not fair,' he shouted, tears and saliva spluttering.

Aiden put his arms around him and pulled him to his chest. 'You're right, it's not fair,' he said. 'It's not fair at all.'

There was something exhausting in their collective grief and Sophia shut her eyes for a moment as they slumped together on the sofa and could almost have dozed, except she felt Grayson stir beside her. Huddled into the seat, he wore a curious lost look on his face. Sophia sighed, got up, and chose a handful of books their mother always read to him, lugged a blanket from her bed and cuddled up beside him. 'Which shall we read first?'

Aiden stood and paced the floor before grabbing the large stone from the shelf and settling to sharpen the flint he used as a hand axe.

'Sophia, keep reading.' Grayson shook the book at her when she faltered, the scratch of stone on flint making it difficult for her to concentrate.

Aiden carefully rubbed his finger across the flint testing its sharpness, frowned, and ran the stone over it again. His eyes darkened with concentration. He had a look of their father about him. Peaceful. Confident. His fringe flopped in his eyes. He pushed it aside and Sophia wondered whether to use his hand axe to give him a haircut. His hair, such a bramble bush of textures, had lifted to a mix of blonds, scorched by the summer sun. He must have been outside more than her for her own remained its usual brown. She tightened her ponytail and twisted the tail of it into a knot.

'Sophia, read.'

'All right, keep it together,' she said, though she knew neither Grayson nor herself were that interested in the story.

The church bell rang. Three peals and then a pause, another three peals, and so it went on repeating. Aiden cast the flint aside impatiently. Tall and wiry he made the room small. 'Come on,' he said. 'There might be news.'

Kasimir

By the time my embryotic state evolves, my father disappears. He is dead. Slaughtered... drowned... my mother knows no details. With eyes now forming, I see her tears. She doesn't cry from love but from loss of familiarity.

Grayson

The clanking brass bell pealed like a death knell. The early promise of sunshine had disappeared, leaving the morning overcast, like when they buried Auntie May, and all Grayson wanted was to stay at home and have things as they were. Instead he followed Aiden along the winding lane that led to the church, listening while he talked at Sophia, spouting words Grayson didn't want to connect with. Horrid words like *abducted* and *snatched*.

Aiden gabbled on about the town council's reluctance to rescue anyone in the past, arguing the risks were too high and the chances too slim. Grayson didn't like those kind of odds. Aiden probably didn't either, for now he was saying, 'Miranda must take our side.' Grayson had never seen him so frantic. 'Because if she doesn't, I'll...' Aiden clenched a fist, as his words petered out.

'Let's just see which way the vote goes, shall we?' Sophia sounded reasonable.

'Voting, huh. That's another load of horse crap.' Contempt coloured the air and Grayson wished Aiden would calm down. 'Sixteen. I'm old enough to fire a gun but not to issue a bloody vote.' And that's when Grayson really wanted to cry.

A black object flew from the eaves just as they arrived at the church door and Sophia started, her face pinched tight. Grayson watched the tiny creases on her lip deepen and hoped she wasn't going to go weird and see stuff that meant other stuff, because he really didn't want to be part of that right now. Just to be sure, he studied the bat until it became a tiny speck and dipped below the tree line.

So far nothing odd, but the strangest things could upset Sophia, a leaf the wrong colour, a double bloom on the head of a flower, a dog with three legs that had once strayed into town. Aiden had no patience with her theories and sometimes poked her just to shut her up, especially when she tried to suggest special links between the two of them because they were twins.

'A bat in the middle of the day...' Sophia looked as though she would say more but Aiden cut her off.

'It was probably startled by the bell, Sophia.' Aiden sounded curt, though he did put his arm around her.

Inside the crammed church Grayson could only shuffle, tiny steps at a time, sandwiched between Aiden pushing his way through the throng of people and Sophia behind, nudging him forward. The place smelled of sweaty bodies and incense, not a good mix for his stomach, though he wasn't the only one suffering. Aiden had the white powdery look around his mouth that always appeared when his belly hurt.

This was only the second council meeting Grayson had ever attended. His parents dragged him to one last spring, not long after his ninth birthday, declaring that it was time to act more responsibly. He hadn't been too impressed then, but at least he knew what to expect now.

Miranda tapped the table for quiet. The last time, it had been Emmet leading the meeting and a stab of anguish caught Grayson by surprise as he realised afresh that Emmet was now one of those missing, like his mum and dad. He wondered if they were in the tent he had been held in. Was his mother's mouth stuffed with a rag so she could hardly breathe? Grayson snatched a mouthful of air to overcome the feeling of suffocation that rose up in him and he squashed against Aiden, wrapping his fingers around his, to reassure himself he really was home.

Miranda coughed into her hand before speaking. 'As you know, there was the threat of a raid last night. What you may not know is that our expedition party has been ambushed. Its members were either killed or taken to a city in the north. Emmet, Annabelle, Seb, and Amelia. They're all gone.'

Shock registered on some of the faces near Grayson and a low murmur of voices hummed through the room. Among the swell of people, he felt as insignificant as an ant. He could hardly match the names Seb and Amelia to his parents. It was as though Miranda was talking of strangers.

'What we have to decide right now is whether we send a rescue party, or not,' Miranda continued. 'I don't feel this is a council decision, so there will be a general vote. Personally, I don't think there's anything we can do for them, and I say this with a heavy heart, but we simply don't have the manpower or firearms. So my vote is we take the hit and protect our homes and families here from whatever is coming.'

Groups of people nodded their agreement. Josiah raised his hand and said, 'That has my vote, too.' Even Hannah, looking red as a boiled buzzard, threw a sideways glance at Sophia before raising her hand to vote against a rescue. After the general vote was cast, people began to leave as though nothing more was required of them, and all the while an anger burned slowly through Grayson, making him want to scream. How dare they go about their lives, forgetting his parents? They always volunteered for every expedition. Surely that deserved something? Some thanks? Loyalty?

Aiden grabbed Grayson's hand and made for the doorway but Miranda stopped him. 'I'm sorry,' she said. 'I wish there were a way to bring your parents back. But you know I can't in good conscience send a rescue party after them, when I know the men and women might not return.'

Aiden nodded at her but said nothing. *What was wrong with him?* Grayson wanted to shout at him. *Tell her she must go. Make her go, Aiden!* A tight band squeezed across Grayson's chest and he was back in the tent with the man's luminous eyes staring at him, and he couldn't breathe. Far away he heard someone shouting. 'Cowards, you're all fucking cowards.' The voice sounded like his own. He felt himself falling backwards in a slow sweeping arc and the last thing he saw was the streaks and patches of the sapphire pigment that coloured the ceiling.

Kasimir

The gulls' incessant cries eat into my mother's spirit. She would shoot them all never to hear them again in this lifetime. Watch them rupture, a mix of blood and feathers, and not feel a pang of remorse.

Their despairing screams reflect the amplification of human suffering, and in a port where slavery is the main trade she is surrounded. Our windows are rarely open, and she hums softly to mask their noise.

Aiden

Aiden sank into the couch. A sharp pain plunged through his stomach. He hadn't eaten since yesterday and his guts protested, but he couldn't eat, not when he felt so full of anxiety and misery. Grayson's voice screaming obscenities at Miranda kept running a loop through his head and he was relieved Hannah had been near enough to sedate him. She'd knocked him out cold with a whiff from one of the concoctions she had whipped from her bag. Primrose oils or some such. Sophia knew all the names. It would have been difficult to get his unconscious brother home but people rallied around to help and, though that wasn't enough for Aiden to forgive their vote, it softened some of his anger towards them. In the end people looked after their own. How could he blame them for not wanting to endanger lives of loved ones? At least it helped him come to a decision. He, too, had loved ones to protect.

He formulated plans while Sophia watched over Grayson. Now all he had to do was tell her. He went into Grayson's bedroom to gage his sister's mood before spilling his ideas to her. She was never one to make things easy, so he knew he would have opposition to overcome. The room was quiet, with Sophia reading, her fingers threaded lightly through Grayson's as he lay exactly where they had placed him several hours before. His face, pale under his tan, had a sick, yellowish tinge, accentuated by his mop of black hair that their father said was a throwback from a great grandfather.

'Any change?'

'No, but Hannah said the longer he slept the better,'

Sophia said. 'He should be out 'til morning.'

'Good, come and eat, I have something to tell you.'

When they finally sat together at the table, Aiden, still uncertain how to begin, found himself swallowing rather than talking. Though his mind was made up, he hesitated at the confrontation ahead.

Sophia tilted her head to one side. 'Well?'

He wondered at how she could make one word sound so belligerent. 'Tomorrow I'll start making my way to the north. Oliver's got his scooter working and it's got gas. I can ride it 'til it dies. Might take me some of the way.'

'That's a really dumb idea, Aiden,' said Sophia. Just the kind of reaction he had expected. 'If you so much as get on that scooter, I'll...'

'You'll what?' he flared.

'I'll push you off the bloody thing and drag you back home.'

'Damn it, Sophia, it's our parents.' Now he was shouting. 'Don't try to stop me, I can't stay here.'

'There's nothing in the world you can do for them.'

'Don't say that.' He thumped the table so hard the bowls rattled and soup spilled over the tablemats. Walking away from the mess, he gazed at the window and saw the symbol for safe travel Sophia had traced with her fingers the day before, dribbling down the pane. He was sure she'd have something to say about the distorted shape and scribbled his hand through the condensation, just to have one less thing to argue about. The pain in his stomach tormented him again with fresh intensity.

'Your stomach?' Sophia said. He didn't answer, he was too sick to go anywhere just yet and she knew it.

Without saying another word, she went through to the kitchen and came back with a glass filled to the brim with an orange liquid.

'Another of Hannah's inspired medicines?' he said. She pushed the glass into his hand and reluctantly he took a sip, then nearly spat for it was so sour. 'Bloody hell, Sophia.'

'Not the most palatable drink but I have a good feeling about this one,' she said. 'There's this, too.' She handed him a morsel of carrot, pappy and bloated. 'I kept it in blessed water for a whole full moon.'

'What the heck is blessed water?'

'Brine water that Hannah blessed.'

Aiden gingerly bit into the carrot, a foamy rubber, only to spit it out into his hand. 'Way too salty.'

Sophia leaned into him, her head against his shoulder. 'Don't go,' she said.

'Can't you see I have to? I'd do the same if it were you on that truck, because we're blood. We're family.'

'What makes you think you'd survive a day out there? You think a gun in your hand will even the odds? Mum and dad had guns. Now they're gone.' Aiden felt her cold hand squeezing his fingers but he said nothing. 'You've made up your mind, haven't you?'

'Yes.'

'Well then, I'm coming with you. You can't do this alone.'

'All right.' Pulling her to his chest, she nestled against him.

***

'Why are you out here?' Grayson stood in the doorway shivering in the early morning cold.

Sophia leapt from the couch and hustled him back to his bedroom. 'Get dressed,' she said. 'Do you want to catch influenza as well as brain fever?'

Dressed and looking like he could sleep another twelve hours, Grayson nibbled at the hunk of hard bread Aiden placed in front of him, while Sophia chopped eggs for them all, but Aiden's appetite had long fled. He didn't relish the next few hours as he thought of the hassle ahead, for now Sophia was coming with him they would have to tell Grayson their plans and find somewhere for him to stay. But first he waited until he was certain Grayson would eat no more before breaking any more bad news to him.

In the wake of his abduction, his young brother had changed, whereas the old Grayson would hardly let him complete a sentence this one just sat and listened, as Aiden told him they were leaving. Grayson made no comment, asked no questions until, unnerved, Aiden asked him if he understood.

'Yeah, you want me to stay with Hannah, while you search for mum and dad.'

'That's right,' Aiden said, hardly believing they had got off so lightly. That's when Grayson told him that though he liked Hannah plenty, he didn't want to live with her. He wanted to stay where he was, at home.

'But Sophia and I will be gone for a while.'

Grayson stared unblinking. 'A while? You don't know if you'll *ever* come back.'

Aiden felt the hairs rise on the back of his neck,

sending a chilly response along his spine, and saw Sophia knocking on the wooden table. For once he agreed some things shouldn't be said aloud. 'We will come back. With mum and dad, I promise.'

'Don't make promises you can't keep.' Grayson made for his room but Aiden seized him by his shoulders.

'That's not an empty promise,' he said.

'Don't lie.' Grayson shrugged him off. 'But you leave me with Hannah and I'll run off.'

'Aw, hell, Grayson, I have to go. Meet me half way here, would you?' Aiden combed his fingers through his young brother's fringe, pushing it from his eyes. 'Who would you stay with?'

'Helen. If I can't stay here with you and Sophia, I'll stay with Helen.'

Aiden considered his request, not finding it in his heart to deny him. He knew Sophia would have preferred Grayson to stay with Hannah, but Helen was the same age as Grayson, the only other nine year old in town, and she lived with her older brother William, a year or two senior to Sophia and himself. 'We could ask them, I suppose, but if they say no, then Hannah it is.'

Sophia frowned but thankfully said nothing, just started packing away the breakfast and readying for their journey, preparing backpacks for each of them. There were two pistols their parents had left behind and she packed those too.

Grayson watched her with a look of revulsion showing on his face but turned away when Aiden tried to explain it was only a precaution.

They found William straddling the fence in his yard

with a hammer in his hand and a nail between his teeth. He straightened his lanky frame when he noticed them, wiping the sweat from his forehead. He wore shorts and Aiden saw his legs were daubed with gaudy colours, streaks of yellow, green and all shades of pink. He wondered at the reason William would colour himself so. Maybe it was a sort of game?

When having told him the reason for their being there, William took the nail from between his teeth and hammered it into the pickets. 'All right,' he said. 'He can stay. But if he becomes a nuisance, he'll have to go someplace else.'

'Fair enough,' said Aiden, and went to hand him one of the packs. 'There's some food here, should last for a while.'

Grim faced, William indicated to the house with his thumb. 'Leave it inside,' he said, and looked as though nothing in the world would make his sour face friendly.

Beyond the doorway, a wet, muck-coloured carpet rotted on the floor. Inside the ceiling leaked. For all Aiden knew it may have been leaking for years and he wondered at his small brother's choice of venue.

'Okay then,' said Sophia as she hugged Grayson. 'We'll be back sooner than you think.'

'Another lie,' was all he said.

Sophia tugged her necklace from under her shirt, before unclasping the chain. 'You know this is precious to me, don't you?' When he didn't answer, she gave him a little shake. 'Grayson?'

'Yeah.'

'Keep it safe for me, little brother. I'll feel happier

knowing it's with you.'

He stared down at the necklace as she placed it in his hands and when his mouth twisted in a funny shape like he was going to cry, Sophia grinned at him and said lightly, 'Don't get too attached to it. I'll want it back,' and he threw himself at her, burying his head in her jacket. Over his head she looked at Aiden, her mask of cheerfulness slipping.

It was then Helen sauntered up the path from the back garden, wearing a crown of withered petals, her bare feet caked in mud and clay. She beamed a welcome at Grayson and Aiden felt a tug of release inside. He clasped hold of Grayson, pulling him into an embrace. 'I *will* keep my promise,' then turned and left, before he changed his mind.

'Okay. Just don't take too long,' Grayson called after them, his voice dying to a whimper, and Aiden had to muster his resolve not to run back.

The gate to Oliver's barnyard opened to a grassy crease in the ground from where the grimy, puppet-like bones of a colt protruded. Oliver's father had bred horses back in the day. Those that hadn't succumbed to vanishing feed died in a hard frost. When he was a kid, Aiden would come to see the bones that a downpour never failed to reveal.

Although it was early, Oliver must already have gone to the lumber mill. Aiden was counting on him not being around for it was safer to take the motorcycle and worry about compensating Oliver later than ask his permission and be refused. He supposed he should now add theft to his growing list of crimes. Also, he knew Oliver wouldn't let Sophia leave. He was too fond of her. Not that he stood a chance in the romantic stakes, Sophia had pledged a vow there would be no one else after her childhood sweetheart had gone missing.

The scooter leaned against the stump of a tree, freshly washed and oiled. Oliver recently got it to work after it had broken down yet again. The damned thing was as unreliable as hell but Aiden hoped it might get them a good way, as long as he didn't push it over forty-five miles per hour, or the engine would give.

They studied the map and decided which path to take. The longer route would suit them better. It was more side road than main and there would be less chance of encountering raiders.

They got on the scooter and Aiden fiddled with the wires to get it started.

'Are you okay?' Sophia shouted against the wind as they left the barnyard.

'I'm fine,' Aiden said. And he was, although they were heading far to the north and it would take a miracle for the scooter to get even a quarter of the way. They rode past the tower at the town square they had scaled as children, past the rusting remains of a tank silhouetted against the shelled derelict school, out of the town they had lived all their lives, and down the deeply rutted trail.

Kasimir

It surprises her. The things she misses. Grey eyes crinkling against the light. The weight of his sideway glances, making the sashay of her hips a little more pronounced. Chewing his food with vigour and appetite. The smell of his hair, newly washed with the sea. He is dead, but not gone, like larvae left under her skin to hatch and hurt when she least expects it.

Sophia

Sophia leaned into Aiden's back, smelling the warm scent of his skin. She knew, even without trying to sift through his thoughts, he was starting to relax. To be doing something active, to take charge, suited him. Never having been one for travelling, she felt uncomfortable leaving all that was familiar. Still she had made the right decision coming. Grayson would be safe enough with Helen and William until their return.

The sunlight flickered through the trees, odd flashes of brilliance, which had Sophia scrunching her eyes shut. Taking a less direct route to avoid any chance meeting with raiders, or those Seafarers, meant the road was a myriad of twists and turns. The scooter whined incessantly and dropped speed at the slightest incline, or whenever Aiden tried to push it above forty-five miles. As each hour passed, the world narrowed around her until it was only the scooter and road, mile after mile.

She began to feel achy, tired of being crouched behind her brother and so prodded him to pull over. 'Let me take a turn.'

'Sure.' Aiden rubbed his face with both hands. Sunburned red, it looked itchy and sore.

'Don't scratch,' she said, pushing his hands away. He rolled his eyes but she could see he did it good-naturedly and an inward grin warmed her. After consulting the map to get the route firmly lodged in her mind, Sophia started the scooter. The wind heaved and swirled with the scents of dry grasses and loam. For a while it was invigorating to have the air rush over her face but soon her skin started to feel stiff and gritty.

When the afternoon tipped towards dusk, the sky turning a deeper shade of grey and the sunny day changing to a drizzly evening, they decided to pull off the road to find shelter. They parked the scooter among the trees growing in clusters away from the road. Aiden placed it facing the road in case of a quick getaway and they walked towards a lone dwelling nestled in a dip. A one-story house with a mock up barn attached alongside. The thatched roof was patchy in places and bald in others with straw lifting on two of the corners. In the yard Sophia could see flowerbeds, dug over, but nothing growing.

The air had the bite of approaching winter in it, like a whisper of things to come. Sophia shivered, tugged up the collar of her coat and snuggled into it. Noticing a familiar sign spread in front of the house reassured her. Seven stones in a ring. The symbol was common enough, a mark to safeguard inhabitants, but the stones themselves were striking, different from anything Sophia had ever seen. So white, they could have been cut from snow. So smooth, they might have been ground and blasted to find the inner gem. She would have liked to pick one up, feel its shiny surface, let it fill her palm, but she contented herself with just looking. No point in creating disharmony for the sake of curiosity.

A skull dangled from string hooked round a nail banged into the eaves. A stark contradiction to the candle burning in the window. This irregular pairing made her hang back and pause to consider her feelings. Reluctance was a feeling to pay attention to.

By the door a pile of rags in mixed colours spilled

onto the step. The bundle moved and Sophia realised it was a girl huddled over her knees. She lifted her head and looked straight at Sophia and Aiden. Her lip quivered. 'Who are you?'

Sophia crouched down level with the child. 'Hello.'

A keening cry came from the open door and the child pushed her hand in her mouth as if to stop herself from joining in. Then, unexpectedly, Sophia heard a man's voice from inside the house.

'Shut your fucking whinging, woman.'

The child's face crumpled. 'Pa doesn't like ma ill.'

'Let's get out of here.' Aiden snatched at Sophia's sleeve, forcing her back towards the scooter.

She jerked free. 'No, Aiden. She might need help.'

'Oh, Sophia,' Aiden groaned the word, dragging out her name. 'Always bloody thinking you can solve everyone's problems.'

He sighed. It was the sigh that did it. That was when she knew he'd stay. Her brother might blow and bluster but she trusted him to choose the right way in the end. Otherwise she'd never have left Grayson to chase this promise of finding their parents. A shout from inside the house startled Sophia with its fierceness. 'Lila, who you talking to?'

The child leapt from the step the same moment the door flung wide. 'Pa, we has visitors.'

The man filled the doorway, square and thick-set, his crop of coarse hair stood like stalks on top of his head and made him appear taller. Catching sight of Sophia, his scowl turned into a leering smile. He eyed her from head to toe, taking his time, his gaze lingered at her breasts long enough to make her uncomfortable. She felt her face flush and stepped nearer to Aiden. The man followed her small movement and shifted his attention to Aiden, his expression changing once more, hardening into something aggressive.

'Well, boy, we've no room for guests.' He shoved the child through the door. 'Lila, go see to your ma. She's ailing.'

Sophia pulled herself upright and stopped leaning into Aiden. Better to face this bully on her own as Aiden seemed to provoke the man just by being there.

Another cry came from inside the house and the sound of something falling. The man made no attempt to move and Sophia started towards the door. 'Is there anything we can do? I'm a healer.'

'Are you now?' The man sneered. He braced his leg in front of the doorway barring the entrance. 'A healer?'

Once more he gave her a weighted stare as if considering his alternatives. Sophia eyed him back determined to show him any of his personal preferences were likely to have a zero outcome. Inside she trembled but must have hidden it well because the man gave a shrug, spat pointedly at her foot before he stood aside and allowed them in.

In the dingy light Sophia's first impressions were someone had tried to make the place cosy with the candle in the window, a pile of clean washing on a cupboard surface, and a small fire burning in the hearth. But the good feeling was overridden by an air of violence dominating the room. A couple of overturned chairs, a smashed dinner plate with lumps of uneaten food stuck to the wall told a different story.

The far corner of the room contained a curtained space used as a bedroom, and on the bed was a woman with the same curly tangle of hair as the child. Her thin frame made her swollen belly seem like an obscene growth. She clutched it and moaned. 'It's too soon, too soon.' It was the same mournful sound Sophia heard earlier. Catching sight of Sophia, the woman managed to gasp, 'The baby's coming,' before continuing to wail.

Aiden stood by the table, white-faced, digging his fingers into his own stomach. Sophia picked up one of the fallen chairs and pushed him into it. 'Sit there,' she ordered.

Lila's hands, wrapped round her head like a shawl, covered her ears. 'Stop it, ma.' She repeated the words almost like a song, but Sophia knew that wouldn't drown her mother's awful groans and she picked up the child and put her on Aiden's lap. Comforting her would take his mind from his own pain.

The man lifted the other chair upright and sat next to Aiden. Sweaty patches leaked through his shirt in two semi-circular stains under his armpit and the odour from him was so pungent it made Sophia's eyes sting. He dragged a glass jug filled with a black, gelatinous liquid across the table and poured a generous dollop of the brew into a mug, finished it in one gulp and then poured another.

Sophia rummaged through the drawer of the dresser for something sharp, but in the end settled for her own hunting knife, finding nothing clean enough for the job she had in mind. Then she placed a pan of water over the fire.

'Could someone bring this through when it's warmed?' she said.

The man barely hid his irritation. 'Who do you think you are? Fucking nag.' He snarled the words through clenched teeth as if they hurt his mouth.

Ignoring him, Sophia searched through the wash pile, until she found a couple of towels and a small rag cloth, which she tucked under her arm. Satisfied she had all that was needed, she went into the bedroom, drawing the curtains to give them both privacy.

'Now,' she said. 'May I have a look at things?'

The woman squirmed as her belly tightened in a contraction. 'There's no saving this one.'

'Well then, let's try and save you.' Sophia spoke confidently. Hannah had told her many times when people have confidence in their healer they almost halve their discomfort. How true, already Sophia could see a difference in the woman. She was calmer and more ready to co-operate. A blessing, as she probably knew more than Sophia in matters of childbirth.

Lifting the coarse blanket that barely gave coverage, let alone warmth, revealed a puddle of blood on the already grubby mattress. A metallic, meaty stench released from its enclosure hit Sophia, nearly making her gag. She quickly schooled her face to hide her momentary disgust and placed one of the towels under the woman and over the mess to give at least the semblance of a semi-clean entrance into the world. She rubbed her hands together to generate warmth while waiting for a lull between contractions before touching the woman's stomach. A bruise formed just under her navel where the edge of an object had dug into it, the corner of a table, or some such. Sophia looked up at the woman's face. Another bruise darkened one of her eyes.

Sophia touched it briefly. 'That's a fresh mark,' she said, but refrained from commenting further and began to prod with a firm touch around the woman's navel, deep into her hips and along the top line of her pubic hair, but there was no answering stir from the child within.

'There's still two full moons before this one's due,' the woman managed to gasp before another contraction took over.

Poor soul, Sophia thought, although if asked she wouldn't have been able to say whether she was referring to the tormented mother or the child who would never take a breath. She pushed the woman's skinny legs apart and probed gently inside her. A nail's worth of finger and she felt the baby's head. 'Nearly time.'

Sophia helped the woman move further down the bed until her feet rested against the wooden foot board to allow some resistance to work against, and propped a pillow into the small of the woman's back. Then she called through the curtain. 'Is the water warm?'

The woman grabbed Sophia's hand. 'Mind my baby, whatever happens. You mind her.'

For a moment Sophia was confused. 'Your baby?'

'My baby girl.'

'You mean Lila?'

Relief crossed the woman's features as she sank back into the pillow. 'Yes, my Lila,' she murmured. She said the child's name with such love Sophia felt a rush of tears burn and tighten her throat and could only nod a response. The woman's ease was short-lived for another contraction, the strongest yet, shook her body. Sophia counted the seconds to see when the next contraction would start but there was hardly a pause between each one, so she re-checked the baby's head position.

'We're ready.'

The curtain pulled back and the man came through with the pan. He placed it on the side table at the same moment the woman grabbed hold of her knees and, in the throes of her first push, uttered a throaty grunt, which sounded as if it was dredged from her very core.

It startled the man and he recoiled as if someone had flung boiling water at him. 'Bloody hell, woman,' he slurred to the room, staring drunkenly at the walls.

Sophia put herself between the couple with her back to the man, thinking what a foul oaf he was, while at the same time murmuring encouraging words to the woman on the bed.

Once the contraction was spent, Sophia bathed the woman's face using the rag soaked in the warm water. The woman closed her eyes taking a momentary respite from her labour. Sophia wished the man would go, his gaze was too intense for such an enclosed space. She could feel it drilling through her back. So it was no surprise when he came behind her and put his hands on her shoulders, letting them slide down her arms in one languorous movement. Goosebumps followed his creepy trail and Sophia shrugged him off. He leaned in closer, nuzzling her ear and she smelt the sourness of his breath. The bastard was so drunk he could hardly stand and Sophia shoved him, harder this time. 'Get off me.'

Reeling backwards, he uttered a curse and clumsily clutched at the curtain, yanking it from its hook. It billowed around him as he fought wildly to free himself, before staggering through to the living area. The curtain fell to his ankles, tripping him. He fell heavily and lay on the floor. A drool of saliva spilled from the corner of his mouth and he cuffed it in an inelegant gesture, before falling into a sleep of coma proportions.

Aiden leapt up with Lila still in his arms. 'You okay, Sis?'

With all pretence of privacy gone with the fallen curtain, Sophia beckoned Aiden to her. He put Lila back on the chair, prising her hands from his neck, and then walked over to his sister.

'Take Lila outside.' Sophia spoke softly. 'Sleep in the barn... and Aiden,' she dipped her voice even lower, 'find something to dig a grave. This baby is dead.'

'You sure?' Doubt clouded his voice and for once Sophia wished she wasn't so sure. She nodded and had the added pain of seeing her brother struggle to manage his emotions. Finally, he just compressed his lips into a tight smile, scooped Lila back into his arms and took her outside, gently closing the door as he left.

The woman braced herself for another push and Sophia focused her attention on the task of delivery. The sheer physicality blotting away the impending sorrow that would surely follow. Night dragged on, hours of endless pushing without result, and the woman slept between bouts, exhaustion etched onto her features. Sophia began to think the baby was reluctant to leave its mother with only the cold ground waiting.

Tiredness took a hold of Sophia, causing her to shiver when the room's temperature chilled. The candle in the window guttered and outside was a blackness with no hint of approaching dawn. Sophia went to replenish the fire. She stepped over the man still prone on the floor. To her relief he didn't move, apart from the occasional jerk, an involuntary twitch in his dreams. She threw the last of the wood onto the embers and rubbed some warmth into her arms as she waited for the twigs to catch.

Her mind wandered to Grayson and instinctively her hand went to her throat, but of course her necklace wasn't there anymore, it was in Grayson's safekeeping. She hoped he would feel part of her was still with him, no matter how far she travelled.

The woman groaned, recalling Sophia to her duties and she retraced her steps towards the improvised bedroom. Skirting around the man, she barely glanced at him, an oversight she instantly regretted when his hand shot forward and grabbed her ankle. She tried to save herself from falling, but couldn't shake free from the firm grip. Tumbling she landed on top of him, the breath knocked from her. Pulverised tobacco puffed from his clothing, dusting the creases of his shirt and trousers, and stuck to her.

'Well, honey, you're a keen one.' His hands went under her shirt, his calloused fingers scratchy against her skin. The spread of his palms almost covered her back as he pressed her hard against him.

'Kiss me.'

Sophia stared at his mouth, at the stubble around it, stained brown in patches where the continuous flow of drink must have trickled from his lips, and she wriggled to get away.

'Let me go.'

The more she wriggled, the more his hands seemed to find access to her body. He gripped her waist and flipped her off him and onto the floor and before she could react had pinned her under him.

'Show me some love,' he said, his hands moving from her waist to her breasts. Rage and embarrassment raced through her, causing her breath to snag. 'You liking it?' he leered.

She made herself compliant in his arms. 'Yes,' she whispered.

Then steeling herself as if for battle, she lifted her face to be kissed. His mouth crushed down hard on hers, his tongue forcing her lips apart. Sophia kissed him back, her hands straying to his hair where she tugged gently. He seemed to lose himself in her softness and allowed her to move from under him. Once free she brought her knee hard up into his groin and had the satisfaction of seeing him topple sideways, his hand clutching his genitals. Jumping to her feet, she stamped down on his hand to cause further pain, and then lifted her foot to do it again.

'No more,' he roared.

'You fucking bastard.' She wiped her mouth, making every effort not to gag. 'You touch me again and you'll be sorry.'

'I'm sorry *now*, you skinny cunt,' he groaned.

Sophia went to the basin and poured some water into a mug. She scrubbed her mouth, sluicing the water over her teeth. She shuddered, still feeling dirty. There were some things no amount of scrubbing would make clean.

Sure the man was no longer a threat, Sophia went to tend to the woman. She had stopped pushing and was gently panting. The baby lay still between her legs. A girl. Perfectly formed, but tiny, and as pale as wax. Sophia drew her hunting knife and cut the cord, cleanly and in one stroke. Then she swaddled the child in a towel, and handed her to her mother. Hannah had taught her even death should have its goodbyes.

Kasimir

Preoccupied with death, the emptiness my father leaves is vast and gaping ever wider. Each day as black as nightfall to my mother. A boat out at sea lurches under an overhang of rock, transporting children, tearing them from their homeland. She hears their cries, smells their misery, and feels guilt her own child is safe within her womb. And I, mere insubstantial matter, can offer no relief.

Aiden

Aiden's stomach kept him in a light sleep most of the night. That, and the responsibility for the girl asleep beside him. He found a blanket to cover her and topped it with his jacket as the night chilled. She was a funny little thing, all hair and eyes. The hair, a mass of twists and knots as wide as her shoulders, framed an elfin face, and from under her fringe her eyes shone like two solemn pools of aquamarine. He couldn't decide if they were blue or green, but whichever colour, were as unfathomable as the sea.

She had followed him to the barn willingly enough and he wondered if it was down to him to tell her about the baby. Still fighting with the shock that his sister had to cope with a stillborn delivery, he decided to delay things until morning. Bad news could wait a while longer.

What the morning did bring, however, was a worsening of pain. It gripped him like a fist squeezing his innards to pulp. He pulled himself upright and in the dawn light was able to see the interior of the barn. The wooden frame was sturdy enough, planks of rough wood nailed together. The builder had been no craftsman. Various tools, with broken handles, were rusting in a pile slung on a work bench that still had clinging remnants of sawdust. He sorted through and found a shovel head he could use. He turned to see Lila sitting up on the makeshift bed, regarding him with her serious expression.

'Lila, your ma's baby...'

'Dead.'

Her blunt answer was unexpected and appalling. Poor kid, he thought. There was no sheltering her from the awful circumstances, so he said it as it was. 'I have to go... dig...' But found himself stopping at the word *grave.*

Lila went and picked out another, smaller, spade. Together they went outside and Lila led him around the rear of the house, over towards the back fence, where he saw three small mounds in the ground. Lila picked at a scab on her lip. 'Those are the others.'

'Babies?'

The girl nodded.

'Poor little orchids,' Aiden murmured. Lila gave him a considered look but said nothing. She probably didn't know what an orchid was but she must have guessed he meant something special because she moved close to him. He squatted down, pushed the shovel head into the damp ground and began to dig. A tear dripped off his nose. He cuffed it away, pretending sweat, hoping Lila hadn't noticed. But the young girl moved closer still. He stopped his digging when her arm touched his, and he looked up into those blue, green eyes of hers to find them filled with such wretchedness, he closed his own for some respite. 'Oh, Lila,' he groaned. 'Some things are just... shit.'

Then together, as if working to an unspoken agreement, they both set to on their unrewarding task. The hole, once dug, was neat, and pared, and... tiny. Aiden lingered by it, reluctant to leave the empty grave. He was determined it wouldn't be him laying the baby in the damp soil, or covering its body with clumps of freshly dug earth. But Lila was braver than that and tugged at his hand, pulling him towards the house.

Inside they found the man pacing helplessly in the middle of the room, his face as pale as ashes. Sophia was bent over the woman. 'Get in here,' she called over her shoulder. 'You might as well make yourself useful.'

Aiden stood rigid. What in hell was going on now? He pushed Lila behind him. The girl had seen enough. But Lila darted away from him, running to the bedroom.

'Ma? Ma?'

He followed her into a space that was a mess of blood and soiled cloths.

'Aiden?' Sophia looked up at him as if she was struggling to bring her thoughts back from a million miles away. She nodded towards Lila. 'Get her out of here.'

But Lila was unstoppable in her determination to be with her mother and Aiden felt no desire to prevent her from reaching her goal. 'Leave her be, Sophia,' he said. 'She needs this.'

The woman on the bed seemed to need it, too. For the first time Aiden really noticed her. It was like seeing a death mask with only the eyes alive, and they were fixed on her living daughter.

Last night the woman had been a complication. He had found it difficult to reconcile her writhing body with something human. But now with the baby swaddled in one arm, and the other held out to encircle Lila, there was a power in her that only those at the end of life can emit.

Sophia shook her head and went over to the man. Aiden followed her, giving Lila and her mother a few private moments. His sister spoke so quietly, he could barely hear her.

'We need to get the afterbirth out and the only way I know is to manipulate her stomach. It needs to be quite rough.' The man's face changed, taking on a sickened expression at the implied brutality. 'Why so shocked?' Sophia added. 'You should be good at rough-handling women.'

'Sophia?' What was his sister saying? Aiden had never heard her speak in such a callous way, especially to someone who has just lost a child and was about to lose his woman.

The man raised an arm in a defeated gesture, his face blanching further, taking on a strange bloodless complexion. 'It's all right,' he said. He was nothing like the stinking drunk Aiden had left under the table the night before.

Sophia pushed back a loose strand of hair that had strayed from her knot. 'Sorry, I'm tired. And it's not over yet. If we don't get the afterbirth from her body, she will die.'

The man sighed. 'You'd best show me what to do.'

He followed Sophia back to the bedroom area where the woman had laid the baby on the bed and was cuddling Lila. 'So honey, let's tell them the plan.'

'No, Ma.'

'Lila will go with Sophia and her brother.' She cast a beseeching look at Sophia and then at Aiden.

Sophia pursed her lips together in a tight fold and Aiden knew she wasn't pleased with this new outcome. He swallowed back any protest. He wasn't about to argue with a dying woman, though he hoped the man would have something to say. Aiden cast a covert glance his way, before deciding he would be useless. The man wore the spaced look of someone who had lost everything.

The woman continued weaving her make-believe

story designed to bring relief to her daughter. 'Then pa can devote himself to looking after me. And when I'm well, we'll send for you. Sophia will let us know somehow.'

'No, Ma. I don't want to.'

'Sure you do. My Lila always wanted adventures.' The woman stroked the girl's wild hair and over the top of her child's head she looked at the man. He nodded his support.

'But, Ma...'

The man cleared his throat. 'You do as your ma says.'

'Yes, Pa.'

A surliness emanated from the girl. Aiden felt it, as tangible as frost. Unexpectedly she threw a filthy look at Sophia.

The woman gave Lila a soft push. 'Go pack your stuff, honey.'

Once she had left to gather her things together, Sophia pulled the covers from the woman and with the help of the man set to work to expel the afterbirth. Aiden stood by, the pain in his own stomach so strong it rendered him useless, and he wondered if Sophia's theories were correct. Maybe the pain did indeed predict a death. He watched as his sister scooped the bloody mess from between the woman's legs, checked the fragments, which were impossible to piece together, and decided they had done all they could. The man pulled his splattered vest over his head and then wiped his face and torso with the soft material.

Sophia leaned against the wall and then sat down, her legs suddenly failing to support her. 'I'm sorry. I'm so sorry.'

'Don't, Sophia, no sorrys.' The woman, breathing heavy, squeezed her lips into the semblance of a smile. 'One last favour… take my baby while she still sees breath in my body. Take my Lila.'

'I can't leave you alone. There must be someone to keep you comfortable.'

The man squatted down beside the bed, taking the woman's hand in his. 'She's not alone.'

Sophia glared at him, and the woman noticing, said, 'He does love me in his own way.'

The man gave a rueful smile, which contorted to a grimace as he fought to gain control of his feelings. Aiden felt like an intruder. He averted his gaze from the man's internal battle so visible on his face, and helped Sophia to her feet. 'Go wash. Pack your things. I'll get Lila.'

'We can't take her…' Sophia started to say.

'We have to.'

Outside, he found Lila by the open grave.

'I don't want to go,' she said.

'I know.'

The drizzle of rain spat down on them, wetting their faces, and saving them both the effort of crying.

Kasimir

My father's brother claims us for his own. There are no options. No get out clauses. His kinship is insidious, it suffocates, the binding heavy as shackles. Dread clenches my mother's heart as she plays her deadly game with skill.

Grayson

Grayson shuffled a deck of tattered cards, practicing some tricks his dad had shown him. This took some improvising with most of the jacks and all of the queens missing. Not that he held Helen's interest. She was too preoccupied mixing and crushing plants she'd soaked in water. Her hands were stained with a thick oily yellow residue. Speedily she daubed the soggy assortment of petals and stems over her legs using the back of a spoon for even coverage, but still managed to leave a streaky stain along her shin bone.

It was only the second morning since Aiden and Sophia had gone and he hadn't slept well. Yesterday his imagination of their whereabouts ran out as the day progressed. Now they might as well have gone to the moon they felt so distant. His hand fumbled for Sophia's pendant around his neck. The metal of the necklace felt warm having rested against his skin since she had left. He wished it was as magical as she seemed to think. Maybe it could make everything all right.

'What are you doing?' he asked. Helen was now running a spoonful of dye across her hairline and her white blonde was fast becoming the colour of straw. 'What's all the artwork?'

She paused and then stared at him as though she just realised he was in the room. 'Grayson,' she spoke in a grave matter-of-fact way that gave weight to her words. When she used that particular tone he would believe anything she said. 'William and I don't want our bodies teeming with lice. Do you want me to colour you, too? I promise the flower pigment only itches a tiny bit.' She spat into her hand and held it out to him.

He pushed it aside gently. 'But your body isn't teeming with any lice.' Then he wondered if lice were invisible.

'William says we can't be too careful. Once they attach to you, there's no getting rid of them.'

A thump on the door, followed by Oliver shouting, stopped any further revelations. Oliver filled the doorway as William let him in. He towered over them all and at that moment was so enraged he appeared colossal to Grayson. He reminded Grayson of a mad bull he'd once seen bellowing up and down an enclosed paddock. The beast had taken the best part of six hours to calm down. Grayson hoped Oliver wasn't going to take as long, although he had no idea what had upset him in the first place. Oliver usually said very little to Grayson whenever they met, and was more interested in chatting with Sophia, but maybe Grayson had insulted him when he'd had his odd outburst at the church.

'I knew I'd find one of you somewhere. Where's your brother?' Oliver shouted as soon as he saw Grayson. 'I know he pinched my scooter.'

'I don't know.' Lying always made Grayson's cheeks tingle.

'Speak louder, damn you.'

'I said I don't know.'

'Don't lie to me, you hear? I know he took it.'

'I'm not lying.' And now Grayson's cheeks felt warm as well as tingly.

'Where's Sophia? I can't find her either.'

'She's with Aiden.'

Oliver frowned. 'What? Your brother's stolen my scooter *and* taken your sister? How bloody irresponsible.'

Grayson felt the room closing in on him. The same feeling of suffocation he'd felt before started to rise in him. Suddenly he was being shaken. William jerked him to his feet. 'Get outside.' He shoved Grayson through the door, passing by Oliver as though he wasn't there.

'He doesn't know where they are, and neither do we,' William said over his shoulder. 'So go home Oliver, and cool off.'

Kasimir

The healer puts a cold rock on her belly. 'Limestone from the seafloor. The ocean produces the best medicine.'

He doesn't know the cause of my mother's abdominal pain, only surmising something is wrong. He probes her stomach low along her pubic bone. Invading fingers touch her skin. I squirm, withdrawing to lie along her spine. My writhing makes her vomit.

'If it comes to choosing, which will it be? Mother or child?'

My uncle doesn't hesitate. 'The mother.'

Aiden

Thirty or so miles along the road, the sun broke through and cleared the rain. Lila wriggled and Aiden felt the scooter rock. He tightened his grip on the handlebars to balance the three of them. 'Not much longer,' he said, but the words were lost on the wind. He urged the scooter on, letting the throttle out slowly, and tried to ignore Lila's feet in his back.

'We should take a break,' Sophia muttered in Aiden's ear, but they continued riding a while longer. Away from any sign of habitation, through woods and out the other side, by which time the sun had sunk low in the west. A large lake pooled beside the road, its water the colour of stained glass in the town church, somnolent red, the blood of martyrs. In the water, Aiden saw tips of spires and edges of roofs. The bombs of the old war had made craters that over the years had filled with rain and river water where the dams had been destroyed.

The road ahead was blocked with mottled army coloured trucks littering the tarmac. The blacks, greens and browns led him to hope some supplies might be hidden. 'Mind the scooter for me,' he told Lila as he parked. He knew little about kids but somehow sensed she required some indication she was connected to them and they needed her.

Together, Sophia and he searched through the trucks, steadily working through them. But there was nothing to salvage. The last truck they checked held more skeletons than they dared count, packed tight, a small pyramid of bones stripped clean. Climbing down, Aiden staggered to the side of the road, dropped to his knees, and threw up.

Lila ran over to the truck. 'What's in there? Can I look?'

'No, you can't,' said Sophia.

Lila threw a resentful glance at her and began to climb into the back of the truck anyway. 'Let me see,' she insisted.

Too ill to move, Aiden could only watch as his sister pulled Lila down. The child lost her grip and fell, tumbling onto her knees. She howled a protest, clutching one of her legs.

'I'm sorry. I didn't mean to make you fall.' Sophia helped her up and checked her for cuts and rubbed her leg gently, but Lila drew away from her grasp, snivelling all the while.

It was the first time Aiden heard her cry. She had been through so much in the last twenty-four hours, without a murmur, and now this little fall created an outpouring. Aiden went over to her. 'Hey, it's not that bad, is it?' Her mouth took a downward turn, a perfect crescent. He thought she looked sweet and hugged her. Surprisingly, she hugged him back, wrapping her skinny arms around him. 'Come on, we'd best get going.'

They rode for a little while longer until the sun had set and black storm clouds flooded the sky. Finally they stopped in front of a house on a low mound. Clay-coloured bricks surrounded the mullioned windows and a dome crowned the roof. The pair of marble pillars standing either side of the large white door served no purpose that Aiden could see, merely projecting the dweller's grandeur. 'I guess that's where we spend the night, if we want shelter from the rain that's coming,' he said.

Sophia seemed less keen. 'What if someone's living here? Someone who wouldn't care for our company?'

Aiden's attention was caught by the tattered remnants of a torn curtain protruding from a window frame, flapping like someone was waving. 'We won't know unless we check.'

'Okay.' She dragged out the word and Aiden pretended not to hear the reluctance in her voice.

They walked the scooter through the soggy, overgrown lawn, and then leaned it against the wall of the house. Anticipating a heavy rain, he desperately wanted to rest the night inside those walls, even if that meant he had to fight for it with whoever dwelt there. But that was the kind of thing raiders would do, force themselves into other people's homes. And he wanted to be nothing like them. If he were not welcome here, he would leave. But then he peered down into Lila's face and wasn't so sure.

Sophia thumped on the door at the exact second a roll of thunder rumbled through the sky. Clearly frightened, Lila buried her head in Aiden's jacket. Again Sophia thumped the door before trying the handle. But the door didn't open. Impatient, Aiden pushed her aside, wiggled his fingers like he was playing the piano, and grinned at his sister. There were not many doors that remained locked to him thanks to the tuition of Miranda. He pulled a pencil case from his backpack, unzipped it, and shuffled through the few tools within, scissors, screwdriver, small pliers, before finally locating a strip of wire. Squatting level with the keyhole, he leaned against the door, inserted the wire, and played scratchily until he felt a purchase. 'Come on, come on,' he murmured. The lock sprung with a satisfying click. The door opened. They were in.

An acrid fragrance of wet earth and cedar wood laced the room, forcing Aiden to breathe through his mouth. Sophia fumbled in her backpack and retrieved a torch and a matchbox. She ignited the fabric at the tip and the torchlight slowly illuminated the place, far too slowly for Aiden's liking. He squinted through the dark, straining his eyes. They were in a hallway. Shiny patches of damp shone on the carpeted floor and mould grew on the walls in scalloped shapes. Water tinkled eerily at the back of the room, where the torchlight did not penetrate. In front of him, a long hall table blocked further entry into the house and at its centre a misshapen object drew Aiden's attention, but he couldn't decide what it was in the murky light.

'Swing the torch here,' he said to Sophia.

'What is it?'

In the pale illumination, Aiden saw holes gouged in the middle of a brown rounded heap, a swollen protrusion at the bottom, a tuft of yellow hair on top. His throat tightened.

'It's someone's head,' he managed to say.

Sophia shuddered. 'You sure?'

Aiden took the torch from her and gazed at the desiccated, crumpled face of a man. 'Oh, yes. There's no mistaking a head, Sophia,' he said.

'Look, it's placed on an embroidered cloth. Some kind of keepsake?'

'Whoever left it here is probably long gone. It's been rotting for some time,' said Aiden. 'Let's see if we're alone in this place.'

'You can't seriously still consider spending the night? Let's get out of here.'

Then he remembered Lila. Swinging the torch away, he sought to shelter her from the monstrosity on the table, but she had vanished. 'Lila,' he called. He cursed himself for not paying attention. The head must have frightened her badly.

Sophia sighed. 'She's through there,' she said, and pointed to double doors opening to a staircase.

Aiden pushed through the doors, the worm-eaten woodwork feeling strange to his touch with its hundreds of holes. Lila stood at the base of the dilapidated staircase, a bemused expression on her face. Aiden peered into the gloom until more accustomed to the dimness. 'What is it? You heard something?' She shook her head. He turned back to Sophia. 'Let's find a room, barricade ourselves in and get some rest.'

'And if we're not alone?'

'I don't see anyone, do you?'

There was no convincing her. Sophia edged closer. 'Please, let's go,' she whispered.

The wind howled and rattled windows like a malicious spirit trying to get in and the front door banged repeatedly. He rushed to secure it, through the double doors and back to the lobby where water tinkled at the far end of the room. He waved the torch, and caught sight of the head in the flare of light. It stared vacantly into the room, a grim reminder they were trespassing.

He wondered if Sophia was right. He trusted her instincts and knowing she was uneasy made him jumpy and his imagination became fired. Rain pelted the windows and he heard the patter of feet in the raindrops hitting the pane and hints of voices in the wind baying through the house. Damn it, Sophia, they needed shelter. He reset the lock on the front door, taking his time with the task to allow his breathing to even. He wasn't ready to leave yet and he scolded himself for being spooked by the creaks of shifting wood.

'Let's just look upstairs, okay?'

'Do we have to?' Sophia placed Lila between her and her brother, resting her hands on the girl's shoulders, while Aiden warily climbed the stairs. Still he managed to stumble on two of the broken treads.

'Be careful here,' he warned as the girls followed him. 'And here.' He paused on the top step, uncertain, as the hallway divided either side of the staircase. The torchlight dimmed beyond the archway to his right but he could see the upstairs was in better repair. They might have a comfortable night after all. He handed the torch back to Sophia and pulled the gun from his belt, deciding to start the search with the room straight ahead. Carved down the middle panel of the door was an exotic creature, birdlike, with a rapier thin beak, the full breasts of a woman, and two snakes as arms, which wrapped back on themselves around its torso. It was not an inviting door and Aiden braced himself to overcome his reluctance to enter the room. Only the gun offered him courage to move forward.

Inside was a well ordered living area. Thick curtains covered the windows and the wind could hardly be heard. Two armchairs were arranged around an unlit fireplace and a picture of a snow scene banged into the wall with a nail.

Wooden carvings were placed on the odd assortment of furniture, mythical creatures so vague Aiden couldn't put a name to them and they created an uneasy tension in him. Lila moved around in the rim of light, touching each carving she saw, running her fingers over the wood. Was she humming? She picked up a smaller one, turning it over in her hands, studying it like it held a memory.

The room smelt of gutted candles. 'Sophia, shine the torch here.' Aiden pointed to a candelabra, which held two stumps of wax, a thin strand of smoke curled from each wick. His pounding heart filled his head.

'Well, we're definitely not alone,' said Sophia.

He stood listening, barely daring to breathe. Damn it. What was he doing here? He glanced at his sister's pale face and then down at Lila who gripped the hem of his jumper.

'Come on, let's go,' he said. More wary now, Aiden checked along the hallway to ensure their safety before leaving the room. Each doorway beckoned menacingly, holding some mystery he had no inclination to discover. He willed himself to caution, although he wanted nothing more than to be out of there. Gripping the balustrade they descended the stairs carefully. No point in risking an accident. At last the front door was in sight, they'd soon be free of the place. But what was this? The door shifted. Hadn't he secured it properly? A draught of cold blew through the lobby. The torch flickered, causing a ripple of shapes to dart across the wall. Shadows loomed in the doorway and moments passed before Aiden realised the strange silhouette he was staring at was a figure swathed in a hooded cloak.

Kasimir

Custom dictates six moons pass before a bereaved woman can be claimed in bed. My mother counts the days. There is no hurry, only safety in the wait, but she is misguided. A mere two moons and my uncle comes to her drunk, unwashed, and smelling of other women.

'I've waited long enough,' he says.

Tucking a wayward strand of hair behind my mother's ear, he uses a light touch but she isn't fooled. He likes to shock and lifts her skirt above her waist and stares. His scrutiny burrows through us both. She smacks him on the face but gently, a half smile on her lips. 'Not tonight.'

She meets his gaze and he is the first to look away. 'I'll wait,' he says and licks her jaw. 'But not forever.'

Sophia

Time stretched for Sophia, its fabric tearing at infinity where she became a spectator with no means of stopping their inevitable discovery.

Aiden moved in front of Lila, his gun primed in his hand, as the woman stamped her feet on the mat by the door. A cascade of raindrops spilled down her cloak in silvery threads. Whatever she held hidden under her cape created an odd shape in the fabric, and with her hands full she kicked the door shut with the ease of a practiced gesture.

Sophia could just make out the face beneath the hood, pretty, but overlarge, as if moulded from a dinner plate when a saucer would have done. Lifting her head, the hood slipped, revealing someone younger than Sophia had first supposed. The woman's assured manner exuded determination and purpose of someone older and the colourful painted pattern on her left cheek, three eyes chained together, intensified her steady gaze as it lingered on the pistol pointing at her.

'You think to scare me with that gun, boy? I've dealt with real men who carried more intimidating firearms than yours.' Amused mockery tinged her tone and the woman parted her cloak to reveal a couple of rabbits in one hand and a shotgun in the other, which was ready to fire with a quick flick of the wrist and a fierce snap of the barrel. There would be no contest if put to the test and with an imperceptible head shake at Aiden, Sophia said quietly, 'Lower your gun.' Aiden slowly did as she asked but kept his finger on the trigger.

'Wise choice.' The woman laid the rabbits beside the severed head as though to emphasise a point. 'I don't take kindly to trespassers.'

'I... my brother and me... we just thought we'd shelter here. We didn't realise this was someone's home.' Sophia heard herself gabbling in an effort to deflect the high tension building within her for the front door seemed a chasm away.

'Now you do know, please make yourselves scarce.'

Relief flooded through Sophia. She never wanted to stay there in the first place. Stepping towards the door, she glanced behind to see if Aiden needed chivvying but he was right at her heels with Lila behind. Seven more steps and they'd be free, small ones so as not to agitate the woman.

A sharp intake of breath made Sophia freeze. Now what? Something was wrong. The blood drained from the woman's cheeks. Her total focus on Lila, who stood silently by Aiden, her turquoise eyes so widened they almost engulfed her face. She leaned closer to Aiden under the woman's deliberate stare.

'Nadine?' The woman staggered forward, confusion rippling across her features. 'You brought *Nadine* home?'

'No, this is Lila,' said Aiden.

'Lila?' She spoke the name awkwardly like it was foreign to her and stepped closer. 'Come here, child. Let me look at you.'

Aiden placed a hand on Lila's shoulder. 'You can look from there.'

'Let the child make up her own mind,' she said sharply. 'Nadine? Sweetheart, don't you remember me?'

Lila clutched at Aiden's hand, dropping the wood

carving she was holding onto the sodden carpet.

'You always loved that little unicorn. Oh, Nadine, it really is you!'

'I'm not Nadine,' Lila said. 'Stop calling me that.'

The woman gave a considered stare at Aiden and Sophia. 'Are you their sister?'

'Yes,' Aiden answered, as Sophia said, 'no.'

'Aiden?' A hot rush of blood mounted Sophia's cheeks in her effort to check her bafflement. She wished she understood his attachment to this girl.

Aiden's jaw tensed. 'She's our responsibility.'

'Let's just go,' said Sophia.

Aiden waved his gun at the woman but she made no attempt to stop them. Her shoulders slumped as if only the fight had been keeping her upright.

'Wait,' she said, breaking open the action of the gun and hooking it over her arm. 'Don't go.'

'We'll be fine. We'll risk the storm.' Aiden eyed the severed head.

The woman followed his stare. 'The head that worries you is a good deterrent, no?'

For the first time Sophia saw the woman's precarious standing, all she had to protect herself with was her gun and her wits.

'Sometimes a gun is not enough. Besides, I didn't kill this poor unfortunate, although he is more use dead than he ever was alive. No, he was slain by one of his own.' Loathing curled from the woman like a physical force. 'He craved something his leader claimed first rights to. Apparently breaking standard codes demanded a high price.'

Sophia waited to see Aiden's reaction to the woman's turnabout but all he said was. 'What did he want?'

'Me,' she answered simply. Directing her gaze at Lila, she continued. 'Nadine, I mean... Lila.' She spoke the name carefully as if it required her absolute concentration. 'I'd like you to stay. For the night. I've a mind to look at your face a while longer.'

'I'm going with Aiden.' Two spots of colour flamed through Lila's cheeks, and Sophia, surprised at the girl's fiery response, found a sudden fondness for the small usurper of her brother's affections.

The woman sighed. 'The boy may stay. The girl, too.' She propped the gun against the wall, shook off her cloak, threw it across a chair before walking over to the head and stared as if noticing it for the first time.

Aiden threw a questioning glance at Sophia and she knew he would do whatever she decided. She searched inside herself for signs of unease but found none. She believed this woman. 'Let's end this or none of us will get any rest. We'll stay here tonight. It's warm and dry.'

Returning his gun to his belt, Aiden didn't look particularly happy with her choice and spoke harshly to the woman. 'If anything happens to my sister, or Lila, I will make you sorry.'

'Let's be assured, Aiden...' the woman extended each syllable of his name, making it sound derogatory. 'You stay only because I want to be sure your Lila, and my Nadine, are not the same person.'

'They're not,' he answered.

Sophia picked up the wooden carving Lila had let fall. She wasn't so sure. She ran her thumb over the engraved wood, feeling the curved flank and chiselled horn of the unicorn, before handing it to Lila. The girl tucked it into her coat pocket without looking at it.

The woman lit a candle and then went to the back of the lobby where the water trickled. Without waiting for a response she called, 'Girls.'

Girls? Was someone hidden there? How remarkable, for that part of the house looked the least habitable. Though that explained the smoking candle they had seen. Whoever lived here had been well drilled on how to hide from trespassers. But it was still a surprise when three girls, none of them any older than Grayson, rushed into the light.

The first girl to emerge clattered over the wooden flooring with a hysterical cry. 'Mother!' Slight to the point of boniness and white as a spectre, she looked so terrified Sophia felt nauseous at causing such distress and shamed at invading their privacy. She tried to quell the girl's fears. 'We won't hurt you. We only wanted shelter from the rain.' Somehow the words seemed insufficient.

A thump of feet and a second, taller girl crashed towards them. She wielded a stick, swiping the air with it, creating a spacious arc around herself. 'Don't worry, Mother,' she shouted.

'Caroline, it's all right,' the woman called to her.

For several seconds Aiden tried to reason with her as he danced out of the way of her stick. When exhausted she finally ceased her chase and stood like a bird of prey hunched and narrow, her hair hanging in dreadlocks touching her waist, and her breath rasping with exertion.

The last girl, the smallest of the three, stuffed the

thumb of one hand in her mouth and wrapped the other hand around the woman's leg. Plump cheeks softened her appearance, although she was as skinny as a broom handle, and she stared at Aiden as if at any moment he would transform into a wolf.

The woman stood among her girls, an arm around each of the younger ones. The older girl close by, her stick held ready to strike again, her stance fiercely protective. The woman directed her gaze at Lila and spoke. 'These are your sisters. Have you no memory of them?'

Sophia gave the girls a measured look. They were nothing like each other. Indeed three more different children would have been hard to find. She frowned trying to make sense of what the woman was saying.

The woman must have noted her confusion for she sighed and said, 'Perhaps one more introduction is needed, Sophia. I'm Crimson Wraith, mother to stray girls.'

The tall girl moved towards Lila. 'Nadine?'

'Her name's Lila,' Aiden said. 'And this is my sister, Sophia.'

The girl took no notice of him. 'Nadine?'

'She is not Nadine.' Aiden spoke sharply.

But the girl persisted. 'Yes she is. I know what Nadine looks like. Nadine, it's me, Caroline.' She pointed at the two other girls. 'And Scaredy Samantha, you remember her, don't you? And Dora was only a baby...' Caroline rolled her eyes. She shook the thumb from Dora's mouth, revealing gaps in her gums where half her baby teeth were missing. 'And still is.'

Lila shrank against Aiden. A disturbance of thoughts crossed her features before she buried her face in his jumper. 'Make them stop,' she cried. Patting her back, Sophia knew Lila was really upset when she didn't pull away from her.

'Shush, child, hush. It's no matter.' Crimson Wraith spoke with a no-nonsense tone, effectively reassuring. She walked to the table and picked up the rabbits. 'I expect you are hungry.' She looked at Aiden. 'Will you skin these while I get a fire going?'

'Sure,' he said.

'Just use the table here. The more blood and guts on it the better.' Crimson Wraith raised an eyebrow, a seamless arch. 'We do our living upstairs.'

The girls clattered up the stairs, neatly dodging all the broken treads that had given Sophia such trouble on her earlier climb. 'Come on, we'll show you where we eat,' they called, and she followed cautiously.

This time they turned right where the stairs divided, opening another carved door. This one depicting a sumptuous bowl of fruits. On closer inspection, Sophia saw the bowl was a voluptuous woman, peel curling seductively around her breasts and through her legs. The fruits were cradled in her stomach, as she lay curved like a foetus, her shoulders and head, thighs and feet, the handles.

Samantha lit candles and Caroline placed one in each corner of the room, while Crimson Wraith started a fire in the grate and set a spit. It was ready just as Aiden appeared with the skinned rabbits, Lila followed behind him. The fat was soon hissing as it dripped into the flames and the scent of roasting meat permeated the room.

After they had eaten, Sophia, warm and well-fed for the first time in days, wandered around the room. Books lined two of the walls. She had never seen so many in one place. Cards that told the future were spread on a table. Skeletal Death wielding a scythe, face up, grinned at everyone. She turned it over and pushed it to the bottom of the pile. Death surrounded them, even here in a cosy room with a full belly.

Sophia studied Lila, the little girl had lost so much in the last few hours. Her home, her parents. But was this the second time she had lost family? Was she, indeed, one of Crimson Wraith's stray children? Lila's father had made no attempt to keep her but Sophia could have sworn her mother had shown such attachment that could only have come from giving birth to her.

Dora gravitated towards Lila, while keeping the greatest distance from Aiden, worming in close. 'Have you come to stay?' She tried to hold Lila's hand. 'Forever?' But Lila sullenly shoved her hand away.

'Lila!' said Sophia.

The girl gave her the usual scowl. 'Leave me alone, you.'

'Dora didn't mean anything,' Samantha said, as Dora put her thumb in her mouth, her lips curving around it as she started to cry.

Crimson Wraith stepped towards Lila, tentatively touching the young girl's cheek as if she might scare her. 'Dora wants to be your friend. That's all.'

'She thinks I'm someone else.'

Crimson Wraith pulled a chair over and sat down. Dora climbed onto her lap and cuddled into her, occasionally reaching up to touch her cheek. Crimson Wraith cuddled her back. 'They might see some of Nadine in you but they would soon love you for who you are.' She took hold of Dora's hand and turned it so it was palm upward, tracing her fingers along her skin. 'Did you know the lines on your hand tell a story? Would you like a reading?'

Lila shook her head. Yet when Aiden sat on a chair next to Crimson Wraith and lifted Lila onto his lap, she turned her face into Aiden's shirt but held out her hand to the woman.

'Oh, how well I know these lines,' Crimson Wraith smiled. 'See the two lines meeting here? We would call it the crow's beak, remember? According to lore it's a sure sign for ingenuity. Below it is this line, see how lengthy it is, Nadine, I mean... Lila, your path in life will be a long one. And precious still are these lines criss-crossing here. Foretelling adventure. Yes, sweetheart, there's so much fortune in the palm of your hand.' She folded her hand around the child's.

'What do your lines say?' Lila's question surprised Sophia, though she was more than a little curious, too.

Crimson Wraith peeled off her gloves finger by finger and stretched her hands. Burned smooth, they did not have one line on them. 'They tell us nothing,' she said sadly.

Sophia thought they told plenty. They spoke of suffering and showed a woman who had somehow won through adversity. 'Such hands can make their own destiny,' she said.

Crimson Wraith looked at Sophia as if really seeing her. 'Thank you for that,' she said, and carefully replaced her gloves. 'Come, I'll show you to your room.'

The room was surprisingly warm and occupied by two rows of beds. The mattresses were thin, stained with dark yellow blotches and smelled putrid. Lila wrinkled her nose and wandered past a few beds, while Sophia claimed the nearest, tiredness overwhelming her now there was a chance to sleep. She lay back against the thin pillow, leaving Aiden to manage Lila.

'So which bed do you want?' Aiden asked her. Lila shrugged. 'Well, I'll have this one and you can sleep between us. Come on, kick off those shoes.'

The little girl was quick to obey him. Tucking the blanket around her there was a softness in her brother Sophia had never seen before and she wondered again at their strange bond. Soon their regular breathing was all she heard. She closed her eyes but sleep eluded her. Overtired, her thoughts spun a tangle of mysteries she searched to unravel. Turning on her side she looked at the occupants in the two beds beside her. 'Aiden?' she whispered so not to wake Lila. 'You awake?'

'I am now. What's up?' He leaned up on his elbow.

'I've been thinking.'

'Yeah?'

'About Crimson Wraith. You can't deny she cares for those girls.'

'So?'

'Well... she's certainly taken a shine to Lila.' It was like watching a shutter pull down over Aiden's face. She recognised his mouth tightening into its hard stubborn line and she knew he wouldn't consider what she had to say, but she whispered it anyway, if only to lay a seed. 'I think we should leave Lila here. It's where she belongs.'

Kasimir

'You should eat,' my uncle says. But she is robbed of appetite, already full with apprehension. He offers her meat the way he likes it, rare, the blood glistening. 'It would please me.'

She takes a piece. He nuzzles into her neck, kissing her earlobe. More kisses down her neck. Down further to her swollen breasts. The leaking colostrum entices him, but she knows better than to push away.

Reluctant to read what he knew would be in Sophia's face, Aiden stared at the ceiling. That didn't discourage her, though. He knew she was still watching him. Finally he glared in her direction, punched the pillow and buried his face in it, hunching his shoulders up to his ears. But she wasn't done yet.

'Hey, Aiden, just a thought. If Miranda and Hannah were one person they'd be Crimson Wraith.'

'Shut up, Sophia.'

Why did she have to say anything? He heard her shuffle under her blanket and in barely two minutes she was asleep, while he was left awake fretting. Did he trust Sophia's judgement? He sometimes thought she sized people up too quickly but had to admit she was rarely wrong and usually astute to strange atmospheres. Tonight though... she seemed too won over by Crimson Wraith for his liking, or maybe, just too tired to take proper notice. His thoughts jumped around keeping him from sleep, as he struggled to judge Sophia's comments fairly.

Sometime in the early hours before dawn, the temperature took a dive. Lila got up sleepily and rolled in beside him, snuggling into his warmth. Scrawny little thing tugged at his heart. He pulled the blanket around her, tucking more into any loose draughty gaps, which left one leg hanging in the cold. He wriggled his toes to prevent them cramping and then went back to his thoughts, though they hardly warmed him. He tried to picture Crimson Wraith through Sophia's eyes. The caring aspect of Hannah and the fearlessness of Miranda, he could see similarities, it certainly made for a formidable combination.

He must have finally dozed because he dreamed of a sea, dark as night. On a rock repeatedly slammed by the waves stood a robed figure, clasping a bloodied dagger. Corpses of boys, grey, bare, bloated with water, borne by the tempestuous surf, bobbed alongside severed heads. A tap on the shoulder woke him with a start, and he opened his eyes to Crimson Wraith leaning over him, fingers on lips, warning him not to wake the others. 'Come,' she whispered. 'I need to talk to you.'

He left Lila splayed over the bed with an abandonment never portrayed when awake and Sophia deep in sleep, her face still managing to look weary. He wondered what she would make of his dream. Then he laughed to himself, she would be in her element, analysing the meanings. He might tell her later, just to give her the enjoyment.

Hail rattled against the windows through a stone coloured sky. Aiden sighed. The last thing he wanted or needed was a chat with this stranger but already Crimson Wraith had turned her attention away, expecting him to follow. She led him to the room where they had eaten the previous evening. On the table was a bowl of dried fruit and nuts, such rarity sparking hunger in him, and she offered him some.

'Aiden, I'd like to talk about Lila,' she said. 'You said yourself she's not your real sister.'

'She's real enough.'

'Won't you even consider the possibility I'm right? It is evident you're travelling. Isn't it best for Lila to stay here with me than journey with you or be *your responsibility*, as you put it? Not the safest thing for a girl, no?'

'Stop,' he whispered. 'She will have to decide for herself. We can't do it for her.'

'All right.'

His appetite vanished. 'I'll talk to her.'

'I will take good care of her. I lost her once. It won't happen again.'

Aiden grabbed a handful of fruit for Lila and returned to the bedroom. Both girls were up and dressed and he said to Sophia to go have breakfast, then handing Lila the fruit, he took her to the end of a narrow hall where they would not be heard. From the full length window they looked down at a stream strewn with rocks, which ran through the woods behind the house. 'It's nice, isn't it?' he said. 'You could play there with the girls. Skip and hop from rock to rock.'

Lila stared at him, like he had said something immodest. 'Do we live here now?'

'This can be your new home, if you want. Crimson Wraith could be your ma and Samantha and the other girls your sisters. Wouldn't you like that?'

Her silence made him uneasy and he reached for her, but she pulled away. 'She calls me Nadine. I'm not Nadine.'

'You're right. You're not. But they really want you to be part of their family.'

'Will she be your ma, too?

'She won't,' he said. 'My mum and dad were taken by bad people. That's why I can't stay, Lila.' Aiden drew in a harsh breath, it hurt, and he suddenly realised he was fighting back tears. 'I'm trying to find them. Bring them home.'

Lila pulled something from her pocket, a small charm in the shape of a shamrock, which she placed in his hand.

'What's this?'

'Ma said the stone glints because there are dreams in it. You have to kiss it every night to have the sparkle in your sleep. Then what you dream about comes true. That's what ma said.'

'Did your dreams come true?'

'Sometimes. When pa didn't drink. But not when ma had a baby inside her.'

He could only marvel at her strength of spirit. 'It's very pretty,' he said, holding it out for her to take back. But all she did was fold his fingers around it with both her hands and kiss his knuckles.

'Oh, Lila. This little rock must mean so much to you. I can't take it. Why don't you keep it safe for me?'

'Ma said when a thing is done with, pass it on. Now you will have the sparkle in *your* sleep.'

What could he say to that? He felt as though the wisdom of the ages spilled from the young girl's lips.

'All right, I'll keep it,' he muttered. 'Thank you. Never had anything quite like this.'

He unfurled his fingers and the silver charm with its frosted green enamel coating twinkled with budding possibilities, so he almost believed it had the potential for all Lila said. Damn it to hell. Lila could come with them if that's what she wanted.

'Listen, you need to tell me if you're okay with the

idea of staying here with Crimson Wraith and the girls.'

Lila frowned and pushed the hair from her eyes. 'It won't matter what I say. You already decided.'

'No, I haven't.' That much was true. 'But you are safer with them. And they have food.'

'Not much.'

'More than I can give you.' His thoughts seesawed between wanting her happy and keeping her from harm. 'Staying here is for your own good.'

'First ma don't want me, and now you.'

'Stop it, Lila. We both have your best interests at heart.'

'Liar.' She burst into tears.

'I'm not lying to you. A few weeks from now, when your mother has been nursed back to health, and can take care of you again, Crimson Wraith will take you back home.'

'Really? Or maybe?'

And he found he couldn't lie to her. Not when she had been through so much already. 'Maybe... But there's always the chance.'

Lila stared listlessly at the floor, sobs shuddering through her long after the tears stopped, so all he wanted to do was hug her and make the hurt go away, like his father had soothed him when he had lost a friend. They stood together, his arm about her, until the hail stopped and tinges of pink shafts of light perforated the racing clouds.

A restlessness aroused within him and he couldn't wait to be on the road again. If Aiden had the choice he would have returned home. He longed for a glimpse of Grayson's cheery face, the way it was before he was taken, when all Grayson thought about was spying and eating berries. But Aiden knew there were no choices and his journey lay in a different direction yet awhile. He turned as he heard a slow tread in the passage.

'You two have been away for so long, I needed to check on you.' Sophia gave him a measured look. Lila huddled against Aiden's side, her fingers digging into his waist. Neither of them spoke. There was nothing to say. Sophia looked through the window. 'They are going down to the stream. Coming?'

They walked into the woods along the stream, where the banks were overgrown with bracken. The earth was thick with puddles from the previous night's storm and Caroline, Samantha and Dora jumped into the big ones. Their giggling and splashing, reminded him of Grayson and Sophia at the river. Was that only two days before. He had lived a lifetime since then.

They came to a pile of rocks. 'The sacred stones. The shrine of our gods,' said Crimson Wraith. Aiden stepped closer and saw the carvings of an eye on each of the rocks. 'They told us to give them sight. So we made the rocks their eyes.'

'They spoke to you?' said Aiden.

'A few times. When I desperately needed guidance, I prayed to them.'

'What did you pray for?'

'Protection and good fortune. To be left alone.'

'Did they hear you?'

'We're still alive, aren't we?'

He couldn't deny her claim.

Crimson Wraith spread a blanket on the ground where there were no puddles, and placed on it the wicker baskets they had been carrying. They contained assorted herbs, roots and applesauce. 'Before we eat, let us offer thanks to the Orphaned Gods.'

Aiden looked at the food and was thankful indeed. All of them were hungry, but Aiden only had a spoonful of the applesauce. He closed his eyes. Apples were such a rarity now. It was cold the first time his parents had brought some back from one of their expeditions to where pockets of fertile land had survived. Those apples had been so beautiful, the colour of embers. He sank his teeth into the hard fruit, so sweet and sour in his mouth. Happy childhood memories were interconnected to this taste.

They knelt on the mossy stones and drank from the stream. Samantha and Dora stepped out of their shoes, tripped into the icy, shallow water, and romped in the pale light that shone through the canopy of leaves. All the while, Lila sat on the bank and watched.

'Let's join them,' said Aiden, poking her with his elbow.

'I don't want to,' she said.

'Why not?'

'I just don't.'

'Don't be shy.' Caroline danced over to her. 'Come and look for pebbles with us. I think you'll find the prettiest ones. Nadine always did.'

Lila didn't answer, she just stood up, and ran behind the shrine of sacred rocks. Aiden moved after her, rounding the shrine, but she had disappeared. He called for her as he pushed through the bushes, thorns grabbing at his clothes and scratching his face. The bushes opened into a shaded glade, where Lila was sitting, hugging her knees.

He sat down beside her, close, touching. 'What happened?'

'Nothing.'

'Then why did you run?'

''Cause...'

'But why? 'Cause they were being kind? 'Cause they like you?'

The girl shrugged. 'There's blood on your face.'

'Yeah. And not a scratch on yours.'

'Ma would love it here,' she said.

Was it acceptance in her voice? Aiden turned and cuffed his tears with his sleeve so she wouldn't see him crying. 'I'll bet,' he said. He couldn't tell her he'd miss her now he could see she wanted to stay.

'Don't be sad,' Lila said.

Before he could answer he noticed Crimson Wraith moving from the shadowy rim of the glade towards them.

Lila looked up at her and the woman cupped the child's face in her strange, smooth hands. 'Hello,' she said quietly. She gazed at Lila the way his mother looked at him. The same kind of love shining from her eyes. Then she hugged the little girl, and to his surprise, Lila returned her embrace.

Kasimir

Death is always there, its all-pervading stench wafts into my mother's dreams. They colour her waking hours, sapping her strength.

She has seen my uncle kill a woman, garrotting her in the port's water, her legs kicking in the luminous ripples. At first she thought it love play, until the thrashing water stills and the woman is cast adrift like flotsam. And through it all, my uncle laughs as though nothing could please him more.

Sophia

The farther north they travelled the more inclement the weather. A blanket of fog slowed them considerably and Aiden pulled over on the bank of a stream to check the map. 'Hopelessly lost,' he muttered. 'Neither this stream or those woods we passed through show on here.'

Sophia took it from him before he tore the map to shreds and had a look herself, but the landscape was too hidden by fog to gage a landmark. 'Let's wait a bit. Grab a bite.' She shared the last of the blackberries Crimson Wraith had given them, less than a handful between them. Now their supplies were down to a wedge of cheese, already crusty and dry, and four strips of dried beef. 'These will have to last,' she said, and somehow saying the words aloud made the quantity seem even less.

How Aiden tasted anything the speed he shoved his share into his mouth was a mystery to her. At any other time she would have laughed at him he reminded her so much of Grayson, but now since saying goodbye to Lila, Aiden carried an air of remorse about him. Sophia sighed. She felt no such attachment to the child and could offer no comfort. It was difficult, particularly as he treated Sophia as if she were somehow to blame for the outcome. Maybe she was, she certainly believed leaving Lila was the right thing to do.

Before she finished eating he shouldered his backpack to indicate it was time to move on. Not to keep him waiting, she scrambled behind him onto the scooter and he kicked the throttle into action. It didn't help he was burdened with most of the driving, for her wounded hand had rebelled against her steering the scooter and started to bleed again. She wondered, not for the first time, if Aiden regretted her being with him.

Two or three miles farther along the road, the sun broke through the fog, thinning it enough to see buildings looming ahead. They forded the stream and headed into a deserted town, where crumbling walls of the houses around them offered a shadowed glimpse of past lives. Machines they had no name for filled every room, appliances from a bygone age. Such abundance and still it wasn't enough.

The scooter gave a final splutter and died. Aiden fiddled with it to try and coax some life back into it but ended up pushing it through the mounds of rubble that littered the streets. It was no help looking back at how far they had come when the journey ahead strained towards infinity and now had to be achieved on foot. Sophia unstrapped the backpacks from the scooter, handing Aiden his. Some things had to be made the best of. 'Let's look on the bright side, shall we.'

'Please tell me there is one.'

'Oh, there is. You always wanted to cross the land with nothing but a backpack, right? Well, now's your chance. So screw the scooter.'

'Yeah, I guess,' was all he said, but at least he sounded friendly.

The fog rolled in again, dragging a grey drizzle in its wake and they sheltered in an abandoned bus, brushing glass off the seats before huddling next to each other.

'Do you think it snows in the north?' she said.

'I don't know.'

'Might be too soon for that.'

'Might be. Another reason to hurry.'

The dismal late afternoon made hurrying an unappealing prospect, as they waited until the fog grew patchier before leaving the protection of the bus.

The barrel of a gun pointing straight at her was the first thing Sophia saw as she stepped onto the road. The man who held it wore a beanie and had his face hidden by a bandana. Bandits. Sophia glanced to see if there were others, all the while inwardly cursing her carelessness.

'Hand me your packs. Be quick,' he said.

'Here, take mine,' said Aiden, pushing the bag hard against the gun, as the man reached for it. Aiden followed through by flinging himself at the man, throwing them both off balance. They fell and scuffled, crunching the broken glass, punching one another until blood spurted.

Sophia grabbed the gun from her belt and cocked it. 'Stop. I *will* shoot.' The pair continued to exchange blows until Sophia parted them by booting the man. 'Stop, I said.'

The man backed away in an awkward crawl, while Aiden picked up the man's gun and stood up. The bandana and the beanie lay discarded on the ground and Sophia saw he was not a man but a boy, roughly her age. To think she could have been shot for a stale wedge of cheese. Was her life worth so little?

A strand of platinum streaked through the boy's long, copper hair, and an unsightly scar ran from his throat to the top of his left cheek. The scar was a new addition but the platinum and copper hair she recognised, and tried to conjure the face from the past and connect it to the one in front of her. 'Tuck?'

Even without the bandana she wouldn't have

recognised him immediately. The boyish curves of his face had become straight, his nose appeared longer, nothing like the button one she remembered, and those sea green eyes that used to light up when they had played together as children were nothing like the grim dark ones, rimmed in red, that looked at her now.

'How? Who are you?' Wiping the blood from his face with the back of his hand, the boy's eyes stretched wide open. 'Sophia? Oh my hell. Would never have recognised you.'

Sophia felt a giggle bubble up inside her. A small burst of happiness. It really was him. He got up feeling his nose with his thumb, wincing and spitting blood, just as the drizzle stopped and the sun threw a weak ray through a break in the cloud. Sophia took it as a sign. He cast a rueful glance at her brother. 'Aiden, right? Sorry about that.'

'That's all right, Tucker. I think I hit you harder.'

Tucker's eyes hooked on Sophia's. 'So, what the bloody hell are you two doing here? Foraging with your parents?'

Sophia wanted to weep and laugh and throw her arms around him but ended up doing none of those. 'We're here on our own.'

'Bit far from home, aren't you?'

'Could say the same about you.'

'Dad and I live in one of the houses here... so technically I am home. Say, have you time to spare? You're the first people I've seen from town since dad and I left. Come back to ours. There's loads I'd like to ask you.'

'We can't really,' Aiden began. Sophia sent him a furtive pleading look. This was an opportunity she never thought possible. Thankfully, Aiden shrugged. 'Sure, why not.'

The clouds, underlit with sullen gold, drifted away. One more hour of sunshine left. If that. Fortune must be smiling on her at last for in the dark they would surely have missed each other. She could not believe he was here. Her childhood love, her dearest friend, risen from a grave she thought him buried in.

'Great.' Tucker led the way and Sophia fell into an easy step beside him. After a while of steady walking, he cleared his throat and took a deep breath. 'How's my mum?'

How should she tell him? There was no easy way to speak of such things. 'She had a skin infection a few years ago but she's well now.'

His mother had been close to death. For several weeks Sophia had applied a bone coloured tincture that had made the poor woman wail at the slightest touch. But even on the darkest days, Sophia had never doubted the healing properties of the tincture. Hannah had told her it would work, and work it did.

'Your mum misses you terribly. You and your dad just disappeared. What happened?'

'My dad did what he had to do to protect me. We ran away. Look, can we talk about this later? For now just tell me about mum. Did she marry again? Have children?'

'No, Tuck, she's on her own,' said Sophia. 'Your mum went searching for you many times but obviously never found you. Eventually, she... well...'

'She what? Tell me, Sophia.'

Perhaps she should just say it plainly, without worrying so much which words to choose, for they were all inadequate. 'She dug a grave for you in the backyard. A small grave fitting for a little boy, where she put all your toys in. I'd come and sit with her beside the hole, but she never covered it up and at some point I stopped visiting. You were either dead or alive. Not both. And in my mind I accepted you were dead.'

'You thought I was dead? For a time I felt the same. I missed home so much.' He tightened his lips together and swallowed as if the pain of his sorrow was a big mouthful, before saying brokenly, 'It was her fault, you know, that we ran away like that, the way we did.'

'Really? Why?'

But Tucker made no reply. Saddened, Sophia thought of the time when they used to tell each other everything. She'd had no secrets from him. But that time was gone.

They came to a house with all walls intact, standing in its own piece of land, and a well-kept garden at the front. 'Here's where we live,' he said. 'Come on, take off your boots. You're going to like what's on the other side.'

Round the back was a pond, where they bathed their feet in the green water, thick with algae that tickled. Aiden was the first to get out, letting his feet dry in the last of the sun. Sophia traced a finger across Tucker's face, down along the scar. 'How did you get this?'

'Wondered if you were going to ask. Not pretty, is it?' To her everything about him was lovely, coloured by affection. The need to pinch herself to prove this wasn't a dream nearly overwhelmed her. Did he feel the same? She thought he did from the way he looked at her, caught hold of her hand and tucked it into his. 'About a year ago,' he said. 'We went to barter in a town to the north-west of here. A real pigsty like you've never seen. The locals reckoned on robbing us. We fled to the countryside and they hounded us like hunting dogs. Finally caught us on the brink of a gorge. A fight broke out.' Tucker rubbed his scar. 'Guess I was too dumb to know when to give up. I didn't have my gun back then, neither did dad, and they quickly overpowered us. As a lesson they gave me this delightful token.' His smile was mirthless and she shuddered thinking what he had been through.

'Can't say I expected company,' said a man coming from the side of the house. Unlike his son, Tucker's father, Arthur, looked much as Sophia remembered him, only with a beard, tangled and tawny.

'This is Aiden and Sophia from back home,' Tucker said, jumping up to meet his father. 'They came alone, Dad. There's nothing to worry about.'

'Are you certain of that?' said Arthur, staring at Sophia as if she were a fox caught in the chicken coop.

'I am.'

'What's their business here?'

'We're heading north,' said Aiden, also rising to his feet. He took a defensive stance, but Sophia shook her head at him. She never remembered Arthur being a threat to them as children. Surely he hadn't changed so fundamentally.

'We're just passing through,' she said. Passing through? How could she leave Tucker now, just as she had found him again?

'Up north there's nothing but trouble.' Arthur laid the bag he was carrying on the table. 'Ferret soup for dinner. You're welcome to dine with us. If you want to rest the night here, that's fine too, but tomorrow morning I expect you to be on your way. Nothing personal, we just don't like company. Now you can set about skinning the animal, if you want to be of help.'

'Sure,' Sophia said. She took the knife Arthur retrieved from his bag and set about peeling the skin off the ferret, then cleaned and sliced it. Meanwhile, Tucker and Aiden set a fire and supported a cooking pot with some rocks. Firelight glowed on Tucker's face as he cooked the chops of meat and Sophia sent covetous glances his way, enjoying just watching him, and all too soon dinner was ready.

'You've been living here all this time?' Aiden asked between gobbling chunks of meat by the mouthful.

Tucker's father grunted. 'No questions, boy. Just eat.'

After the meal, Arthur led Aiden and Sophia to a small room where they would sleep. The two mattresses were the colour of rotten cabbage but Sophia didn't mind, they smelled clean and she dozed off immediately.

When she opened her eyes it was dark and she shivered with the cold, wondering what had woken her. A tall figure in the doorway leaned against the doorframe. It was Tucker. He whispered her name and motioned her to follow him. Quickly she threw on her shirt and trousers, careful not to wake Aiden, and followed Tucker outside, behind the house.

'Why are you awake?' she whispered.

'I was thinking of you.'

Excitement clawed through her. So many times she

had wondered about him, now here he was thinking of her.

Tucker picked up a rock, skimming it over the pond's surface so it skipped lightly two, three times. 'I wanted to show you something.' He gestured towards the water. 'There is this beautiful light in there that gets so bright, you think it might suck you in.'

Sophia squinted and leaned forward. 'I can't see any light.' She didn't want to disappoint him but there was nothing there.

'You will, soon enough. It comes and goes but for some reason only at night. Dad says it's submerged putrefaction, something to do with the underwater vegetation. I don't really know.'

She waited patiently, happy just to be in his company, when a dim glow appeared in the water, as though someone lit a blazing fire at the bottom of the pond. Bathed with its amethyst glow, the water glittered restlessly in the light. Sophia gasped. Even decay had its own loveliness.

'You're going tomorrow, aren't you?' he said.

'Yes.'

'I don't want you to.'

Warmth stole over Sophia and she clasped his hand. 'I don't know what caused your dad to leave town with you. But it's been seven years. Can't you come back now?'

'Most of my memories from back home are rotten, Sophia.' His gaze wandered over her face. 'The only good ones are of you.'

'What about your mum? Don't you want to see her again?' Tucker shook his head, looking away.

'Do you remember Prosper?' he said. 'The guy who was always chasing us off the commons, as though it was his land? We used to reckon he was drunk.'

A memory trickled back and Sophia nodded. 'I remember him. But there's something you don't know. He was murdered sometime after you and your dad disappeared.'

'Actually, he was killed the same night we left. My dad strangled him.'

'What?'

'I saw it happen.'

Sophia shivered. 'But why would he?'

Tucker breathed deeply. 'Prosper used to come over when dad was away. He and mum would fuck in the back room but after a while they didn't mind doing it where I could see them. She'd groan and moan and wriggle beneath him, wink at me to be quiet and not spoil her fun. Prosper wasn't the first fella mum whored with. There were a couple of other guys but he was the one who beat me, swore he'd kill me if I told dad. To make his point he'd take off his belt and whip me on my back, which was pretty dumb, because it left the marks that dad eventually saw.'

'Well, he got what he deserved then,' said Sophia.

'It wouldn't have fixed my family if he had died a hundred times over,' said Tucker. He stared into the water, eyes dreamful. 'You know, there's this little valley beyond the hills,' he pointed in a vague direction over to his left. 'There's a meadow there, nothing much else, but earth and squirrels that skitter from here to there and a clump of ancient, sweet smelling pines. Some hollyhocks, too. In the trees there's a cabin with one big room. No one in the whole world knows of it except me. We could live there safely, you and I, and at nights we could come here, feast our eyes on this violet spectacle. What more is there to want?' *What more, indeed?* 'I've often had those thoughts, Sophia, of you... here... with me. It kept me going, kept me sane.'

A lump filled her throat and she forced herself to speak. 'Oh, Tuck, don't say any more... I can't stay, you know.'

Tucker let go of her hand like it burned him. 'Of course. I'm a complete stranger really. After all these years.'

'Don't be silly. That's not the reason.'

His face twisted into a sullen expression. 'So what is it?'

'Mum and dad were on a bartering expedition when their truck was ambushed. Now they might be kept as slaves somewhere in a city to the north.' Sophia felt her voice hitch as her fears rushed back. 'Or they're dead. I don't know.'

'Why didn't you tell me this sooner? Listen, let me come with you. You might need help.'

'I can't ask that of you.'

'You don't need to.' Tucker leaned towards her to kiss her lips, a sour sweetness on his breath. How dare he make her feel such delight when she should be miserable? A smile tugged her mouth and she tried to quash it, but Tucker had already seen it. 'I don't know why you mean so much to me, Sophia. But you feel it too, don't you?' He cupped her face between his hands and brushed her lips with his once more and she felt safe, precious to him.

They sat until the band of ashen light from the moon appeared on the hilltop. 'I'd better go,' Sophia said, but was reluctant to leave the warmth of his arms. He stood and pulled her up and they walked back to the house. Sophia crept into her bed and lay under the blanket for a long hour before she slept.

She awoke to Aiden shaking her shoulders. 'Sleepy head. It's noon already.'

She propped herself on her elbow, feeling she had not slept at all. Then excitement coursed through her as she remembered Tucker. 'Why didn't you wake me sooner?'

'I woke up late as well. Decided to let you sleep some more while I scouted around.'

'Found anything?' she asked, rubbing her eyes.

'Nothing good. The river to the north has overflowed. The flooding's widespread. I should have anticipated this.' Aiden frowned. 'The nearby bridge is totally submerged. Nothing we can do but wait for the water level to fall.'

Waiting in Tucker's home didn't sound such a terrible idea. Sophia felt a pang of guilt. Surely they shouldn't let a submerged bridge slow them down. 'Can't we swim for it?'

'Current's too strong. And you swim like a rock.'

'How about a raft?'

'I've thought about that but don't think we can build one. I've searched the place, found a bundle of rope in the attic but that's hardly enough. And I couldn't find an axe anywhere.'

'Why didn't you just ask Tucker for the tools?'

Aiden looked uncomfortable. 'Yeah, Sophia, about Tucker...'

'What about him?'

'He's gone. So is his dad. They weren't here when I

woke up and they're still not here.'

Jerked into wakefulness, Sophia tried to assemble her thoughts. Tucker couldn't be gone. 'He must be here somewhere. I mean, he *must* be.'

'Well, unless they're in a huddle under the sink...'

'Maybe they went hunting early.'

'Maybe.'

Sophia pulled back the blanket, got up and tucked her shirt into her trousers. 'We can't just wait for them to get back.'

'What do you want to do?'

'I don't know, go look for them?'

'I don't know about that,' said Aiden clutching his stomach with his hand.

If his stomach hurt that was usually a sure sign of trouble. Maybe Tucker was in danger. Sophia then worried she was reading too much into it and Aiden hated when she went on and on about signs and premonitions. 'Are you feeling all right?'

He evaded making eye contact, a sure sign he was thinking up a lie. 'Just hungry,' he said. 'Let's finish the cheese. One more day and it'll spoil.' He removed the cheese from the bag and split it into rough halves. Despite any stomach troubles he still managed to wolf his portion at his usual speed, at least now he wasn't a hungry liar.

With her mind on Tucker, Sophia nibbled small bites. Maybe nothing he had said was true. Maybe he'd had no intention of coming with her and this was his cowardly way of telling her. Why did it hurt so much to think that?

'How long do you reckon we'll have to be here?' she said.

Aiden glanced outside. 'Hard to say. Another day, maybe.'

The day dragged on with nothing to do but sit and worry. 'If they had gone hunting, shouldn't they have returned by now? What do you think?' Sophia finally said.

'You know as well as I do, hunting can take a while.'

'They might be in trouble.' She wanted to go look for them, despite Aiden hating the idea, no doubt he would ramble on about how Tucker wasn't blood, so they should leave him be. But Tucker and his dad had offered them food and shelter and that meant plenty. She rose and strode over to the door.

Aiden followed her. 'They could be anywhere,' he said, grabbing her arm. She shook him free, resisting the urge to punch him.

'I'm going to go look. We should help if we can. They helped us.' The door at the back of the house opened and a tread through the hall interrupted her.

Tucker and his father came into the living area, mud and blood splattered on their clothes. More on Tucker's. He peeled off his coat and lay his rifle against the wall without glancing at her, and she knew something had changed.

'Are you hurt?'

'It's not his blood,' Arthur said in a low voice. He placed a large leather satchel on the table. 'Why are you still here?'

'We can't cross the river. The bridge is underwater,' said Sophia.

'No worries, you can stay here,' Tucker said.

Tucker's father stopped going through the contents

of his backpack, a weary expression crossed his face and he pinched the bridge of his nose. 'You dumb kid. We can't have strangers in the house, least of all from that fucking town. We didn't leave trouble behind just so it could follow us here.'

'Hey, don't get mad at him,' Aiden said.

'Please,' said Sophia. 'We won't stay longer than we have to.'

'You can stay tonight,' said Arthur. 'Then if the bridge isn't clear you take the mountain pass. Either way, you are out of my house tomorrow.'

'But, Dad...'

'No buts, Tucker. Tomorrow I want them gone.' Then Arthur left the house, slamming doors behind him.

'I'm so sorry,' said Sophia.

'It's nothing,' said Tucker, but evidently it was because he looked embarrassed. 'Dad don't mean half of what he says. He's not usually like that.' Tucker raised his head to meet their gaze. 'It's just he's under a lot of pressure. Some people expect goods from us, you see, and recently goods have been hard to come by.' He drew off his gloves and hurled them down on the kitchen counter. 'Let's just eat. I bet you're hungry.' From a large holdall, Tucker drew out three small bundles wrapped in muslin and shared them. In each bundle was half a loaf of bread and a pear, already turning brown.

'Just where did you get bread?' said Aiden, sinking his teeth into it.

'We bartered with some travellers from the east,' Tucker said.

Remembering how they met, Sophia pushed the

bundle aside. Tucker had pointed a rifle at her. Would have robbed her. No doubt the bread in front of them was stolen, and if he killed in the process he wasn't any better than the people who had taken her parents.

'You should eat, Sophia,' Aiden said, already half finished with the loaf. She gave him her share.

Later Sophia followed Tucker to the back yard, where he sat on a stool and began cleaning his rifle with an oily rag. Aiden had gone to check the bridge again. He couldn't just sit and do nothing.

Tucker slotted the bullets back into the chamber. 'You didn't eat much. Not hungry?'

Sophia thought the question was more loaded than the gun that Tucker's concentration appeared focused on. 'Those people you spoke about... they make you steal for them, don't they?'

'Yes.' He rose and paced about.

'Do you also kill for them?'

'Hell, Sophia, how can you think that?'

'There was all that blood.'

'I do get into a scuffle every now and then.'

'A scuffle? Is what you call it?'

'You know what, Sophia? I wish this was a dream I could wake up from just by snapping my fingers. Find myself back in town, with a loving mother who cared more for me than the random blokes she took her knickers off for. And not have the threat of being hung from a tree, or beheaded if I don't rob for the people who really own this land. Yeah, I wish all that. But that's not my life.'

His face flushed and she forced herself not to dwell on the atrocities she believed he committed. 'You don't have to stay here and do as they tell you. When the water level falls, come with us,' she said. 'I need to find my parents first and bring them home but then I'll go with you to that cabin in the woods. You will be free from those people.'

He slipped a hand behind her neck and pulled her mouth to his. He smelled of oil and sweat and sodden wood. His voice came in a whisper. 'I can't come with you, Sophia.' He kissed her before she could say anything. 'We had news this morning that makes this impossible.'

'What news?' she said in a small voice.

'The men we provide goods for said they want more. Now we need to do other things for them. They are building a small army to fight a group of men coming from the northeast. So, in a few days, dad and I are going with them.'

'Why don't you pack up and run away?'

'Dad won't listen. He says everywhere you go there are people you must serve. Refuse and you're as good as dead. He thinks it's better to stay and serve the evil you know.'

Sophia touched her fingers to the red and brown scar on his throat and cheek, the long line of ruin that made this sweet boy fearsome. 'Hey, if that's what you have to do. I can't ask you to stay if your dad's going. Just be careful. And come back to me.'

Tucker leaned towards her and kissed her. 'I might never see you again.'

After thinking him dead all these years was she to mourn him again? 'Please, don't say that,' she whispered. He cut her off, kissing harder, probing her lips apart with his tongue.

She pulled him to her and his hands roamed over her as though he didn't know where to start. His fingers unbuttoned her jacket and she felt his heavy breath warm on her skin as his hand stole under her shirt, cupping her breast. Bending his head over her, he took her nipple in his mouth. She arched back over his arm, giving in to sensations she'd never felt before. Tucker had always been the one. She had known that way back when she was young. Kindred spirits. If she were ever to give herself to someone, Tucker would be the one and now would be the moment.

He clumsily fumbled to undo her belt and she giggled, delighting in her freedom to laugh even at this moment of intimacy, and he laughed, too, and pulled her to the ground where they lay on the prickly fir needles. She felt him harden against her and power rolled through her at his passion. She wanted him to explore her, touch her body like she wanted to feel his.

Spreading her legs apart, he gently positioned himself between them. Her fingers burrowed into his hair as he pushed inside her. 'Does it hurt?' he said.

'No.'

He moaned and pushed harder, fondling and tonguing her nipples until she wanted to scream her pleasure.

When he pulled out, she felt his warm wetness between her legs and she kissed him, biting his lips. Whatever happened, they would have this memory. The boy who pillaged and maimed would forever mean the world to her.

***

The cold woke her, the white cloud of her breath, leaking from her lips. She looked out of the window towards the woods where frosted brushwood gleamed like a galaxy of gems, and billowing clouds spilled across the sky as far as the eye could see. Aiden returned from the river. It was time. With his father's consent, Tucker supplied Sophia and Aiden with two jars of buckwheat porridge and four loaves of bread plundered from a nearby farm.

'I'll come after you as soon as I can, Sophia,' Tucker told her.

Later in the gloomy radiance of sunset, Aiden got a fire going on the bank of yet another stream, making the distance between her and Tucker insurmountable. Only then did Sophia allow herself to cry. She sobbed until she thought her heart would break, and all the while, Aiden held her close and rocked her, and told her this wasn't the end.

Kasimir

My mother washes his clothes in a shallow stream, scrubs each garment hoping to remove the smell of death my uncle wears. One shirt flows from her, snagging on a rock, bothersome like its owner. She wades in after it, the cool water lapping her legs and I paddle in my own pool of life.

I kick the wall of her stomach and for the first time she feels the pressure of my foot. She drops the shirt and lets it drift. Now she thinks of *me*. 'Easy,' she says, putting her hand on her belly. 'Be kind.'

Grayson

Another dawn and the recurring nightmare woke him, the knife nicking at the skin of his throat, the anguish of being taken from those he loved. His heart thumped noisily in his chest and Grayson whispered to himself that everything was all right, he was safe. He used words his mother would say if she were here to comfort him. He kicked off the blanket saturated with his sweat, the tiny hair fibres clinging to his skin in dirty patches and stared around the room he still found so strange to be in.

Waking brought its own nightmares. He struggled to put from his mind the loss of his whole family and resentment flared as he remembered how Sophia and Aiden had chosen to leave him.

Both Helen and her brother were not early risers and usually he, too, was unaccustomed to early starts. It was only since his abduction his sleeping habits had changed. Now he found it impossible to lie quietly once awake. He rose quickly, hitting his head on the steep slope of the ceiling, the crisp blue sky calling him outside through the window cut in the roof. Rubbing his head and chiding himself for forgetting the room's layout, he dressed, pulling on enough layers to brave the morning chill.

Outside, the air had that damp, burned smell that could only be autumn. He remembered the trail, although Helen had only taken him there that one time. Over the far side of the woods where everything grew denser and through a grove where an abundance of yews dimmed the dawn to a bronze twilight. It was restful walking at his own pace with no need to talk to anyone, taking his time to look around. He was busy thinking and breathing the lush greenery, a stark contrast to the smallholdings of his home, when something bright glanced from the ravine. Hopping off the mossy ramp, careful not to skid on the slippery rocks, he stole towards the peculiar light. *This was a real spy adventure,* but when he came to the spot where he had seen the brightness, there was nothing there. How could it have disappeared so fast, whatever it was? Was it a trick of light?

A movement of colour caught his attention, a handful of green fire fluttered like a plastic bag caught in a tree, slowly hovering towards him. His instinct was to run. But he forced himself to be brave. If Helen wasn't frightened of the light, and she was only a girl, then he shouldn't be either.

The fire lingered before him for a moment or two and he saw a pair of eyes looking at him from within. Should he try and speak to it? What could he say? He was pretty sure Helen had names for them but he couldn't remember if she had told him or not. Certainly he had never believed he would come face to face with whatever was there. The fire dispersed and he was left sheathed in a thin layer of cold sweat, his heart galloping like a wild mare.

So Helen had told the truth. There really was something in the woods. He couldn't wait to tell his brother, not that he could now that Aiden had gone, and besides, his brother would never have believed him. Aiden was always scoffing at Sophia when she started prattling about supernatural stuff. *Prattling* was Aiden's word, not his. Then Sophia would say it was Aiden's disability to perceive the world with only his senses and not with his spirit, too.

Disability was her word. So was *spirit*, come to think of it.

Curiosity pressed him forward. He staggered slightly, losing his footing and nearly stumbled into the muddy ravine. It was then he saw the metal drum, the rim catching the light. The sign on it such a bright yellow, even though it must have been buried there for years. He tried to read the words on it but it was too far in the distance. All he knew was they commanded attention and gave him a bad feeling. After that he was more careful where he trod.

He realised he must have gone further afield than he had thought for it took forever to get back to Helen's house, especially as he went the long way through the town to avoid the barn where the Seafarer, Jake, was held. The thought of him so close made Grayson queasy. As he approached the yard, shouting pierced the silence. It was William and he sounded angry.

Immediately Grayson hung back, reluctant to enter the house. It was bad enough when fighting broke out between members of his own family but quarrels among strangers were best avoided. Unfortunately, there was no escape from this one as he lived here now, so he braced himself and pushed open the door. Inside he found Helen sitting on the floor, tugging a comb through the wool hair of her doll, apparently mindless of her brother. Grayson had to admire her, she was fearless.

'I won't tell you again, you stupid girl. Get rid of this witches' plaything.'

'Marigold is not a witches' plaything,' said Helen, without so much as raising her head to meet her brother's gaze. 'She's my good friend.'

William's face flared an ugly red and his stringy

beard whooshed from side to side as he spoke. Even Grayson could see his temper was being stretched to the thinnest of threads. The doll hung limply over Helen's arm and William made a grab at it, but catching sight of Grayson, vented his anger at him instead. 'Don't you go snitching to people.' He stared at Grayson from haggard eyes so red, like he hadn't slept in a month or had been crying. While all Grayson could think was what could possibly make William cry, him being so sour and grouchy all the time?

'I won't say anything.' Grayson stumbled over the words and wanted to say more to reassure William but wasn't given the chance. William snatched the doll, hauling Helen across the floor as she clung to it until forced to let go. But even as the doll was torn from her grip she didn't submit and followed William as he tramped outside.

'You give her back. Marigold's mine. She's my friend.'

'It's not right to call a doll a friend. That's crazy,' William shouted back.

'It's *not* crazy. Mum gave her to me. So give her back right now.' Clenching her lips tight made Helen look oddly commanding until Grayson realised it was to prevent herself from crying.

For a moment William appeared as though he was mellowing down, giving his sister a tender look, but then it was gone. 'No, I won't give it back. This bloody thing will bring us trouble. Now stay inside and don't dare follow me or I'll give you such a clout.'

Grayson moved towards Helen. He'd never seen her so upset. Perhaps if he had spent the last two years with only William for company he too might have begun a friendship with some doll that would grow to be so dear to him he'd be devastated at its loss. William was far too intimidating to follow into the woodland, even though Grayson was tempted, just to see what William had in mind. Still maybe it wasn't such a risk. Someone like William wouldn't dream of being disobeyed. Grayson nudged Helen with his shoulder. 'Don't be sad,' he said. 'We'll get Marigold back.'

Helen struggled to stem her tears. 'Thank you.' She cast him a look of complete trust that he felt compelled to live up to. Why didn't he keep his mouth shut? 'Come on,' he said, before he could change his mind. 'Keep behind me.' It was no good being a spy if he baulked at the first sign of nerves.

Helen was a willing accomplice. She was on his tail before he had finished his sentence holding onto the edge of his jacket, wrapping her skinny fingers around the material and tightly squeezing it into creases.

William strode with purpose and Grayson wondered what kind of punishments William would deal out if they were discovered. They dodged puddles, pools of polished onyx. Helen lightly skipping over them, hardly making a dint in the mud while he got caught out and had to splash his way through. And this was the easiest part. Some areas still remained boggy from last winter when the dam higher up the slope had burst, flooding the lowland. The overflowing had been a real thrill as Grayson joined in the efforts to reinforce the dykes and make sure they held. It had been proper man's work and his father had praised him.

Now Grayson followed what he thought were William's footsteps but soon had to admit to Helen he wasn't so sure. She leaned over a particularly clear shoe imprint and stated emphatically it was William's and *yes*, Grayson was still on the right path. He had no evidence to argue with, so he shrugged away the doubts and continued to follow the prints. They led to a part of the woods he was familiar with but where he never really played except when he had spied on his brother a couple of times.

Cuckoo Zara lay spread-eagled by the front door. A young man bobbed on top of her making noises like a rutting pig. Grayson paused but not soon enough. The thump of their feet must have alerted the young man for he leapt up holding his trousers and scooted over the fence through the thicket, his shirt-tail flapping loosely and his strawberry blond hair streaming behind him as he headed towards town.

Cuckoo Zara's nakedness filled Grayson's sight, his eyes drawn to the thatch of hair between her legs. Heaving herself upright he watched lumps of wetness trickle down her thigh. She stared straight at him, scooped up the trail with her finger and sucked it with a deliberate noisiness. An involuntary grimace wrinkled his nose. Everyone knew Cuckoo Zara had disgusting habits, although he had never seen anything like that before and from the look on Helen's face neither had she. He wished Aiden was around. He was good at explaining the mysteries of adult behaviour especially when it was just the two of them and his mother and Sophia weren't about.

Pointing the offending finger at him, Cuckoo Zara offered a taste. When he pulled back she let out a great bellow of laughter as though he was the funniest thing she had seen in a long while. Still laughing, she picked up her clump of clothes and wiped herself with her rag of a dress before ramming it over her head. It was too short for her plump frame, elaborately patterned with huge, colourful flowers, disguising stains Grayson knew must be hidden there.

Slowly she cricked her neck this way and that. 'Maybe Zara knows what you're looking for,' she said, pausing on the threshold, half in and half out of her door and she beckoned them over, casting a knowing look that Grayson didn't trust for one heartbeat. 'Your brother has robbed you of something precious, hasn't he? Zara sees...' Cuckoo Zara tapped the side of her nose, '...everything.' The shrewd sidelong glance made Grayson think of her as sly and he wanted nothing more than to get away. But Helen had other ideas. Finding Marigold was her driving force and overrode any sense of caution.

'If there's a chance she knows something, I'm going in.'

Grayson caught hold of Helen's hand but she moved so he was left holding the edge of her sleeve. Still he held on to the thin material not wanting Helen any nearer to the proffered door.

'William's footsteps go this way, not inside her cabin,' he said. 'She's lying to you.'

'We can't be sure those are William's footsteps, can we? You said so yourself. They could be anyone's.'

Helen gently unravelled his fingers from her sleeve. 'You coming?' He was sure she asked just to be polite and would go ahead with or without him. He tried to sound confident. 'All right. Let's go.'

They followed Cuckoo Zara into the gloom of her cabin. A dead garland of crumpled foxgloves disintegrated where it fell, a dry crunchy hoop that crackled under their feet. Once the walls had been painted violet but were now so covered in cow splats the colour was barely distinguishable.

'Out of the way, Baps,' Cuckoo Zara gave the cow's skinny haunches a thump and pushed her towards the door. Baps didn't look bothered enough to move.

Helen's eyes were two round circles of surprise and she grabbed his hand. The woman wandered into her bedroom where an oil lamp burned its flame, a weak flicker.

'Please would you tell us what you've seen?' Helen asked.

Cuckoo Zara sat on the unkempt bed and scratched her head like a mangy dog, making the sand and pine needles fall from her hair and scatter on the bed. 'I saw him put something in a tree hollow when I was coming home with the lad you two just scared off.'

Grayson couldn't tell if she was angry or not. He found crazy people hard to read but when she twirled a finger through her hair, and said, 'It was a doll,' Grayson figured she wasn't too upset.

Cuckoo Zara leaned forward and jabbed Helen with her finger. It was supposed to be a friendly gesture from the couple of winks she gave. 'Yours? You the little sister?'

Helen's mouth fell open. 'How did you know?'

'I've seen you and your brother about. Besides, he talks about you.' She did another wink. 'From time to time.'

'William talks about me? With... *you*?'

'Sometimes, when he doesn't doze off right away.' Cuckoo Zara smiled, showing blackened stubs where her bottom teeth should have been. 'Lovemaking does that to a man and your brother is just a boy.' A rosy tint flushed Helen's face and she looked at the floor. Grayson wished the woman would stop talking, everything coming from her mouth was stuff he didn't want to hear but she didn't. 'He touches me like he can't get enough, here and here.' Her hands stroked her breasts and between her legs.

Helen's voice fell to a mumble. 'I never... noticed you.'

'You get so absorbed with your flower picking, didn't think you'd notice me if I walked right up to you. Anyway, you want that doll back?'

'Yes.'

'Going to tell Zara what's so special about it?'

Before Grayson had time to think whether Helen would hold back, the girl already blurted out, 'Marigold speaks to me.'

If Grayson hadn't seen the light phenomenon that morning he would have had trouble believing Helen, but to Cuckoo Zara's credit she just nodded as though a talking doll was the most natural thing in the world.

'You'll find your Marigold a hundred yards to the right, past the outhouse.'

'Really? You're not just saying?'

For the first time Grayson saw a genuine kindly look from the woman. 'Really,' she said. 'You can't miss it. The tree stands alone and the leaves are as rusty as a tin can.'

'Thank you,' Helen said softly. Her fingers entwined

Grayson's. 'Come on,' she said and they left.

They found the doll where Cuckoo Zara had said to look. Grayson thought Marigold hadn't improved with her adventure, as now one of the arms hung loose. 'She's here,' he said.

'Brilliant.' Helen looked jubilant. 'Now William's in *big* trouble. Marigold warned him she'd bewitch him if he tried to separate her from me again.'

Kasimir

My mother travels often. It is dangerous, but my uncle likes her at his side. He tells her she is always on his mind. So now she knows. While he rapes and murders *she is always on his mind.*

Aiden

The view from the hilltop revealed verdant meadows, russet trails, and to the east, the snowy slopes of the mountains. Nothing to the west but flooded lowlands. Brackish water cloaked field after field all the way to the horizon. Only the top of a Ferris wheel broke the surface.

'We'll go east and then north. Find a pass through the mountains,' Aiden said. His finger traced a line on the map. 'See, here's a way.'

Sophia leaned over his shoulder, followed his finger with her own and sighed. 'I guess.'

'I can't see a better route, can you?' He didn't mean to sound so snappy.

'No, Aiden, I can't.' She sighed again and he caught her in a headlock and rubbed her nose. She hated rough play but it always made her laugh, like now.

'Stop it.' She pushed him away. Then, as if changing her mind, she grabbed him back by the sleeve. 'Thanks, Aiden,' she whispered.

There was nothing else to do but journey on. They trudged until the sludge and rocky grass gave way to snow and then they turned north. Freezing fog rolled down the mountainside, engulfing them. Aiden hunched into his jacket, the hood grasped tight with a fist to keep it close to his head. His aching legs buckled. 'No more today,' he said, and slumped in a grave of snow.

A needle point of pain stabbed his side. Reaching into his pocket, his hand bunched around Lila's shamrock of dreams and he wondered how she was doing. He remembered her telling him something about the charm.

What was it she did? Kiss it or some such nonsense. Three days now and not once had he tested its magic. Best do it now. Lila would want him to have the spark of the jewel in his dreams. Aiden brought the charm to his lips, before closing his eyes and sinking into the enveloping blackness.

A voice spoke to him, an urgent whisper, dragging him from his reverie to unforgiving coldness. His teeth clattered together, so noisy inside his head he barely heard the words uttered.

'Get up, Aiden. We can't stop here.' Sophia's palm felt cold on his brow, which was vaguely unsettling as he felt icy inside. 'You're burning up.' She patted his cheeks with her hands and pushed some snow between his lips. 'Aiden, we have to move. Do you think you can? We need somewhere sheltered.' He nodded and leaned heavily on her to get himself upright.

A jaundiced crescent moon peered through the mist, a wry smile mocking him. 'Not far now,' Sophia said. 'Nearly there.' Desperation edged her soothing words and Aiden shuffled along the path, panting with exertion, his breath spurting milky clouds into the murkiness. *Nearly where?* He wanted nothing more than to lie down.

Off to the side of the road they sheltered in a narrow cavern deep enough to wedge themselves in. Aiden leaned against the stony wall as his sister made a fire beyond the entrance. Sparks rose one foot in the air, then died in the cold, consumed by the dampness. Sophia took out a handful of yarrow from her pouch, soaked it in snow and washed his face and wrists with the infusion. Aiden drifted towards sleep.

He woke in the night, sweating and kicking his way

from covers Sophia had placed around him. The fire burned and sputtered and he stared, mesmerised by the warm, flickering colours. Deep within the blaze he saw a face, feminine and childlike and horned. She sang in a sweet voice words he didn't understand, but how he wanted to. Reaching out to her, he willed her to be still. Heat seared his hand before being snatched back by Sophia. 'Don't,' he mumbled, pointing at the fire. 'Lila's here. Can you see her?'

Sophia stared into the fire. 'It's your fever talking.' She fed him more snow, settled him against the rock wall, then sat across the entrance, barring his exit.

Stirring to consciousness, the remnants of dreams lingered, predominantly of his mother. The smell of her breath as she kissed him, the feel of her arms in a hug, anxiety wove through his thoughts when he failed to conjure her smile, banishing the last traces of sleep and he opened his eyes to a dreary morning.

Bustling in the small space, Sophia performed her little rituals as though she was on her own. A pan placed in the embers of the fire with some snow thrown in, a sprig of hawthorn added to the flames. Then the fanning to cast the fumes and a muttered prayer. Aiden never knew how he felt about this spiritual side to his sister. Most of the time he ignored it. Sophia rooted through her medicine pouch. He guessed she was searching for some concoction for him but already he knew his fever had broken.

He rubbed his hands together for warmth and saw his palms nicked with tiny slices, a strange injury that had him stupefied at how it occurred. Lifting his hands above the covers he turned them, studying them, perplexed. Offering him a cup of warmed water, Sophia shook Lila's charm at him. 'I had to peel it from you. It was carving your skin.' She passed it to him. 'Best keep it in your pocket.' Sophia hovered by his side and he waited for her to speak but then she just shook her head and patted his shoulder. 'Ready to leave?'

He stamped out the fire and shouldered his backpack in preparation for the steep ascent. Long before half a morning passed, Aiden craved rest. A sheen of sweat covered his skin and he barely had the strength to wipe the moisture gathered above his lip and across his forehead. The whole world narrowed down to the pathway he walked on. Later when it snowed they huddled for shelter in the hollow of a tree and slept.

The following morning came soon enough and they continued their journey. The daylight bringing no relief to Aiden, the cold air burning his throat and lungs. They travelled in silence, saving their energy for the climb, but stopping often, if only for a few moments. When they came to a fork in the road he chose the steepest pathway in the hope the sooner they scaled the mountain, the sooner they would be on the descent to the shore. Pincer-faced birds with cruel beaks sailed above them, floating on the air currents, their wing span the length of two arms, their keening cry echoing into the valley below like a compilation of sorrow. Then over their cries he heard the faint murmurings of people. Sophia stopped walking and listened, too. A few piercing whistles reverberated down the path. They moved in the direction of the sound. Ahead of them the road extended under an archway cut into the mountain.

A white stone plinth either side of the arch had a

crudely etched bird on top. Despite their inexact appearance, they were the same type of bird Aiden had seen circling overhead. These faced away from each other, wings folded, like custodians on guard.

A pain shot through his stomach, familiar, but intense, and for a moment he struggled to walk. Already ahead, Sophia passed under the arch. Slowly he followed.

A man in a trench coat, the material straining around the middle button, stood at the entrance, smoking a pipe. His fingers protruded from holes in fraying gloves, with which he stroked his bristly chin. Tremulous light illuminated the concave wall behind him and the voices of a crowd roared and howled from deep inside.

The man stared at them with the pale eyes of the dead and motioned them closer. 'Where's everyone else?'

'Everyone else?' said Sophia.

'The rest of your group?'

'It's just us.'

The man scratched his chin. 'You two climbed the mountain all by yourselves?'

Aiden felt his feet going numb. 'We're just passing through.' He peered into the cave behind the man. 'What's all the noise about?'

The man half turned his head. 'Public whipping. Never fails to rouse the crowd.'

'Who's getting whipped?'

'Common thieves. Brawlers. Adulterers. There's always some sinner.'

'Doesn't sound like a very safe place.' Sophia turned to leave. 'Come on, Aiden.' She grabbed him. 'Let's go.'

Unenthusiastically, Aiden followed her and they

began climbing down, the wind blowing in their faces.

'Wait,' the man called out. Aiden turned to face him as he walked towards them. 'There's only one place you're going to in this snow, and that's an early grave. Look, I'll give you red ribbons to wear on your arms. That will make you mine and the others won't touch you.'

'Make us yours?' said Aiden.

'That means no one will mess with you.'

Aiden and Sophia exchanged looks. They couldn't afford to trust the wrong man, but Aiden felt he could barely carry the weight of his own bones. 'There's nothing we can give you in return,' he said.

'Worry about that later.'

'Later is not going be any different,' said Aiden.

'You have no reason to trust me.' Snowflakes brushed the man's cheeks and he scrubbed them away. 'But go down that slope and in a day, two at the most, your corpses will be a permanent part of this mountainside.'

'Better to take our chances with the elements than with you people,' said Sophia. Again she grabbed Aiden but he would not budge.

'I can't feel my feet. Let's go inside and sit by the fire.'

The man fumbled in his pocket and retrieved a pair of red ribbons and shook them at Aiden. 'Go ahead. Take.'

Aiden stared at the ribbons. 'Why are you helping us?'

The man coughed and spat a mouthful of blood. 'I have kids myself. Now take the damned ribbons before I have to saw your feet off.'

Aiden tied one around his wrist and waved the

other feebly in front of Sophia. Her disapproval seeped from every pore and he almost gave up. 'Please. Tie it. I can't walk anymore.'

Sophia grunted but took the ribbon. 'All right. We do as you say,' she said in a tight voice. She jerked her head towards the man. 'But if he tricks us, he'll be sorry.'

'Aren't you the fiery one?' the man said. 'The name's Joel and I won't trick you.' He gave a bellow of a laugh. 'Not today, anyway.'

They followed him through a cave passageway connecting the outer wall of the mountain to the inner courtyards that made this mountain town. Shadows from the fire built in the entrance swayed on the wall, swooping and dipping as though they were birds of prey. Walking through the shelter of the cave passage made the brightness on the far side all the more surprising. Startling white buildings on a slope looked clean and inviting with a gleaming brass bell on top of a tower. Excited voices carried in the air. Men, women and children milled about, chattering, pointing to something Aiden couldn't see. He strained on tip-toe just as the crowd parted to reveal gallows with a body hanging, a couple of bloody gouges where the eyes should have been. The pain in his stomach eased just when he should be sickened the most, and he wondered if Sophia was right after all that his pain was a prelude to death. A pen, like those used to hold sheep or cattle, detained a man, a couple of women and a girl, all chained to wooden stakes banged into the ground. No one took heed of Aiden or his sister as they moved closer to the gallows. He then carefully looked over at the people in the pen and saw they each had a green ribbon tied to their wrist. Around the girl's neck the words *liar* and *thief* were scrawled across a slate, the string attached to it sawing at her skin.

'What does the green ribbon mean?' he asked.

'They are trash.'

A man made his way from the tower towards the gallows. The crowd cheered frantically and all the while the bell rang. The man climbed the gallows chanting loudly, the skin of an animal dyed the colour of saffron draped across his shoulders. Small, white stone ornamentations hung from his belt and chinked together as he moved. Aiden couldn't decide on the shapes of them, though one was in the same likeness as the bird on the arched entrance.

Behind him a boy followed, carefully pacing his steps to remain at the same distance for the whole route. He, too, wore a draped skin and his hair, a halo of curls, seemed like spun gold to Aiden. He had never seen such fairness. The boy carried a stone orb, white as snowdrifts newly fallen, the sheen, flawless satin, where someone had polished it smooth.

'A Guardian Spirit lies within the orb, cleansing people of their sins,' Joel said.

The boy stopped and lifted the orb for all to see. 'Be silent for the Protector of the Orb,' he said, his voice holding the curious flat quality of the deaf. 'Be silent.' But the crowd would not quieten.

The man on the gallows extended his arms as if embracing all the people in the square. 'Oh, Spirit of the Orb, forgive us for the blood we are about to shed.' The square thundered as all the men and women joined him.

The man on the gallows scanned the crowd,

skimming over every face. Then he pointed his hand to the people in the pen. 'There are thieves among us. People who have given in to temptation and committed adultery or are pregnant out of wedlock. What shall be done with them?'

'Whip 'em! Stone 'em!' roared the crowd.

Aiden watched the people in the pen withdraw from the gate, the man whimpering. Aiden's gaze flickered to the girl, her face visibly pale, white to her lips, smudged dirt and traces of tears, long dried, tracked down her cheeks like bruising. Aiden clenched his fist, digging his nails into his palms as he studied her, feeling the blood drain from his own face, her fear affecting him like a virus. He suddenly felt as if swept by a tidal wave as he realised he recognised the girl in the pen.

She regarded him with a serious expression while the man on the gallows continued, his voice rising to a bellow. 'Bring the girl.' The crowd couldn't contain its delirious fervour.

'She's pregnant but not married. Can a girl be more sinful?'

'No,' shouted the crowd.

'This one can. For she was caught stealing, as well.'

'Thief! Thief!'

'Can't you do anything for her?' Aiden asked Joel.

'She's pregnant out of wedlock. Nothing can be done for her.'

Aiden made for the pen, elbowing through the crowd.

'What are you doing?' he could hear Sophia asking as she followed him.

Two men climbed down from the gallows and went

towards the pen, opening the gate. The girl recoiled from them, losing her balance and falling over.

'Everybody's looking, Aiden.' Sophia said. 'We better walk away.' But seeing his expression, she faltered. 'Do you *know* her?'

The girl's face seemed fuller than he recollected, her dark hair thicker and longer, but yes, he knew her. He even remembered her name. *Cassandra.* The girl who had moved and disturbed him when his brother had been taken by her people, stirred something in him now. Cassandra's eyes flickered with recognition.

Aiden nodded. 'It's Cassandra.'

'*Cassandra?* Cassandra who?'

'We need to get her out of there,' he said.

'And how do you suggest we do that?'

'I'm thinking.'

'We can't intervene on her behalf,' said Joel, coming over to them.

'But they'll whip her.'

'That's according to custom. She's both a thief and a fornicator.' The men who had climbed down from the gallows grabbed Cassandra and dragged her through the dirt in the pen and up to the gallows.

'What if I say I'm her husband?' Aiden whispered to Joel. 'Then she's done nothing wrong.'

Sophia glared at him, as he knew she would, but he was determined. 'She's still a thief,' she said.

'Not exactly,' said Joel. 'If you say you're her husband, then you're responsible for her. You'll be whipped for her thievery.'

'Instead of her?' said Aiden.

'Yes.'

'All right. Then I'll say I'm her husband.'

'No, Aiden. That's madness,' said Sophia. 'You're ill. Your body won't take the whipping.'

An inner force thrust Aiden up the gallows to face the man, who frowned and opened his mouth to speak, but it was Aiden who spoke first. 'She belongs to me. I'm her husband and the baby inside her is mine.'

Standing behind him, Aiden could not see Sophia's expression, but could well feel the heat of her gaze burning through his back. For a moment there was silence, then hisses rent the air. 'Whip him! Whip him!'

The man eyed the ribbon on Aiden's wrist and pondered before he spoke. 'As her man you're responsible for her actions. You will be whipped ten lashes for her thievery. Grab him!' The cheering and whooping of the men deafened Aiden but through the tumultuous din all he was aware of was Cassandra.

Kasimir

The boy comes for his brother, she sees the similarity, but it is the look he gives her that surprises. Part lust, part pity. It is the pity that wrenches at her pride. She blames the moonlight, the flicker of the fire, anything to feel she is mistaken. She tells herself he's merely a boy, but wonders about him long after he has gone.

Sophia

'Make them stop,' Sophia screamed at Joel.

The crowd surged forward animated by this unexpected turn to the day's events, and would have swept Sophia off her feet and into its midst but for Joel pulling at her jacket, jerking her back to him.

The whipping post dominated the whole of Sophia's attention as the man led Aiden towards it. That and the weighty man who stood beside it, a whip curled around his hand, his arm muscles flexed, and bulging.

A group of youths stood on the first rung of the fence, catcalling and heckling. The man with the whip stretched his arms and performed an elaborate volley, sweeping the whip into a figure of eight, inciting further excitement from the crowd.

Sophia shouted to Aiden. 'Tell them you made a mistake.'

'Too late for that,' Joel said. 'Don't undo his good deed or they'll both suffer.'

A man escorted Cassandra down from the gallows, cut the ribbon from her arm, handed her a bag with clothes spilling from it and shoved her into the crowd. At that moment Sophia would have snapped every bone in the girl's body if it meant Aiden would be safe. She gripped hold of her and drew her own face in close. 'Don't even think of disappearing,' she said.

One of the men dragged Aiden's shirt from his shoulders before tying his hands to the post. The sleeves hung limply from his waistband down either leg, revealing his bare back, white and unprotected.

The man wielding the whip took a stand a few feet away. His first strike was surprisingly underplayed but the quick flick found its mark nevertheless and Aiden's whole body bucked at the impact of the blow.

Cassandra closed her eyes and turned her face away. Sophia nudged her with her elbow. 'You only have to watch. Nothing else,' she hissed. 'So fucking look. It's the least you can do.'

The next cut was swung overhand and elicited a moan from Aiden that churned Sophia's stomach into loops. The long, scarlet rip of skin glistened wetly.

'Don't look,' said Joel. But look she did, unable to take her gaze from Aiden. The third lash crackled through the air. The man liked an audience and showed her brother no mercy. He played them, eking out the pauses between the whip cuts, giving Aiden time to recover so as to hit him all the harder.

The crowd quietened, holding a collective breath as they waited, then howled as one voice when the lash fell, the youths on the wooden fence hollering the loudest. Sophia bit into her knuckles, her fingers skidding against her wet palms.

The fourth and fifth lashes came in quick succession. Her brother moaned, straining at the rope, his body tautened with pain. Sophia went towards the steps but strong hands grabbed her, enveloped her, pulling her back.

'Don't be foolish, girl,' said Joel. 'There's nothing you can do for him.'

Sophia struggled against his hold, her face heating as she strained to stem her tears and anger, then as suddenly as it started the fight abandoned her and she stopped resisting. Numb and spent she watched the whip fall a seventh and eighth time, drawing blood and tearing flesh.

Cassandra glanced at Sophia apprehensively. 'I only took a hunk of bread.'

Anger suffocated Sophia. How she kept her hands from hurting the girl she didn't know. Cassandra definitely wasn't anyone who had ever lived in their town, so how come her brother knew her?

The whip slashed Aiden's back a ninth and then final time.

'More! More!' the crowd hollered but their enthusiasm turned to jeering when the man on the gallows ordered Aiden to be untied. A couple of men dragged his him down the steps and shoved him into the crowd. Sophia rushed to Aiden's crumpled body but was unsure where to hold him without hurting. Joel pushed his way forward and heaved Aiden up onto his back.

'Now for the other thieves and fornicators among us,' shouted the man on the platform. The crowd cheered. 'Thieves and whores! String 'em up!'

Joel made his way through the crowd with Aiden slung over him and Sophia followed. Her eyes locked on to Aiden's back, her mind in turmoil. She had decisions to make. People backed away from Joel but pushed into her, deliberately jostling her, and threw the odd spit at Cassandra. Finally they left the crowd and came to a deserted side alley where Joel carefully placed Aiden on the ground. 'Come on, boy, start coming round.'

Fumbling through her dwindling medical supplies, Sophia wondered what herb or seed to use on his wounds but couldn't find anything. If only she had lavender oil. How she wished Hannah were here.

A woman's voice shouted down the alley. 'Oi, where do you think you're going?' Joel froze and Sophia turned to see a small, red-headed woman steaming towards them. 'Our children need their dad at home, not here in the square, befriending these ratty waifs, giving them ribbons like they deserves them.' She flailed her arms at Joel, striking blows at his cheeks and ears. He made no attempt to answer her or raise his hands to protect his face. 'What if something happened to you? What if they dragged *you* onto the gallows? Who would take care of our children? There's not an ounce of sense in you. Come home right now.'

Joel looked embarrassed. 'I must go.' He delved into his pockets and pulled out a slip of paper. 'Here's a couple of favours. They will buy you a meal at least. Sorry it's not more.'

Glowering at Sophia, the woman made a snatch at the paper but Joel grabbed her wrist. 'No, Lizzie, let it be.' He spoke to Sophia again. 'Tomorrow try Ma Wilkins down by the quarry. Her place will be full of revellers tonight so you won't have a chance of a bed.'

Sophia realised just how kind a man Joel was and stammered a thank you. Lizzie rolled her eyes and prodded him.

'I'm coming,' Joel muttered and allowed himself to be dragged from the alley, soon disappearing into the crowd.

'We'll get by without him,' said Cassandra. 'There's a cave nearby. I sheltered there. We can go there now, and tomorrow seek lodging at that place he mentioned. Do you think these favours will really get us food?'

'Do you have anything else in case they don't?' said Sophia.

'Only this, though I meant to keep it for a midwife.' Rummaging through her own meagre pile of belongings, Cassandra pulled out a necklace. 'Will this get us anything? It means nothing to me.' And dangling from a leather throng hung one of Emmet's buttons. Not as shiny as before, undeniably missing Emmet's loving care.

Sophia snatched it from Cassandra's hand, the girl's words stinging in her mind. It might mean nothing to her but it meant plenty to Sophia. She remembered how sometimes she had tugged at them, heavy-handedly, but rather than push her away Emmet sewed them tighter, looping strong twine through the metal ring soldered to their back. There was no way this button could have worked loose.

'Just where did you get this?' said Sophia. Pregnant or not, she wanted to hurt her, and stepped towards the girl. Cassandra stood her ground, staring back defiantly, which only inflamed Sophia more.

'Sophia,' came a voice at her back. She turned to see her brother scarcely able to straighten his back. 'She's the key.' Aiden groaned.

'The key to fucking what?'

'Finding mum and dad.'

Any question regarding the identity of the girl would have to wait as crimson seeped through Aiden's shirt. His wounds needed redressing. She spoke curtly to Cassandra. 'Is this cave nearby?'

'It is. I'll show you.'

They helped Aiden up, each looping one of his arms across their shoulders to support him. He moaned, his stiffening back causing him to move with an odd gait.

'It's not far,' Cassandra said.

The end of the alley led away from the town centre down a track and into a cave set aside from the main drag of the pathway. They laid Aiden on the damp floor. His shirt clung to this back and Sophia could not peel it off without a sharp cry of pain wrenching out of him. Some of the cuts ran deep into his flesh like bear claw marks. She searched her pack for a small paper bag in which she had kept powdered alum. The bag felt strangely light in her hand and she found a hole in it. The backpack had a hole too. Most of the powder had gone and now there was so little left to clean and wash Aiden's wounds. 'This needs disinfecting,' she said.

'Is gin any good?' said Cassandra.

Sophia stared at her thoughtfully. 'Yes.'

'Shall I go get some?'

Sophia felt torn between letting Cassandra go or making her stay with Aiden and doing it herself. She toyed with the options. Not being able to trust the girl created a problem but if she stayed what was to stop Cassandra stealing from their belongings?

'I know the town better than you.' Cassandra bit into her lip. 'Whatever you think of me, I *will* come back. I will see him all right before I'm gone.'

'Here, take this and get some food too.' Sophia pounded Joel's favours into Cassandra's hand. 'And keep your light fingers weighted. The last thing we need now is you pinching stuff again.' The look Cassandra gave showed she had little intention of using Joel's favours if an easier option presented itself.

'If you get caught, I won't help you,' said Sophia and Cassandra left with speed not typical for a girl in that advanced stage of pregnancy.

Sophia waited until she couldn't hear Cassandra's footsteps before saying, 'Who the hell is she, Aiden?'

'I saw her at the camp where they kept Grayson,' he said wearily. 'She must have escaped her people.'

'If I'd known that, I would have exposed your lie before everyone. You're such a fool.' She sighed. 'Why take her punishment on yourself?'

'She could tell us where they keep mum and dad. Besides, it was the right thing to do.' Something shifted in her mind as the words echoed. *Was it the right thing to do?*

'Wish I could agree.' The cave darkened as though someone had drawn a curtain around the entrance and Sophia peered outside. Black clouds amassed, blotting all traces of blue from the sky. 'There's a storm coming,' she whispered. Nodding, Aiden closed his eyes.

The wait for Cassandra's return became an interminable delay and anxiety bubbled inside Sophia. Without the gin wash she could do no more for Aiden. A clap of thunder rumbled overhead like a portent of disaster.

'She's not coming back, is she?'

Aiden gave a weak shrug.

'Such little faith,' came the thief's voice through the entrance. Cassandra shoved a jug into Sophia's hands, the precious liquid swilling in the bottom.

'It's all I could get. Hope it's enough. Had to help myself through a window, door was rusted solid.' Cassandra gave a short bark of laughter. 'Oh, there were these left over meats too.' The sweet smell of cooked goat trickled into the air as Cassandra unravelled the cloth it was wrapped in.

Sophia felt her temper rise from nought degrees to boiling. Her hand shook and she put down the jug so as not to spill the contents, before turning to Cassandra. 'You thieving tramp. Why didn't you use the favours? I hope no one followed you. You'll get us *all* dragged onto the gallows.' Sophia went to the cave entrance and sneaked a quick look outside but the track was deserted.

'I was careful. And using that note would have taken much, much longer.' Cassandra had the cheek to look affronted. Bloody girl was a liability.

Sophia soaked a rag from her pack with the gin and dabbed each whip cut. Aiden tensed before she even touched him, his shoulders nearly touching his ears, and while she worked on his flayed skin, trying not to let her anger make her rough, Cassandra came and stood beside her. Ignoring Sophia, she made a sympathetic kind of grimace at Aiden.

'Thank you,' she said. She stroked her stomach, a soft, tender touch. 'My baby and I wouldn't have survived. I know that.'

My brother is barely surviving, and for what? Sophia worked quickly and efficiently, sprinkling what little she had left of the powdered alum on his wounds to reduce the pain and inflammation, and then bound his back with a cloth.

For a while he attempted to pretend he was okay. Of course he did. He was the son their mum and dad adored. But his face became red and he began to perspire and soon dropped the pretence. 'It burns bad, Sophia.'

'The burning will pass,' she said. She hoped that was the truth but didn't really know. There might not have been enough powder left to do him any good.

***

Sophia awoke to a violent crash of thunder and flashes of lightning washed through the cave in a continuous motion as the storm moved directly overhead. Darkness. Then in the streaks of blue and white she saw on the ceiling a majestic chimera of a stag and a boar. The chimera was being hunted. The alternating dark and light of the lightning created a moving quality to the picture. A man clung to the wild beast jabbing his spear into its gut. If ever such an animal existed she didn't know. Darkness again.

Checking on her brother she couldn't tell whether he breathed or not. He lay so unmoving, like a corpse. She held her own breath thinking how would she live without him? She placed her hand over his heart and waited, heaving a long drawn sigh when she felt a muted thump.

At dawn she left the cave. The town square was empty, not a sound except the wind and the swaying back and forth of the hanged man on the gallows. She hopped over the crumbly wooden fence and stood on the ridge, gazing down the slope to a stream, an effervescent seam trickling alongside the foothills of the mountain range.

A door opened behind her. A short and flabby old woman hobbled outside and began to sweep the doorway. Sophia approached her and inquired for lodging. A room for three people. The woman looked at her shrewdly before asking for payment.

'Of course.' Sophia delved into her pocket and handed the woman Joel's favour paper, which she straightened to read but quickly dismissed. 'Maybe this, then?' Sophia reached into her pocket again and handed the woman the only other item she had hoped would get her a room.

The woman took the green, glinting rock, turned it in her hand and brought it close to her bloodshot eye. 'Now that's a lovely thing, although I don't know what it's good for. Can't make me supper with a rock. What is it, exactly?'

'A dream rock,' said Sophia. 'You kiss it before bed and it makes your dreams come true.'

'Does it now? Have your dreams ever come true, lassie?'

'Oh, yes. Plenty of times. Can't count all the times they did, so many they were.'

The woman kissed the rock and put it in her pocket. 'Don't lie, lassie. You wouldn't have ended up here if your dreams had come true. But I fancy the shining, so you got yourself a room.'

Kasimir

Ruby's star maps have more than a hundred constellations sketched out. My mother knows all the names by heart. Romping Bear. Sneezing Ladybug. Trilling Frog. Ruby has a name for the dimmest sparkle. She is a source of fresh brightness in a joyless world. But when my mother returns from one of the slave trade expeditions, Ruby has gone. A typhus, her father says.

The intensity of the grief surprises my mother. The void Ruby leaves is as vast as the night sky she delighted in mapping.

Aiden

The girl slept propped upright against the cave wall. With her mouth open slightly, her face had a sweet blankness she was far too sharp to show when awake. Aware the terrible burning in his back had abated, Aiden shifted a little, testing for damage. Immediately the pain from his cuts burrowed deep through his muscles and nerves to a point at the centre of his body. He tentatively fingered the thin dressing covering his wounds, feeling welts of skin steely rigid, like corrugated fencing, and he took his hands away not wanting to explore further. His body had become something he didn't recognise. His stifled groan sounded loud in the quiet of the room but Cassandra slept on. Only her belly moved under her clothing, the baby within her stirring and stretching. Aiden found a strange satisfaction in being privy to this moment. All the while her name danced a melody through his mind. Cassandra. Her steady breath puffed out gently and he sank back against the covers content to watch her.

The peace didn't last for long as Sophia bustled through the entrance, bringing a movement of air through the cave and scent of outdoor freshness in her clothes.

'I've found us somewhere for us to stay,' she said.

'How have you managed that?'

'Oh, Joel's favours. I gave them to a woman in exchange for a room and she can get food with it.'

His sister's breezy manner worked upon his suspicious mind. Whenever she was like this he knew things were skirted over or left unsaid. 'And that's enough?'

'Yes.' She nudged Cassandra's foot with her own.

'Come on, move yourself.'

Cassandra glowered. She felt the wall to gain a purchase and moaned softly as she hauled herself up. Aiden watched her touch her stomach and murmur. 'Be good. Don't kick so much.' And he looked away feeling like an intruder now she was awake.

Sophia gathered their belongings into a pile. She folded Aiden's blood soaked shirt, dry now, and neatly placed it in his pack. 'We'd best go. I don't trust that woman not to sell our room to someone else if we don't turn up soon.'

Struggling with his jacket, his back too sore to give the leverage needed to shrug it on properly, Aiden stood helplessly. He did not wish to communicate the severity of the pain to his sister, she was unhappy enough he had taken the beating in the first place. He then felt gentle fingers on his neck as Cassandra caught hold of the coat and pulled it into place. The weight and stiffness of the jacket hemmed him in, suffocating with its pressure against his soreness and he wanted to shake it off again, but Cassandra's hand lingered on his collar lifting it higher to cover more of his neck. When satisfied it would stay in place she gave his shoulder a soft stroke. 'It's cold outside,' was all she said.

Feeling his breath hitch at her nearness, he fastened the buttons to occupy himself before plunging his hands deep into the pockets. Empty. 'Hang on, Sophia, I've lost Lila's charm.'

He crouched over the spot where his jacket had lain, scrutinising the floor of the cave. It was dusty and stony but a green shamrock would have stood out. He spread his search. Cassandra came beside him, walking alongside and staring at the ground. 'What are we looking for?'

'A little green charm, the shape of a leaf.' He felt stupid saying it but when she didn't mock him, he added, 'It's dear to me.'

Sophia tapped her foot. 'Aiden, it could be anywhere. Maybe it fell when Joel carried you, who knows?' She shrugged impatiently. 'We have to go.'

Their walk to the new lodgings was a slow one with every few steps sending a ripple of pain through his back. The wind blew directly into Aiden's face, icy blasts from the night's rain that made his eyes smart. He blinked and pinched the bridge of his nose to clear his vision and wiped his hand across his eyes. The wind tugged at the backpack in his other hand, causing it to rear up unwieldly and jerk his shoulder. Cassandra offered to carry the pack but some kind of false pride, which often got the better of him, stopped him accepting her offer. Besides, he required her to feel indebted to him, so when he sought answers to the many questions he wanted to ask she would be obliged to tell him. The questions burned in him, niggling to be asked, but not out here where the wind snatched conversation from his lips before the words were fully formed.

Sophia stopped outside the last house on a row of terraced cottages. Brown, serpentine cracks split the bulk of the walls into brittle lumps. A few of the windows were broken or boarded up with rotting planks, but most were intact. Someone moved in the shadow of one, before the door opened to reveal a squat, flabby woman of indeterminate age. 'Ah good, I've been keeping an eye out for you.'

Sophia skittered in front of the woman as though to hide Aiden from her view and he wondered how bad he looked. Cassandra cast a sharp glance at Sophia but he had no strength to ponder on it, even though his sister was babbling in a false upbeat tone.

'Yes,' she was saying. 'If you can just show us where to go, we'll be out of your way.'

They followed the woman through a dimly lit hallway, smelling of leek and boiled turnip. Oak wainscoting lined the stairwell and provided a curious richness to the otherwise shabby interior, but felt sticky to the touch. They filed up the narrow staircase and the wood creaked a protest. If he hadn't seen for himself Aiden would never have believed the woman's bulk could have fitted through so small a passageway.

At the top of the stairs was a large loft space. Its high ceiling, open to the eaves of the roof, allowed them to stand upright without fear of banging their heads on the beams. A tin wash basin and three makeshift beds were on the floor with a couple of blankets apiece. The grimy wallpaper peeled in curled strips edged with a greasy residue.

The woman fingered something on the front of her blouse. 'You're paid up for the week. Lodgings only, this room and that smaller one adjacent to it. The outhouse is down in the yard. No drunken disorderlies. And I don't take kindly to too much comings and goings.' She glared at Cassandra as if she alone would be a nuisance but the girl just glared back at her.

'Lie down and rest,' Sophia told him. 'I'm going to get medicine and food.' She followed the woman from the room, closing the door behind her.

Alone with Cassandra, Aiden dropped his backpack by the side of a bed and watched as she kicked the bed beside his away from the others. Perhaps it was her way of saying she was not one of them. Glancing over at him she went to the door, stooped and pressed her right ear to listen at the keyhole. Her cheek rested against the wooden hole, her lips parted, oh so slightly, eyes down staring over her left shoulder with intense concentration.

'Hey? Cassandra?' Standing in a shaft of wintry light, the lines on her face deepened and she appeared much older as she regarded him with her solemn expression. 'You know where my parents are, don't you?' said Aiden.

'I might.'

'Can you show me the way on a map?'

'No,' she said.

'You owe me that.'

'You don't know my people. They would put a bullet in your head before you knew they were watching. Forget about your parents.'

Anger fired his nerves. He fumbled weakly with his jacket and at last took out the map from an inner pocket. 'Here,' he tapped the map on a point to the west of the city. 'Jake said your people would want to put them on a boat. They should be somewhere around the docks. Here, right?'

Cassandra's gaze veered away from the map, driving a spear of heat through him. 'Will you look, damn you?' She flinched. Clenching his fist to a tight ball, Aiden swallowed a deep breath to cool his temper. 'I only want you to look. Is that so difficult? Well?'

'No, it's not difficult.' Cassandra pushed the map away. 'I am looking. The north on your map isn't accurate.'

Aiden needed to reconsider how she could help. 'You could come with us? Show us the way?'

She lifted her head and stared at him defiantly. 'I risked my life running away from that place. I'm not going back.'

Aiden sensed her holding something back. Secrets she would not let him probe. But probe he had to. 'I thought they were family to you? Who runs away from family?'

The evening crept into the room playing on her sombre face. 'Not you, obviously.' She sat down on one of the beds. 'Look, I know what you're going through. My mum was taken from me, same as yours.' The window rattled in its frame and she pulled the covers over her legs. 'Long time ago, but some things you remember like they just happened.' Her voice fell to a whisper, clogged with memory. 'I remember kicking a ball on the shore among the rocks, my feet black with tar. I was only little.' Cassandra put her fingers to her lips miming to an action her recollection had immersed her in. 'Shush, be quiet, my mother said. Keep to the rocks and I'll catch us a big fish for dinner. She hugged me then, before leaving. A moment later I heard the screams. I peeked from behind the rocks. Men had surrounded her on the steps of the quay, dragging her away.' Cassandra stopped. Her face held the bewildered appearance of the newly bereaved.

Aiden swallowed the lump in his throat. Somehow she had drawn him along with her. 'I'm sorry,' he muttered.

'I wanted to run after her but I couldn't move. That was the last time I saw my mum.'

'Think you'll see her again?'

'No. Don't suppose I'd even recognise her if I did.'

'So no one is family to you?'

Cassandra's face changed, hardened. 'No.'

He waited for her to continue but she said nothing else. It started to rain and the room became dark as night-time. Aiden struck a match and lit a piece of candle on the window sill.

'Are your parents like you and your sister?' she said.

'How do you mean?'

'You know, can they read and write? Are they book learned?'

'Yes.' Aiden thought of the map he had just shown her. The map his father had taken great pains over and risked much to provide a semblance of accuracy.

'Then they will still be alive. My people make use of those with knowledge.'

'Maybe you've seen them?'

'Maybe. What do they look like? Any distinguishing features?'

How could he tell her their distinguishing features when the ones he valued the most were invisible to the eye? Their kindness, their strength, their love. The image of his parents sprang to mind and with it the sting of tears at the back of his throat. But whether the tears were for seeing his father's face in its entirety or because his mother's was only a blur, he had no way of knowing. 'They're just ordinary. Nothing special.'

'Names then? I'm good with names.'

'Seb...'

Cassandra tipped her head to one side and frowned.

'No. Sorry.'

'Amelia?' A wave of melancholy hit him. So long as he didn't speak their names Aiden could refrain from considering the worst. That his parents might no longer be alive. Now the sound of their names robbed him of his pretence.

'Amelia? I know Amelia!'

'You do?' His breath caught.

Cassandra nodded, rapid little shakes as she spoke quickly. 'She's lovely. She cares for the children, makes puppets out of old, torn socks and spins such stories.' Cassandra sighed, a bemused expression crossing her features.

A sense that all was not lost crossed through Aiden. That sounded like his mother. It was just the kind of thing she would do. 'Do you have many children there?'

'Yes. We do.' A shadow passed over her face. 'It's not a good place for children. The boys are raised to be soldiers. They are taught to fight as soon as they can run.'

They sat for a while not a word uttered between them, but sometimes words were not needed. Aiden heard his breath ragged in the quiet and hoped the girl would put it down to pain rather than the unfamiliar sensation which moved inside him.

A couple of hours later Sophia clattered into the room, her face animated. She held a bag of twigs and a small phial of clear fluid. 'Witch hazel.' She wriggled the phial at Aiden. 'Enough for two applications.'

Cassandra stood in her slow, careful way. 'How did you manage to steal that?'

Sophia glanced at Cassandra as though she was

nothing more than a repellent maggot. 'I'm not a thief. I helped the local healer prepare remedies. Might get something to eat tomorrow too, he said, if I prove myself. You could come with me and do some work yourself. That's what decent people do.'

'I don't know anything about making remedies.'

'You'll just need to watch me. We might be paid a jar of soup. I say it's worth it. Now let's put this medicine to good use.'

Aiden shouldered out of his jacket and took off his shirt. Sophia washed his wounds with the liquid and he wriggled under her touch, biting his lips to keep from crying out when the pain rekindled.

Trailing a finger across each cut, she prodded and probed. 'They are crusted over and feel firm. The area around the scabs doesn't look too red and the heat is dying.' She poked her face into his. 'Although you won't think so for a few days yet.'

She was still mad at him, he could tell. He grabbed her hands in his. 'Sophia, mum's alive.'

'What?' Half glancing at Cassandra by his side she added, 'What are you saying?'

'I know Amelia,' Cassandra said. 'She was alive when I left. She's of use. They won't kill her.'

Sophia's lip trembled and she bit down hard into it, so hard it bled, then she went and sat on the empty bed.

'Sophia?' Aiden didn't understand her reaction. She should be elated.

'Get some rest.' She turned into the covers.

Sometime later Aiden awoke. He brought his hand to his pocket but, of course, the rock had gone. Uneasy and worrying that its loss meant he had somehow betrayed Lila he fidgeted with the covers. It would break her heart, if she ever found out. He got up to shut the window. Caught in a draught, he struggled to close it, fighting against the wind. Returning to his bed he saw Cassandra watching him, her head pillowed on the palm of her hand. She yawned and then turned over onto her other side. He got under the covers, his thoughts filled with her. Who was this girl that encroached on his feelings? Someone's wife or lover? Someone's property that was for certain. But he had never met anyone so their own person. Would it be fair to drag her back with him? Sophia would have no qualms doing that. He knew his sister, sometimes there was no reasoning with her. She would expect a price to be paid for his suffering.

Tiredness overtook him and he closed his eyes. The pretty face of Cassandra imprinted on his mind's eye lightened his spirit and he fell into a peaceful sleep.

Kasimir

Tinker Caldry is a survivor. He survived the ending of one way of life and the beginning of another and wanders freely between coast and mountains. His heart holds music and he plays the accordion that is always strapped to his back, like a body part. My mother is won over when he plays a lyrical tune to her stomach. ‘For the wee laddie,’ he grins.

I kick my pleasure and she smiles at Tinker Caldry. Her heart lightens for the first time since my father died.

Sophia

An ache low in her back penetrated Sophia's sleep. She groaned not ready to wake, turning this way and that but the pain persisted, pulling her towards consciousness. Her stomach roiled, a familiar surging she recognised as the start of her monthly bleed. Opening her eyes, she gazed unseeing at the ceiling. Relief was there that Tucker's seed hadn't caught, but sadness too, now all traces of their union had gone. She longed to believe someday they might be together again.

The other two were still asleep. She felt a stab of envy, watching Cassandra's stomach stretch beyond the covers, her bellyful of baby mocking her own flat one. Aiden lay face down, his blanket rucked beneath him. His relaxed limbs spilled over the sides of the bed, heavy and peaceful.

Sophia kicked off her blanket wondering how long she had slept. Must be early, the waxing moon still hung in the dawn light waiting to set. She pulled a roll of rags from her pack and separated a few strips from the wodge to take with her to the outhouse. Then she tapped Cassandra's shoulder until the girl turned to her. 'Get up,' she whispered.

'What?'

'We're going to work.'

Cassandra pulled the cover over her head. 'Let me sleep.'

'Don't make me drag you out of bed,' Sophia warned, knowing there was little chance she could make good the threat, feeling as she did.

The girl grunted. 'Soph, for the sake of Amelia I'm

trying hard to like you, so piss off and give yourself a fighting chance.' She turned back to face the wall.

That the girl could allude to her mother and be so downright defiant in the same breath made Sophia want to clout her, shake her, and make her teeth rattle, but her stomach had other ideas. Confronting Cassandra would have to wait. Sophia crept down the stairs holding her breath against the indeterminate smells lurking under the constant stench of boiled vegetables that permeated the scullery. Aggressive snores blasted from the living area and Sophia saw the woman sprawled on a couch. Lila's charm twinkled from the woman's saggy breast. She was obviously taken with the jewel but how Sophia wished she could snatch it back, replay the moment and change the outcome.

The yard must have been something of a sun trap for the paintwork on the outhouse door was blistered into crisp flakes of paint which followed the contours of the wood. Fragments stuck to Sophia's fingers as she pulled it open. Hurrying now, Sophia undid her trousers and sat on the wooden seat of the toilet. Already she knew this bleed was going to be a bad one. Panic flooded through her, increasing her discomfort. If only she hadn't used the last of her supply of cramp bark on Lila's mother. She leaned her forehead against the cross strut of the door willing her stomach to stop its pulsing when a thump on the other side made her jump.

'How much longer you going to be?' Cassandra rattled the metal latch.

'Just coming,' Sophia answered and made herself stand. Clutching the wodge of rags, she pressed against the door for support but the latch sprang and the last thing she heard was Cassandra saying, 'Oh fuck, you look like shit.'

Cold water flicked over her face and Sophia came round flapping her hands to stop the unpleasant sensation. The water was icy. Goosebumps stood along her forearms and her shirt was untucked sending chilly breezes along her back. Looking up she saw she was under the spout of the outside tap. Its piping, crudely lashed together with black tape, pressed into the side of her head. A comforting pad of rag was wedged between her legs and she felt her face flush, remembering she hadn't placed it there herself. Bent over her Cassandra looked heated, sweaty and awkward. She let out a sigh that puffed through her cheeks. 'Bloody hell, Soph. That was one fright. Can you get up?'

Nodding, she grasped Cassandra's hands and was jerked to her feet. The girl was a lot stronger than her appearance suggested. 'Thanks,' she muttered. 'How long was I out?'

Cassandra shrugged. 'Long enough.'

'I'm sorry. My first day tends to be this way.' Struggling to stand, her mind felt shrouded in fog. 'I must get going. Promised the healer I'd be there first thing this morning.'

'Sit for a moment. Give yourself a chance to recover, will you?'

'Can't be late.' Swaying a little on wobbly legs, she almost fell again.

Cassandra grabbed hold of her, linking her arm through Sophia's. 'Careful.' She raised an eyebrow. 'I suppose I'd better come with you to the healer. Bit extreme behaviour just to get your own way.'

Sophia felt a weak smile curve her lips. 'Yeah, that's

the truth.'

'Will he pay us with more food if the two of us work?'

'He ought to. But I don't know.'

Putting her hands under the tap, Sophia rinsed them and swooshed her mouth of the foul tart taste, and then they slowly walked back inside the house. The woman's snores still drilled through the air and Sophia was relieved to note she had turned her back to them. Cassandra was more than capable of noticing the jewel and linking it to Aiden's description of the missing shamrock, and that was one trouble she could do without.

Upstairs Aiden sat on the edge of his bed, awake, but only just. 'Try to rest. We'll be gone awhile,' Sophia told him. He looked more than happy to oblige by lying down again.

They left and walked among the houses on the wind-swept ridge, the gold streaked slope rolling westward like a wave. Gouged into the mountainside, the valley below was hidden by mist but where it was thinnest a fire shone through.

'There's a town in the foothills at the edge of the marsh,' said Cassandra. 'The fire serves as a beacon for the hunters. Guides them home.'

'How do you know that?'

'I came that way,' she said. 'You okay?'

'What?'

'You look upset.'

Sophia dragged in a lungful of air. 'I need to ask you something.'

'Go on, then. But come back a bit. You're walking

way too closely to the edge.'

'It's been a week or so. Do you think my parents are still at your... *that* city?'

'I don't know. When I left they were still there.'

Sophia took a breath but felt no relief. It was the uncertainty that stifled her.

The healer had a shack of a place away from the main drag of the town, with wooden barrels lined along the outside wall collecting rainfall. A small perforated keg raised up on blocks dripped lye into a glass bowl placed underneath. It tilted precariously on a wonky flagstone and Sophia edged it, very carefully, onto even ground with the toe of her shoe. She pushed the door. A bell rang loudly, trailing the chime through to the back of the shop where it tinkled faintly.

'Hello, Mr. Pepin,' she called.

The wooden floor sounded hollow underfoot and the air reeked of noxious odours competing with each other. Cassandra wrinkled her nose and pretended to gag. Sophia frowned at her but wanted to laugh. She hid her smile by looking away but had to admit for all the girl had been through she managed to keep a sense of fun about her.

A thin man came from the back room. The whiff of a pungent concoction emanated from his clothing. His tapered sideburns and deep lines carved either side of his nose could have given him a supercilious air except for the one eyebrow singed to a frizz, creating a comical lopsidedness. His hands were speckled with splatter burns. Cassandra studied him. He must have felt the strength of her gaze for he returned her look but spoke to Sophia.

'The payment is still a jug of soup no matter how

many friends you bring.'

Cassandra stared pointedly at his jumper riddled with scorch marks. 'Are you sure it's safe here?'

Sophia felt a wave of nausea sweep over her. Why was everything such a bloody fight? 'A jug of soup *and* a couple of jars of pickled eggs.'

He pushed his hands through his hair in a distracted manner but then his stance sharpened as he scrutinised Sophia. 'Looks like you're in need of a remedy yourself. May I?' Gently he took her face in his hands feeling along her neck with his thumbs. Then he pulled down her bottom eye lids. 'Very pale,' he muttered. 'Blood loss?'

She felt herself redden but before she could answer Cassandra nodded a yes. 'Loads,' she said gruesomely. Sophia didn't argue.

'Hmm, I see.'

The man wandered over to a long counter that ran the length of the wall and lifted a hinged flap that allowed passage through. On the wall behind the counter were shelves of dark glass bottles. His hand hovered along the middle shelf until he came to a tubby green flask which he pulled down and unscrewed the lid. Then he poured thirty drops of pale liquid into a phial, added a teaspoon of sugar alcohol and shook it vigorously.

'We'll double the dosage until the effects are noted,' he said and handed her a small cup. 'And it's one jar of pickled eggs,' he added.

Cassandra wandered over to the counter and ran her finger along the wood. 'You live alone?' She made the movement sexy, though Sophia could see this was unintentional.

The man peered down his long nose. His eyes sunk into the pouches beneath them, making them small and mean. 'What business is it of yours?'

'Have you seen the state of it in here?' Cassandra held up the phial he had just used to the light. It clearly showed a greasy residual on the glass. 'Needs a woman's touch.'

'Indeed.'

'Well, I'm not clever like Soph here but I could scrub this place up good. Got to be worth an extra jar of eggs. No?'

'Maybe.'

'No maybe about it.' She held out her hands as though they were a pair of scales and she was measuring. 'What's a jar of eggs against several hours of hard work?' She tipped the imaginary scales in his favour. 'I think you got yourself a bargain.'

Sophia closed her eyes. Did this girl ever stop arguing? Cassandra nudged her. 'Come on Soph. Don't look so tragic.'

The day passed in a flurry of activity. Cassandra must have enjoyed it for most of the day the girl sang to herself, or maybe to the baby, as she scoured the counter and washed pipettes in hot tubs of bubbly water. At the end of the day Mr. Pepin managed a smile, as he gave them their payment. One jug of soup and two jars of pickled eggs, although one of the jars was decidedly smaller than the other.

When they returned to their lodging they found Aiden sitting on the bed looking so rigid he might have been carved from stone. Sophia rushed forward thinking pain had got the better of him. 'Here let me help—'

'Don't touch me.'

She stopped, realising his pinched expression was the white heat of fury and in the silence that followed all she heard was the window rattling as the wind's icy blasts hit against the glass.

'What's wrong?'

Aiden stared at her hard-eyed, his hair plastered to the sides of his head. 'You took Lila's shamrock and gave it to that woman. I saw her wearing it.'

It was as though the same icy blasts from outside had reached into the room and chilled her through. 'I'm sorry. I had to pay for the room with something.'

'You should have given her something of yours.' He spoke the words quietly, which made her feel worse than if he'd shouted.

'I didn't have anything. Not anything someone would want.'

'It was a gift, Sophia. You don't get to trade other people's gifts. Worse still, when I was looking for it you let me think it was lost. You're bloody unbelievable.'

His bewilderment cut through her. 'I'm sorry. I thought you'd never know.' As soon as the words left her mouth she knew she'd said it wrong but it was too late to backtrack now.

Cassandra grimaced and shook her head at Sophia, then wandered over to her bed, kicking off her shoes. 'What's so special about this shamrock anyway?' she asked. 'This Lila? She a girlfriend?'

Aiden threw her a slanted sideways look. 'No.' He

paused, suddenly preoccupied with his shoe. 'She was just a brave little girl.'

What had she done? Sophia stared at Aiden. 'Oh, Aiden. I'm sorry. Really.'

The room went still. Sophia felt they were locked into a moment where every little detail was brought to the foreground, like the blend of emotions flitting across Cassandra's face as she stared at Aiden. Jealousy, regret, and something else Sophia couldn't put a name to but was disturbed by the depth of feeling it carried. Time pressed on her like a lead weight and she urged Aiden to undress so she could wash and apply the witch hazel to his back. 'Please Aiden, I know you are mad but let me.' He shrugged her away.

Cassandra lowered herself onto her bed with a sigh. 'For fuck's sake Aiden, do as she says. We've worked hard for that gloopy shit. And the sooner you mend, the sooner we can go our separate ways.' She eyeballed them both. 'You twins are something else.' But just what they were she didn't expand on.

Sophia held out the bottle and Aiden silently removed his shirt. Opening it, she realised Mr. bloody Pepin had only given her half the quantity he had the day before. 'What a cheating...'

Words failed her as anger licked hot against her insides. Shrugging it aside she washed Aiden's back, stopping whenever he shouted about how his back was on fire, but at least the flesh around his wounds was less swollen now and Sophia allowed herself an inward sigh of relief. Afterwards he towelled away the sheen of sweat covering his skin. Sophia wanted to help him put his shirt back on but he pushed her away and she knew he would take his time forgiving her.

She pried open the jug of soup and pale and unappetising though it was, her imagination conjured up the smell of onions and parsley and she felt the tang of vinegar on her lips. 'You first,' she said, handing the jug to Aiden. He drank a couple of glugs and then climbed back into bed, drawing the blanket up to his chin. 'There are pickled eggs, too,' Sophia said but he had already dozed off.

Having finished eating, Sophia went to fill a bucket with water from the tap and carried it inside. She took the basin near to her bed and wandered through to the adjacent room and emptied half the bucket into the basin. She undressed, stepped inside it and sat. Raising the bucket above her head she tipped it, letting the icy water wash her body. She removed the rag and rubbed her hand between her legs to clean the dark stain of blood. She did a quick body check, the healer in her noted her hand was mending and the stomach cramps had abated. If only the bad taste of deceiving Aiden could be easily dismissed and her heart wasn't so saddened with missing Tucker. Tears of self-pity welled up and she sat in the red puddle of water until Cassandra banged on the door asking what the hell she was doing in there.

The decision to stay for the week proved a good one, for each day saw Aiden's strength rebuilding. Little by little he moved with more ease although he wouldn't be able to lay on his back fully for a few weeks yet. Mr. Pepin continued to offer work and Sophia lived with the hope he would pay them fairly but Cassandra told her not to be such a dreamer. Journeying to and fro each morning and evening, listening to Cassandra's breezy chatter, allowed Sophia to gain a better understanding about the society that had stolen her parents. It didn't fill her with hope for a positive outcome but her respect for Cassandra grew as she got to know her and what she had run from. Sophia also knew they would part company soon and she for one would be sad, but there was no way she could ask Cassandra to go back with them.

The last evening coming back from the healer, Sophia pushed open the door to find Aiden waiting with their backpacks ready to be filled.

'Here, add this to your stockpile.' Cassandra handed him a full phial of arnica and a pile of fresh strips of cloth.

Sophia gasped. 'When did you steal that?'

'Last thing. He'll not miss it. Old fool had no idea of half his stock, living in that squalor. Would have got you an extra jar of eggs but they were too damn heavy.'

Sophia snorted a laugh. 'You are impossible.' She stored everything away carefully in her backpack, along with some rations she had managed to gather together.

Aiden cast a sidelong glance at Cassandra. 'You coming with us?'

'My plan is to go as far south as I can. All the way to the south shore. There's a few fishing towns I've heard still exist. I'll settle in one. Unless there's a boat, then I'll ask to be ferried to the land across the water.'

'Is that a good idea? You don't know what people overseas are like.'

Cassandra shrugged. She looked at the twins, her face heavy with sadness. 'I have to protect my baby.'

She started to turn away but Aiden moved forward and grabbed her wrist to pull her to him but then dropped them to his side. 'We won't stop you from leaving.'

'I know.'

The mood of the evening changed and the room felt heavy with partings, each of them isolated, huddling in their own pocket of misery. Sophia went to wash. The adjacent room had become a haven for her, somewhere to do her thinking, the fractured glass in the window and the chilled water caused no distraction to her reeling thoughts.

The door opened. Sophia started from her musings. 'Yeah?'

'Only me.' Cassandra came into the room and sat on the floor. A meagre shaft of moonlight broke through the clouds cloaking the sky and encircled them. Sophia took it as a sign.

'You're coming with us, aren't you?'

'Yes.'

'Weren't you going the other way?'

Cassandra gave a wry grin. 'I was. But I feel I'm in your debt. If it weren't for Aiden, I would have lost my baby already. And thanks to you I've had food and shelter the last few days. I liked your mother and now there is a chance for her rescue... well... I'll go with you some of the way. Show you the road down the mountain and into the woods and marshes. Then we'll see.'

'Thank you, Cassandra.' Surprised at how lighter she felt, the words seemed inadequate somehow and Sophia was compelled to give Cassandra a way out. 'Are you sure about this?'

Cassandra looked down at her stomach and gave it

a tender rub. 'I'm sure.'

Even in the half-light Sophia could feel the love there. But some things just didn't add up. 'Where's the father? Do you mind me asking?'

'No Soph, I don't mind. He died shortly after I got pregnant.'

'I'm sorry.'

'Me too.' She had a pinched look between her eyes. 'He was a good man. But I'm running away from another and he has the means to search everywhere.'

'Sounds like you'd be better with us.' Sophia stepped from the basin and dried herself. 'Right under his nose where he least expects it.'

Cassandra smiled wryly. 'Maybe.'

Sophia reached out and touched Cassandra's arm, tugging her sleeve gently. 'Let's go tell Aiden. It'll make his day.'

Kasimir

To my uncle my future is decided. He speaks openly but has sorely misjudged my mother.

Down at the shore, the sea shimmers in solitude. A single white wave washes my mother's bare feet. She will miss the sea but makes her decision. Secretly, at dead of night she leaves, quietly, without fuss. She packs enough but worries at its lack. To stay where there is plenty is no longer a choice, there is no future at the port.

I kick softly, my toes scrape her ribcage, wiggling with approval. I know she understands. She allows herself to smile.

Aiden

They left town moving down a road fringed with deadwood that often dipped sharply into deep ruts. Looking back, Aiden could no longer see the bell tower, only the wavy rim of the ridge silhouetted against the sky.

He still couldn't believe Cassandra was here with them, showing the way. He had dreaded parting from her. All morning he had been so at peace watching her gooning around as she packed the jug of soup, the jar half filled with pickled eggs and the lump of hard onion bread she pretended to crack her teeth on before putting it in the bag. His gaze followed her now as she wandered over to him, took his hand in hers, closing his fingers around a small item.

'What...?' He frowned but opening his hand and seeing Lila's shamrock there, wanted to hug her.

Cassandra grinned at him. 'Happy now?' He was. He had thought Lila's precious gift was lost to him. 'It's a pretty thing, best keep it away from Soph,' she added slyly.

Sophia answered with a wry smile. 'Never thought I'd be grateful to a low-born thief, but I am.'

A shout of laughter exploded from Cassandra and all at once they were friends. Aiden wondered at her skill in deflecting anger as he pocketed the charm. 'Thanks,' he said.

A column of light streaked the mountainside as the sun broke through the cloud cover, showering them in goldenness. Cassandra laughed delightedly at the sudden warmth. She sounded so young and carefree, and with her spray of freckles across her nose, some blurred into others, he had to look away to stop himself from touching them, unexpectedly struck by how beautiful she was to him.

At the side of the road a cart half-buried in snow was turned on its side. Aiden tore the tarp from the top and rummaged through the contents, pulling out the one object that wasn't complete junk, a frayed blanket worked with seashells.

'So pretty,' Cassandra murmured. 'My mum sewed a quilt like this when her sister gave birth. It had colourful patterns and ribbon tabs.' She sighed dreamily. 'How personal random junk can feel.'

The ground changed underfoot. From snowy to stony shingle, becoming damper and muddier as they drew closer to the fens. An overpowering earthiness rose thickly as they crushed the spongy carpet of peat bog where the ground levelled out. By evening they stood at the foothills and all around them the marsh smelled of mildew and moss. In the distance a fire burned.

'We're getting close,' said Cassandra. 'Now we need to decide if we go through the woodland to get to the city, or around it.'

'Should we go around?' said Aiden.

'That will extend our journey by a couple of days.'

'Then we'll go through them,' said Sophia. 'We'll also be less visible.'

'Well, we can't be sure about that,' said Cassandra. 'My people sometimes go there to hunt.'

At nightfall they camped on a soft tuft of mossy turf. Resting their heads on their packs they spread the blanket with seashells over them. The trees surrounding them like ancient sentinels, grey and contorted, as though protesting the betrayal of a once nurturing land. Aiden's back tensed and felt raw with the increase of exercise and he moved to sit up. His sister had dozed off but Cassandra was still awake, watching him. He tucked the blanket around her protruding belly wishing his hand could linger there. What he really wanted was to tear the clothes from her, feel her body against his. He smiled at her, feeling foolish, glad she couldn't read his thoughts. She smiled back, kissed two of her fingers and placed them on his lips before snuggling into the blanket and closing her eyes. His hand traced over his lips trying to capture her touch. He was so taken with her, so captivated... when had that happened? It was a long while before he slept.

A hand tugged at his shirt, pulling him from his dream. 'People are coming.' Cassandra's voice came from the darkness. 'Sounds like hunters.'

'Your people?'

'Could be.'

He pushed aside the blanket and got to his feet when a shot roared. His heart bounded violently. Then he saw the flickering light of torches. Sophia grabbed his arm. 'Come. This way.'

They ran in the opposite direction to the lights but when Aiden glanced behind him, the torches were always there, floating in the gloom like fireflies, hot and golden. The ground sank sharply under their feet sending them rolling into prickly underwood. Concern for Cassandra and the baby jolted through him.

'Are you all right?'

'Just got a bloody nose.'

'Sure you didn't hit your belly?'

'Positively sure.'

'Better to stay in the ditch,' said Sophia.

He agreed. They took their pistols from their belts and hunkered down. A tread in the dark along the ditch had him holding his breath. The light of a torch pierced the gloom and two men appeared at the edge of the ditch, so close Aiden could smell their sullied feet.

'Anything?'

'Nothing.'

'Reckon she's gone?'

'The dogs will find her.' The nearest man, lean and tall with a moustache, peered into the dark behind Aiden. 'They'll eat her alive.'

The man standing further away sounded doubtful. 'That girl's smart, you know.'

'Is she now?'

'She let the dogs have her dinners all through summer. Can you believe that? Even gave them a ball to chase, no idea where she found that. They won't betray her, not these mutts.'

'The traps will get her. The place is littered with them.' As if to satisfy his curiosity, the nearest man cast one last look into the ditch, his scornful eyes meeting Aiden's.

'What in the devil?' A gunshot rang out. Blood squirted from the man's cheek and he tumbled.

'Run,' Sophia shouted, her smoking gun pointed at the man and the world exploded into a frenzy of action. Aiden grabbed Cassandra's hand and they clambered out of the ditch and ran, the immenseness of the swamp working against them. Cassandra stumbled and fell with a cry of pain. He hauled her up and they hunched behind a fallen log, watching the torches bob in the dark.

'Can you run?'

'I've hurt my leg.'

'Fuck, okay.' He turned to his sister for some help but Sophia wasn't with them. He called her name just as a peal of thunder rang through the valley and his voice drowned in the rumble. A sheet of electricity branched through a patchwork sky of tattered clouds, pursuing a downward plunge into the earth. Another rumble, directly overhead, and then a cloud burst. The abrupt evacuation cascaded over the land and drenched them. Aiden felt as though the weight of every possible destructive energy was conspiring against them.

'Come on.' He helped Cassandra to her feet and together they staggered to a cluster of trees, moving further into the woods, only stopping when the tree line thinned to a clearing. Reluctant to push out into the open, they struggled to catch their breath.

Cassandra spoke between gasps. 'Don't worry, we'll find her.'

Even now, she could read his thoughts and offer him hope. 'Of course we will,' he said, taking his cue from her and trying to stem the fear engulfing him.

Guttural shouts ripped through the night and mingled with the hurried stamp of feet. Men called to one another. 'Over here, this way.' And more sinisterly, singing out one name, dragging the syllables. 'Martha.'

Noise surrounded them. The sounds near one moment, distant the next, made it difficult to gauge their number but they moved with purpose and had a set goal. 'Martha, come on girl, give yourself up.'

At one point Aiden was convinced he heard the hoarse rasp of a dog straining against a leash. He pulled Cassandra back into the shadows against him, glad the rain had saturated their clothing and hoping the dampness of the air would deflect their scent.

A slosh of muddy footsteps, followed by a rich stream of expletives. 'Bloody soaked. *Fucking* cunt. You wait bitch, 'til I get hold of you...'

Cassandra's eyes widened. *She knew that voice.* Aiden squeezed her hand, offering a reassurance he didn't own.

From a different direction came the patter of feet. Then a cry. A thick branch prone on the woodland floor sprang into life with more sibilance than twang like the tree had gasped its resurrection. The net attached swung freely from its new height and within something writhed, a feral bundle of hands and feet clawing for an exit. Cassandra stumbled backwards into Aiden, the force almost knocking him off-balance. He steadied himself and prevented her from falling, his arms encircling her and holding her to him.

Inside the net a woman thrashed at the unforgiving cord, her cries more animal than human. Below her stood a man with a dog. He took no more notice of her distress than he might have considered a rabbit caught in a trap. He called to his companions. 'She's here.'

Aiden recognised his voice as the one who had cussed so explicitly and wished the light was better so as to see his face clearer and commit it to memory. His stomach churned a warning. The familiar ache shooting through his gut. He rested his cheek against the top of Cassandra's head.

Within moments two others joined the man and he ordered them to cut the woman down. One of the men used his weight to drop the branch, tugging it down, so the other could reach the net and cut it free, but the woman cringed away from their hands, causing it to swing and behave awkwardly. The man cutting the holding rope had to move aside to save being knocked. After three failed attempts he punched randomly at the net. 'Fucks' sake, Martha.'

Her only answer was a keening cry drenched with terror and more wriggling. Her sheer helplessness made Aiden want to vomit and he felt soiled by the scene.

Once on the ground, the net was cut away and the woman pulled roughly from it. Undernourished, she was older than first glance suggested. Her face lined and her skin sallow in the torchlight the men beamed on her, any youthful bloom long washed away with suffering and enforced fear. Held either side by two of the men, she faced the man with the dog. He patted the animal's head in a casual gesture before he moved in close to her. 'Look at the state of my shoes, you filthy bitch.'

She whimpered through chattering teeth. 'Please, Ray, I didn't mean anything.'

'You didn't, huh?' He combed his fingers through his hair. 'Two days you've been gone. Two fucking days I've had to make camp in this shit hole of a swamp.'

She cringed, flinching at his words like they were wounding her flesh.

'Oh, Martha.' He sounded almost loving. Then taking his time, he straightened her dishevelled clothing, a thin shirtdress, by tugging at the hemline to un-rumple the creased material. 'Look at you,' he said softly before tearing the front of the dress apart in one vicious wrench. The buttons flew into the air, a shower of pearl, leaving the dress gaping and exposing the girl's naked body beneath. She squirmed but the men held her while Ray clutched at her breasts, pinching hard until she cried out.

'You cost me a lot of time, cunt. Only fair I get some compensation.'

Then he nodded at the men and they pushed her to the ground. She tried to escape, alternating between kicking out and pleading with them to leave her but in the end she was held, pinned either side, arms above her head and her legs sprawled apart.

Appreciation for Cassandra's courage took a huge leap in that moment, as Aiden realised the horror she had run from. Had she suffered like this? Was the baby the result of rape? The thought sickened him. No, it couldn't be. He had seen the love on her face when she thought no one was looking. Then it occurred to him there was love there on his part too, and he would willingly die for her and the child that wasn't his.

Ray jerked his belt loose and unzipped his fly and leaned in over the woman. He nuzzled her breasts and dragged his tongue over her nipples, tilting his head to look at her face before he rammed into her, claiming ownership of her body.

A tear trickled from under her lashes and trailed along her cheek. Ray swept it away with his tongue, licking her like a dog. He grunted through each thrust, her body jerking to his rhythm, until he groaned his satisfaction and pulled out from her, leaving the other two men to scrabble for a share. Zipping his fly, he walked over to his dog, who leapt up and gave a tail wag at the attention.

The woman stopped protesting. She lay there legs akimbo even when they were done with her and no longer holding her in position. Her open eyes stared up at the sky and her lips moved. Aiden heard a broken bar of music. She was singing quietly, mouthing words to a song playing in her head.

Ray pulled a knife from his belt and went over to her. He caught her hair with his free hand and swiped the knife across her bare throat. Her blood gushed, a coagulated shade of shale in the semi dark, her lips still caught in her half song.

'Stupid bitch. She never was good for much,' he said by way of an explanation as he let her fall from his grasp. 'Come on, I've had enough of this stinking place.' The other two shuffled after him.

For an age Aiden remained where he was, just holding Cassandra who made no attempt to move away. Seeing the kind of people he was dealing with warred intermittently with thoughts on how he could possibly overcome any opposition. They had chased this woman into the swamp for two days, only to kill her at the end. How relentless was that? She lay in front of them now, a painful reality they couldn't ignore.

Muffled sobs shook through Cassandra and Aiden twisted her round to face him and pulled her to his chest. He felt her baby move against his own stomach, an unlikely sign of life among this human wastage and felt a peculiar easing of the physical pain in his abdomen.

'We will get through this,' he whispered, more for his own benefit than hers. She raised her face to look at him and he saw anger sparkle in her glance and realised her tears were more fury than sorrow.

'Oh yes, Aiden, we will.' A flash of something crossed her features, a transitory memory, unpleasant whatever it was. 'I won't be beaten by that fucker.'

An inward smile lit within him for a fleeting moment, then reality snuffed it out. 'Come on, we have to find Sophia.

Kasimir

The sea billows. Hilly and strewn in driftwood, it ruffles to the shore. Shade and light, like sheets of satin shaking in the wind. Each wave brings fresh breath, washing our spirits free of my uncle's corruption. From the clifftops, with her back to the port, my mother walks away. In time she will feel home-sick. But where is home?

Sophia

If this was the end, Sophia didn't accept it. A ditch, a boulder or a mound was all she needed to face those men, shoot at them until she was overpowered. But there were no boulders, or ditches, or mounds and the slender trees offered no protection. There was only the swampy lakes with their stagnant water. So she ran.

She shrugged off her backpack feeling trapped on all sides when a gunshot ripped the air. Without hesitation she dived into one of the lakes just as another shot went off. She dived lower and lower, until her lungs, desperately straining for air, forced her back up to the surface. Gunshots crackled and bullets whizzed by her head and she flinched, sinking underwater once more for cover. A fiery sensation burned down her left arm. She'd been hit. Sour water filled her mouth, stifling her scream of pain and she bubbled to the surface. Gasping and choking, she managed to hook herself onto a slimy, moss-grown rock, where she waved her gun in the general direction of the torches, squeezing the trigger a couple of times before losing her hold on the rock and sinking again.

The sliver of moon hardly penetrated the underside of the water, holding no promise in its scanty light. She had failed everyone. Faces of her family swam in front of her, trickling in and out of focus. Grayson waiting, watching for her return... her parents gone... Aiden lost to her...

Fighting to stay conscious, Sophia kicked to propel herself to the surface and with her last bit of strength swam to the bank, clambered onto the soggy strip of land and lay on her back in the muck. Her attention shifted away from the trees to beyond the bank and back again, while moonlit shadows flitted and quivered, causing her to start at every tremble. Struggling to raise her arm she aimed her gun at the dark, swinging it in random arcs, but no one came for her.

Heaving a sigh, every breath stung into her lungs. She sat up, leaned against a tree for support, then pushed her fingers down her throat and forced herself to vomit, wrenching the putrid slurry from inside her. How she longed for some clean water to wash her mouth. She checked her arm. A flesh wound. The bullet had coursed a burn from the back of her wrist to her elbow and hurt like hell. Now what? Her backpack had gone. All she had were the clothes on her body, and they were wet through, her gun, and her knife tucked into her belt, which she pulled free. She stabbed into her shirt, creating a hole, making it easier to tear a strip to bind her wound. Although the bleeding was minimal she would need to disinfect it soon. Her mind felt leaden and cloudy, just like when she had woken from her drugged stupor at Hannah's home, only this time there was no drug, just the hopelessness of circumstances weighing her down.

She searched inside herself for a sign, some spark to show whether Aiden was alive, but couldn't tell. Straining to listen she heard nothing stirring and so stayed propped against the tree in the wet dirt until exhaustion brought her sleep, but even then she was aware of the rigidity of her muscles and the pain in her arm. Her dreams took on a wild quality where she went back and shot the bastards and the dogs only to find Aiden dead. His grime caked body strewn on the path for the vultures to feast on his innards. Her sobbing woke her and she covered her mouth with her hand to muffle the sound.

She staggered behind a boulder and crouched in the bracken. Misery clung to her throat and lungs and bones not to be shaken, making it hard to breathe without crying. In front of her was the rust coloured lake she had almost drowned in. On the edge, a stoat peeked from inside a rotting stump, stretching its neck around the decaying wood. It stared blindly, its milky eyes secreting pus.

Dawn sifted down. She should go back and find Aiden now there was enough light for her to see she wasn't going round in circles. If Cassandra and he had been captured, trussed and shoved in the back of some truck, she couldn't do anything for them. But she should check.

In the thin light, a cluster of bloated mushrooms, an appetising bulge, beckoned to her until she recognised them as poisonous yellow-stainers. She squashed her disappointment at the ready meal stolen from her. Was there nothing wholesome to be found in these woods? She walked into a small glade, bending to use her knife to cut through the vines that reached for her feet to trip her, or clawed and snatched at strands of her hair whenever she stood upright.

Among the trees an indistinct sound of low voices trailed from the gloom. Sophia picked up a smattering of exchanges as they approached.

'Wasn't worth coming just for Martha.'

'No. Whore wasn't worth the trouble.'

Two men stepped from the trees, dirty and bearded but young, perhaps early twenties. They saw her and reached for their shotguns. Sophia took aim and shot. One of the men hissed through his pain, faltered a step backward and crashed into the mud. The other quickly shouldered his gun and fired. The pellets hit the tree to her left, spraying bark and splinters on Sophia's head. She fired twice but missed, then threw herself backward and hid behind the tree just as the man fired again.

He shouted to her. 'Come out now and I'll let you live.'

'That's a lie.'

'Fine. Come out and I won't gouge your fucking eyes out, you cunt.'

Sophia scooped a handful of dirt, rounded it in the shape of a ball. 'Give me a moment.'

She threw the ball to her right and when the man fired she leaned from behind the tree and shot. The bullet tore a hole in his neck. A rivulet of blood forded his beard and he collapsed. Cautiously she approached him, the gun smoke stinging her eyes and lingering in her nose, as the man wheezed and gasped. Kicking the shotgun from his grasp she stared into his bearded face. She knew she had to. The man gurgled, his fingers poking holes in the mud as though trying to crawl his way back to life. His face twitched and went still. She knew the image of his death would colour all her future nightmares.

Voices came from behind and she ran. Now she was really lost, unable to retrace her steps to where she had last seen Aiden. She might never find him in this forsaken piece of land. Never had she felt so alone or in such doubt as to what to do next. Crying quietly and stumbling through undergrowth, only stopping to puke, she felt a mild surprise and a sudden lift of spirit when she came to a blacktop road going through the trees.

The wind pushed dark clouds speedily across the sky, its strength making her eyes water. She wiped them and peered about apprehensively. There didn't seem to be anyone nearby, only a truck parked at an angle with the back facing her. She sidestepped around the trees for a better view and was caught by a fresh gust, blowing her hair into her face. She tied it into a knot quickly, never taking her sights from the truck. The eroded tinwork glittered with dew. She thought she saw the shadow of someone in the driver's seat and was proved right when a man emerged from the side of the road and called to the driver. 'Start her up. Let's get them to the port.'

Did they mean Aiden? Imagined scenes filled her head, all without a happy ending. Spurred into action, she ran along the road where traces of tyre tracks had slithered over the asphalt.

Panting shallow spurts of breath, each inhalation burned her chest with the exertion, but she couldn't stop, this was her only chance. Nearing the truck she lifted the hem to throw herself into the back. Her feet scrabbled along the tarmac and just when she thought she'd have to let go, a hand from inside caught hold of her and yanked her further into the truck.

Kasimir

A light dusting of snow greets us at the foothills. Drowsy with its monotonous creaking underfoot, my mother's eyes close and her knees buckle. The playful shadows of the mountain edge closer towards her as she wakes. She clutches her belly, afraid she has lost me. But I'm there, keeping her warm. She laughs and cries at the same time.

Grayson

The hushed muttering woke Grayson. He raised his head from the pillow shoving his unruly hair from his eyes and listened to the muffled whispering. 'Don't be afraid.'

What was Helen doing up so late? Was she speaking to William? Cautiously he got out of bed and tiptoed across the hall. He peered through the open door into her room and saw Helen cramming clothes into a small bag. Marigold was propped against the bedpost wearing such a menacing expression in the half gloom light, it made him gasp. Her mouth dropped crookedly and her one eye seemed to follow him.

'There's nothing to be afraid of,' said Helen and for a moment Grayson thought she was speaking to him. 'I don't like the forest in the dark either, Marigold. The trees are spookier in the moonlight.'

'What are you doing?' said Grayson.

Helen's hands froze in the middle of pressing a shirt into her bag. 'Shush Grayson, keep your voice down.'

'But you're packing. Where are you going?'

'I'm going to find mum.' Helen struggled with the zipper but the bag was obviously over-stuffed so she opened it and began rifling through the clothes, tossing socks onto the bed. 'Don't need so many. Might be lucky and find mum quick.' Then she smothered her doll in three sets of clothes, rags with holes cut in for the head and the hands. 'Marigold doesn't like it when it's cold. Don't know if three layers are enough to keep her warm, though.'

He pushed down the bad feeling that was rising in him. 'You're going where I saw that dumped drum, aren't you?'

She was barely listening. 'Hmm? Yes.'

He wanted to shake her. 'I've already told you being around that stuff could make you very, very sick.'

Helen giggled. 'No, it can't, you silly thing. That's where the spectral children live.'

He curbed his need to yell at her, grab hold of her and keep her safe. 'I don't think going there is a good idea.'

'You're wrong. Mum is there and I want to stay with her. I'm going there to tell her she's been with them long enough and it's time she became my mum again.'

'What about William? How will he feel you leaving him like this?'

'He'll never let me go where mum is so he mustn't know.' Helen stopped her packing. The stern look she gave told him nothing he said would make her change her mind. 'I need to find her.' Every word she spoke resonated with a feeling of longing. 'Besides, I don't fit here. William doesn't either. But he won't leave. He's too used to the place.'

'What do you mean, you don't fit?'

'You think I don't hear what people say about William and me? That we are filthy *inbreds*, whatever that means. That William and mum would sneak into the pigsty at night to mate with the pigs and suckle the sows. They must think I'm deaf as well as mute because they say it right in front of me. We don't belong here. Nobody likes us.'

Grayson had indeed heard the stories and now felt ashamed that he'd even listened. Helen swung the bag on her back and tucked Marigold under her arm but Grayson barred the way. 'Please don't go there.'

Helen shoved him aside. 'You should know how I feel after what happened to *your* mum and dad.' For a moment Grayson could think of nothing to say. Had she really said that? 'And don't you dare follow me, Grayson.' Helen sniffed and rubbed her eyes. 'I thought you were my friend.' She left the room and he heard her step down the stairs and the front door creak open and then close.

'I am your friend, you silly goose,' he muttered.

Quickly Grayson put on his sweater and trousers and shoved his feet into his boots. He stared out the window and glimpsed Helen disappearing into the woods. He didn't relish the thought of waking William. It was bad enough betraying Helen's confidences without the effort of explaining everything to her brother. He knocked on William's bedroom door and then again harder but there was no reply.

'William? Wake up.' Uneasily he pushed the door open and saw William sprawled on the bed. The air was stuffy, smelling powerfully of unwashed socks, underwear and male sourness. William turned and burrowed deeper under the blankets, some dream making him resist surfacing from sleep. Grayson shook his shoulder. 'Helen's gone.'

William awoke with a start. Disorientated he stared at Grayson as if he didn't know him before glowering. 'What are you doing here?'

'It's Helen. She's gone.'

'Gone?'

'Yeah, to find her mum. I mean your mum. But I saw a drum of really bad stuff out there. Why would your mum go there? Doesn't she know it's dangerous?'

'Mum never went there. It was just a story she told Helen.'

'Do you know the place?'

'Not exactly,' said William and began to dress.

'I do.'

William sighed. It was a weary sound and Grayson felt responsible for his sudden weariness. If he had told William before like he had wanted to, Helen would be safe now. People kept disappearing from his life. Was there no end to it? First his parents, then Aiden and Sophia, now Helen. He couldn't help but think he was to blame. If he hadn't complained about being hungry all the time, his parents might never have gone to the city so soon after the last foraging and nothing bad would have happened to them. Everything bad seemed to follow on from that.

'Come on,' William said. 'Let's go find my sister.'

Creaks in night sounded loud and foreign. Somewhere a dog howled. Owls hooted above him, their wings a silent swoosh as they swooped on unsuspecting prey, and shadows skittered along the edge of moonlight. Grayson whimpered, the dark of the woods closing in around him and he rushed to hold William's hand. The warm stickiness brought a comfort and thankfully William was kind enough not to shake his hand free. So much for being a daring spy.

The night lightened and through the yew trees a bronzed dawn dusted the pebbly forest floor. They climbed the swell of ground before them and stared down the ravine where a mossy trickle of water weaved between rocks as smooth as glass. Now they were closer, Grayson could see there was more than the one drum he had seen from a distance. Cracked and chipped they protruded from an overgrown clump of weeds. A yellow circle with three strange trapezoids were painted on them. The redolence of burning gunpowder wafted from below and the air around the drums was tinted tawny, rippling into green. And there was Helen, ambling towards the clump of weeds with the bag that was far too big for her.

'Stop,' shouted William and launched himself down the ravine. His long skinny legs covering ground with a speed that had Grayson holding his breath. Helen must have thought so too for she just stood still as her brother pounded towards her and even allowed herself to be pulled back up the ravine without any resistance. It was only when they reached the top did she burst into tears. 'I don't want to wait for mum to return any longer. Why doesn't she come back?'

William bent down, his face level with hers. 'Oh Helen, I'm so sorry,' he said. 'I should have told you this sooner.'

She looked back at him. 'Where's mum, William?'

'Let's get away from here first.' He stood up and held out his hand to her. She took it and together they wandered further away from the ravine with all its dangers. As they walked William spoke to her, his voice low and soft. 'I'm going to tell you a story. It's a bit sad in places.' He lifted her hand to his lips and gave her fingers a big heartfelt kiss. 'There was a man who had a wife and four children. By all accounts he was a no good drunk who never took care of them. One day, his wife said she'd had enough and walked out on him, taking the children with her. A while later the man left his town and came to live here, in ours. He met a young, innocent girl who fell in love with him. They married and soon had two children. A boy and a girl. Some years passed and the man got news from his first wife that she was willing to have him back. And so he left his second wife and their two children to reunite with his first family. Helen, that man was our father. Mum couldn't bear to be parted from him so she left us, choosing to be his mistress rather than our mum. She never meant to come back for us, Helen. She left for good.'

'That story is *all* sad.' Helen hugged Marigold close to her chest and began to sob. Her brother took her in his arms pressing his cheek on the top of her hair.

'Well, not all, 'cause the little girl had a brother who promised to always be there for her.' William looked over her head towards Grayson. 'She also had a good friend who put his own fears aside to do the right thing. So maybe she had plenty to be thankful for. What do you reckon?'

Kasimir

The mountain people are pious. They bow their heads low but their spirit is proud, their hearts are stone. My mother cannot understand the gods they answer to. They come in countless guises and deal in ambiguities. She can't abide their fickleness. Humming a lullaby, she wishes for someone to take her burdens, a god of her own to pray to... no one listens. She whispers to me. 'There's only you, baby mine, only you'.

Aiden

The truck belched billows of exhaust, revving away with a gassy rumble. Aiden watched helplessly. Had he really just seen Sophia scramble into the back? *What was she thinking?* They had been this close to catching up with her, only to miss one another. His thoughts, a mix of staccato notes, jabbed through his brain and not one held a solution.

Cassandra stood beside him, gawping, bug-eyed, as the truck disappeared, winding around the curved road. They said nothing to each other. Aiden felt caught in some hideous time loop that would only replay the previous few seconds. *What was she thinking?* The sentence reverberated around his head. 'What was she thinking?' he said aloud. His fists curled, like he was making up his mind to punch something. Cassandra grabbed hold of them, stilling them against her.

'Let's get our brains in gear and do some thinking ourselves.' She sighed. 'Look, we just have to trust Soph will do okay. We shouldn't underestimate her. We'll meet her at the city.' She bent awkwardly to rub her sore leg. 'And you'll move a lot quicker without me to hamper you.'

Her challenge arrested his racing thoughts, making decisions easier. That she should even consider he would abandon her here appalled him. Did she think so little of him?

'I'm not leaving you here alone, so you can forget that. You're right, we just keep going.'

Her eyes locked with his. Was it trust he read in them? She nodded and they walked along the track until Aiden pulled them off the main drag of road.

By late morning when the pain in Cassandra's shin rendered her pace down to a slow trudge, they paused to rest in a thicket where they could not be seen. 'Wish we were all on that bloody truck,' Cassandra muttered as she rucked up her skirt. The fall had left a nasty graze surrounded by deep purplish bruises. Aiden winced at the sight. Cassandra couldn't go any faster. He hated to admit it to himself but her slow pace irritated him. Patience was never a strong point. Cassandra touched her leg where the skin had chafed. 'I'm slowing you down.'

Immediately he regretted his transparency. 'You're not. I need to rest myself.'

'Because of your back?'

'Yeah.'

'That's my fault, too.'

'Don't be stupid.'

When she put her arms gently around him he did not expect it. Much like him, she was sticky with dirt and sweat but the undeniable feminine scent of her body enveloped him and for a precious instant pulled him from his gloomy thoughts. He felt her hands steal under his shirt, lightly touching his ruined back. 'We'll find Soph. Soon.'

'I hope so.'

'And then we'll find where your parents are kept and free them.'

He sighed. 'It feels half done when you say it.'

'You got this far, didn't you?'

This far? This far suddenly became not far enough but before he became lost in the futility of it, Cassandra kissed the hollow of his throat. She had him. He held her close.

A tread of boots on tangled weed stopped his breath and he prepared himself to spring from the clump of bushes and shoot whoever came their way.

'No,' she whispered. Her freckles like dark stains against her blanched white face. 'They'll kill you.'

'I can take them.'

'No, Aiden.'

'You don't think I can take them.'

'You can take them.'

'Then let me do it.'

'No.' And with that it was settled.

The men passed by them soon enough. Aiden inched forward to keep them in his sight, ready to follow when they disappeared. But Cassandra held his sleeve, staying his movement. 'Wait a bit.'

When they finally emerged, Aiden's back had seized up from crouching for so long and Cassandra jiggled her feet, complaining of cramp. She cupped her hand around her belly as though to keep it from rolling off. Its roundness, like a separate entity, fascinated him, striking him as almost supernatural that Cassandra sustained precious life within her, when they could barely endure themselves.

His own mother hadn't produced sufficient milk for Sophia and him, coming so soon after the war, and Aiden had nearly died a dozen times over, so his mother had told him. It was only thanks to his Aunt Maggie, whose birth of her own child prevented both Sophia and him from suffering an ill-fated death in infancy. 'No graves were needed for our precious orchids,' his aunt would snort and laugh in her loud flamboyant manner. 'I had enough milk to feed a herd.'

Only when he was older, did he find his aunt's flower choice surprising after reading about orchids in one of Sophia's fancy books. He would wonder how his outspoken and sometimes coarse aunt had latched onto so rare a plant. He never asked her although he heard the story many times and regretted the lost opportunity when she died. Especially when he always felt he fell short of the expectations she had unintentionally placed on him.

'Can you walk?' he asked Cassandra.

'I can manage.'

'But it's still some distance, isn't it?'

'I know. I'll manage.'

A lustrous glow washed over them when they left the shelter of the trees, the sun midway in the sky. The path between the rippling grasses like a seam between two immense waves.

'Your parents and Soph are beyond these slopes. Another day's walking and we'll be there.' Cassandra sounded weary. 'I'm sorry, Aiden. I don't like holding you back like this.'

'Don't think like that.' The sun shone on his face and for one moment he let go of his anxieties. He gave in to the urge to grab Cassandra's hand and brought her small fist to his lips. That she didn't pull away encouraged him. 'Don't be sad, pretty lady,' he said. 'You're the one good thing to come out of this whole mess.'

The autumnal chill returned as soon as the sun dipped and it was with some relief they found an assortment of houses, long deserted and in poor repair, but shelter all the same. They camped in one.

A wind chime hung tenaciously on the part of the

porch still standing. Inside soot and wet ash piled against the crumbled wall, blown into heaps through the gaps in the masonry. On the sturdy wall in the hallway was a crude chalk graffiti of a boy sketched onto the powdery mortar. From top to bottom it was about four and half feet and beside it was a message scrawled in round childish writing. *I'm this big now*. For no other reason than the pure cheekiness of the sentiment, Grayson sprang to mind, and an incredible longing to see him gripped Aiden like a physical ache.

He saw Cassandra was not untouched. 'I hope my baby gets to be *this big*,' she said so wistfully he would have laid down his life right then if it meant it was so. She sat near the fireless grate while Aiden went for wood. When he returned with brushwood, he found her sitting in the exact same place as though there had been no lapse in time, staring at a shadowy corner with a blank expression on her face, and if she was aware of him she gave no sign, so lost in her own thoughts.

He put the twigs in the grate, fumbled in his backpack for the tinderbox, then struck stone against steel for a spark and lit a fire. He tapped her shoulder and she started, no recognition on her face. 'Come closer,' he said.

'What?' Slowly, as though returning from a far off place, she focused on him. 'Oh, okay.' She came beside him and gazed into the flames.

Her silence unnerved him. 'What you thinking?'

'I was thinking about the woman we saw... Martha.'

'Did you know her?' *Please don't let her be a friend.* Somehow that would have made it worse that they hadn't intervened.

'No. No, it was the man who brutalised her. That's who I know.'

The firelight emphasised her worry lines, the little fold between the brows, and the tiny downward stroke just by her eyes. He longed to wipe them away and give her peace, but he was only adding to her worries, dragging her back to where she had just run from. 'You'd be miles away if it wasn't for me.'

A weak smile creased her lip. 'Now who's being daft? I'd be dead if it wasn't for you.'

They ate some of the onion bread and eggs, which he divided up making sure she had the bigger share. 'When this is all over...' He paused seeing her raised eyebrow. 'What? It will be over, Cassandra, I promise you that, and when it is, come and live with us... me. I'd hate to go back home without you. Can't imagine doing that.'

She sat silently, staring at the fire once more.

'Is that okay that I say it? That I want you with me?' Once again her silence had an unnerving quality. He was so used to her chatter. Maybe she didn't feel the same. 'Only if you want to. I'd like you to...' His words trailed away.

Turning to face him, she touched her own mouth and then pointed to his. 'You got crumbs.' She reached over and gently brushed at the few stray hairs that made his small beard. Then, unexpectedly, she kissed him and leaned back with a satisfied smile. She looked full of baby and dinner and that softened some of the tension in his head. Her stomach rippled and once again he was struck by the wonder of the life within. She caught his hand in hers and slowly guided it to her belly. 'Someone's woken up,' she said.

The baby kicked against Aiden's palm, surprising him with the strength and at the same time delighting him. He placed both his hands on the beautiful domed mound of unborn baby, feeling it wriggle and turn. The movements had him guessing at the limbs and he almost forgot Cassandra, so taken he was in the enchantment of the moment. He felt a trickle of hope blossom in his chest, like the small white flowers he had seen once at the start of springtime, bursting through dry, unlikely soil. 'So amazing,' and he heard the awe in his voice, like he'd seen a divine spirit, or something.

The narrow smile wedged onto Cassandra's lips tore at his heart. 'Yes. He is.'

Then just as suddenly as it had come, hope dissipated. Say Cassandra were to give birth now or, worse yet, at the port. He didn't know the first thing about delivering a baby and that was the least of his worries.

Gusts of wind whined at the top of the chimney and along the collapsed corridor, rattling loose boards and setting the wind chimes playing an eerie tinkle. Aiden spread the blanket over them, snuggling under its soft weightiness and with the exception of the firelight and its pale reflection on the window panes, the room was dark.

Cassandra patted his cheek, her hand lingering on his jawline. 'Goodnight,' she whispered and turned away. He meant to catch her hand but accidently brushed over her breasts swelling from her blouse and he felt his face flush and was glad of the dark.

Long into the night he lay awake until the fire had fallen to embers, issuing a last gasp of light. Cassandra's steady breathing and nearness made him restless, and thoughts of Sophia lost somewhere made sleeping impossible. If anything happened to her he would know, wouldn't he? Sharing the same womb must count for something. Sophia always said it did. And his stomach didn't hurt. It always had before someone's death. Premonition Sophia called it. So she must be safe.

Eventually Aiden did sleep for an hour or two but when he awoke, Cassandra wasn't there. He looked for her in each part of the house. The scullery, the tiny room under the stairs, half filled with a box of puzzle pieces, a pair of shoes, several sizes too small to fit either Cassandra or him, and a stack of books, the top one had a page bookmarked as though any moment the owner would return and pick up where they had left off. Some of the stairs were broken, so it was out of the question she was upstairs. Outside, he checked the shed, nothing there, but a shovel and a rake.

At the back of the house he saw her sitting in a tub filled with rainwater, scrubbing under her arms. A hint of rosiness stained her cheeks and the desire to embrace her, touch her, nearly overwhelmed him. He decided she was an exceptional thief because somewhere along the way she had stolen his heart.

'Good morning,' she called to him.

'Good morning.'

'You were talking in your sleep.'

'Was I? Did I give away any secrets?'

'It was mostly incomprehensible but you did say *no* a number of times.'

'Oh.'

'Could have wakened you, but it didn't seem right to cut your sleep short.'

'Probably for the best.'

'Turn around now, I want to get out.'

Facing away from her he didn't move until she stood beside him dressed. She scooped up her jacket and shoved her feet into her boots.

'Once in the city I'll show you where they hold your mum and dad. There's a bunch of warehouses where they keep everybody. But what then?'

'I don't know. How many guards are there?'

'In the entire city? Can't really say. But at the warehouses at least a dozen armed men.'

A dozen men. The number rang in his mind like an astronomical figure. *What was he thinking by going there?* 'First we find Sophia.'

'Of course.'

'Then I'll think of something.'

'Well, I do know a way in.'

'I'm not having you take chances. You'll tell me where to go and then you steer clear of the place.'

'We'll see.'

'No, we won't bloody see. You'll do as I tell you.'

Cassandra gave him a crisp, mocking salute. 'Yes, sir.'

They walked along the tangled marsh at the edge of town. The Quaking-grass rasped dryly against their clothes and created dust as they brushed against the seed heads. Aiden hoped to find some wildlife in the grassland for they were hungry again and when they heard the honking of a goose he almost supposed it was his imagination at first, until they saw it walking this way and that as though desperately looking for something.

'Oh my, a goose. What can we give it?' Cassandra made a friendly clicking sound as she riffled through her backpack and pulled out the hard remains of onion bread. 'I knew this would have a purpose.' She crumbled a few pieces and threw it near her feet. The hungry bird gambolled towards her for the chance of something to eat. Edging near, Cassandra threw her jacket over the bird and herself on top of the jacket. Meanwhile Aiden fumbled with the wire he used for picking locks, bending it onto a stick he pulled from the hedge.

'Bloody hell Aiden, get a move on.' Cassandra's legs wide apart as she wrestled with the trapped bird.

'Okay, I'm going to loop this around its neck. Be ready.'

Aiden pulled down the jacket exposing the goose, looped the wire around its neck and garrotted the bird, while Cassandra hung on tightly, ducking to avoid its vicious beak. Then they both lay back, panting, with the dead bird between them. They plucked the goose, made a fire and cooked it, eating some and keeping the rest in a shirt.

Having such a rich meal tired them and they sat for a while. Aiden, indulging in daydreams, visualised the child inside Cassandra as a boy his brother's age, running and rolling in the grasses until exhausted, and himself holding the boy, lifting him high into the air. Aiden started to laugh as another memory crashed his thoughts, Cassandra sprawled over the bird.

'What?' Cassandra laughed up at him and suddenly he wanted to kiss her. Lick the goose fat from her lips.

The smell of limestone dust tickled his nose and the

tang of saltiness hung in the air long before he caught a glimpse of the sea. It matted Cassandra's hair and lingered on his mouth. He chewed his lips, tasting their dryness, and a hint of the surf. Soon the road dipped into a hollow and the sea spread before them, a long grey swell that heaved and shimmered. A high rolling wave broke on the rocky coast showering spray over a cluster of houses. The sun broke through a cloud and the sea glittered like a million jewels. One boat sailed upon it, so tiny in the vastness of the ocean. *Could his parents be on it?* He could hardly keep from sprinting down to the shore. Sweat leaked across his forehead, clammy and wet and he wiped it away, wondering whether he was too late to save them.

Kasimir

The man ladles stew, greasy, redolent of nutmeg, it stirs a hunger in my mother. Never one to beg, she searches her belongings and pulls her mother's shawl, the only thing she values. She passes it with reluctant fingers but the man has no use for such things, or her. 'I don't care for that. The food is for us, not you, foreigner.' He waves a dismissive hand.

She leaves but returns at nightfall and tries her luck when the vendor turns from the pot. Furtively she fills a jug, then skulks away and finds a cave to sit and eat. Tonight we don't go hungry. But what of tomorrow?

Sophia

Sophia landed face down on the floor of the truck as it rumbled down the road. All her focus pinpointed down to the hand that gripped her arm. The span was wide, fingers fat, the thumbs digging right through to her bones. She felt her gun wound tear in jagged edges, as it split a zigzag course up from her wrist. She struggled to free her gun. The man pulled her upright with a sharp jerk. Her head snapped forward and she recognised him at once and halted her frantic scrabbling.

'Joel?'

'*You!*' His hold barely softened as he regarded her. The frown creasing his forehead made him fierce. 'What the devil are you playing at?' He shook her and she pulled a face, feeling the warm trickle of blood through her fingers. After what seemed an age he lessened his grip and patted the wooden bench seat that ran the length of the truck. 'Sit,' he said.

'What are you doing *here*?' She couldn't reconcile the Joel of the mountains with the one sitting beside her.

He didn't answer, instead his scrutiny switched to the driver's cabin. He seated himself by the small window and tapped on the glass. 'Go careful, Rudy, you'll have a wheel off.'

'You're with *them*?'

'Right now, hothead, all you need to know is I'm the man saving your life.' His eyes held a warmth encouraging her to trust him. She had done so before and he had seen her out of trouble.

Bouncing uncomfortably as the truck lurched over

the ruts in the road she asked, 'Where are we going?'

'To a safe place.' Joel's breath smelled putrid and he blinked with the concentration of a drunk pretending to be sober. 'You'll see soon enough.'

'I need to get to the port.'

'Why would you want to go there?'

'That's where my brother was taken.'

Joel coughed aggressively into his fist. 'You dumb kids, the port's no place for you. Don't you realise the danger you're in?' He kept his voice low, its mellow timbre and occasional slur taking any sting away from what damage his words might have caused.

'I have to get to my parents before they are taken overseas.'

'When were they captured?' he asked.

Something in the way Joel looked at her told Sophia her efforts might be too late. No matter. She would still go. 'I lost track of time. About ten days ago.'

'Then they might no longer be there, kid. Might already be overseas by now.'

A sense of loss took hold of Sophia. 'I have to see for myself.'

Joel rummaged through the contents of a small box he pulled from under the seat. 'Right.' He twirled his index finger to indicate Sophia should roll up her sleeve and he proceeded to rub a strange smelling salve over her wound.

'What's that? I've never smelled anything like this.'

'Ground herbs mixed with alcohol to prevent infection. Comes from overseas.' Joel gave her a shrewd look she couldn't quite interpret, then patted her arm before pulling her sleeve back down. The pungent smell wafted through the material, burning her eyes.

Sophia lifted the back flap of the truck and looked out. They were no longer in the swamp but for all she could tell they were no nearer to the sea either. Tangled grass and shrubs dominated the countryside. Farther away wooded hillocks stood stark against the skyline and a stone wall dropped into a downhill stretch. When the truck stopped Joel unclasped the bolts, letting the back crash down. 'We get out here.'

All Sophia could see was a cabin. 'I thought you were taking me to the sea,' she said.

'We'll get there.'

'Hell, Joel, I thought it'd at least be in sight.'

'Damn it, girl, there are things I need to take care of first.'

He handed her a bread roll as though she were some child who could easily be appeased. 'What things?' she asked, pushing the bread into her pocket.

'I'm transporting some people.'

The idea that Joel worked with the Seafarers had floated intangibly through her consciousness while she sat in the truck, but Sophia had disregarded it. After all, he had aided her twice and that counted for something. But right now she wasn't so sure.

Two people jumped down from the front of the truck. She recognised the first as the deaf boy from the mountain town, despite his blond curls lying flat and lifeless now and his skin being a great deal grimier. A spattering of mud sprayed his overcoat and he brushed at it clumsily, making it worse. Lines of fatigue around his mouth and eyes gave a bleary look of having just woken up. He mumbled a hello.

The second person was a much older man, a head shorter than Joel. His thin lips held a snarl and Sophia didn't like the way he stared at her. 'Who's this?' he asked Joel curtly.

'No one to interest you, Rudy.' Joel answered just as curtly. Judging by the reply, and the resentful expression, Sophia surmised Rudy wasn't in charge and watched as the older man went into the cabin.

She heard a scuffle, and two people, a man and a woman, shuffled through the doorway of the cabin, preceded by Rudy who tugged at the ties on their wrists.

Sophia turned to Joel. 'What are you doing? Who are these people?'

'None of your concern, little girl.'

Joel's shifty expression made her suspicious. 'Are you working for the Seafarers?' When he didn't answer, she knew. 'You are, aren't you?' She grabbed hold of Joel's arm. 'Let them go. Say they jumped you and ran away.'

He shrugged her arm away. 'Someone will find them and then it's my home the Seafarers will raid,' he yelled. 'My wife and kids they will take.'

'Okay. So say they surprised you when you loaded them onto the truck and you shot them to save your life, then buried the bodies. Nobody will look for dead people.' She was talking too much and his uneasy gaze told her he wasn't happy about this.

'No one will believe a fancy story like that.'

'Why not? Damn it, Joel, you don't have to do this.'

'Yes, I do. My children need food and clothes for winter and the Seafarers have those to give. I'm doing this for them.' He pushed past her with a violent thump that jolted through her.

'What's wrong with you?' she said, leaning back to allow the captives to scramble aboard. 'No need to behave like a pig.'

The man clambered up unaided. Square and heavy, even his face was thickset with his bulbous nose off centre where it had been broken at some point in his life and mended badly. His eyes, two slits of dark, stared at Sophia blatantly sizing her up.

The woman beside him possessed a fragile toughness. Her skin brown and wrinkled as dried fruit. She struggled to gain entry onto the truck and no one made any attempt to help her. Instinctively Sophia offered her arm but the woman pulled away, scowling before spitting in Sophia's face. The direct hit of spittle caught the edge of Sophia's mouth and she wanted to cry out and say she was not part of this, but of course, at that moment, she was.

Joel lumbered beside her and answered the look she gave him with a bluster. 'Don't judge me. It's my family or these nobodies.'

'These nobodies may have a family, too.'

Inside the truck, Rudy pulled at their tied arms, testing the knot. The woman complained he was hurting her and he answered her by tugging the rope harder and hooking it through a metal ring on the truck's side to fasten it.

'No need for that,' Joel said. 'I'll do this, Rudy. You go start the truck.'

The bound man sat on one bench seat by himself and filled the space. 'Lean closer,' he told Sophia who sat opposite him. 'I won't harm you.' She leaned towards him. 'You live up on the mountain?' he asked.

'I come from the south.'

'Foraging?'

'No. Nothing like that.'

The man spread his legs leaving only his crotch to focus on and although she looked elsewhere, there was only so much staring at the roof and far corner of the truck she could do. He knew it, for whenever her gaze drifted back to him, he'd wink suggestively and open his legs still further.

The woman had the hollow-eyed appearance of near starvation. Her face dry and broken up like sandstone, as though her body no longer held a drop of moisture. She panted softly, her mouth pursing as she swallowed repeatedly in a nervous tic.

'Are you hungry?' said Sophia. She retrieved the roll of bread from her pocket, a small hunk, enough for a couple of mouthfuls. 'Wish there was more to offer.'

The woman eyed the bread distrustfully as though Sophia was somehow out to hoodwink her but hunger must have overridden fear for she took the bread, casting another baleful glance at Sophia. Her hand, black with bruises, shook when she crammed a chunk of the bread into her mouth, letting her few remaining teeth sink into it. Then just as suddenly as she'd started eating, she stopped. Pushing the bread away from her as though she might vomit, she let it fall from her hands onto her lap. It was like someone had sucked the life force from the woman.

'What is it?' Sophia asked.

'How can I eat when my own little girl is lost to me?' She gave the bread a look of disgust.

Sophia drew in closer. 'You have a child?'

'Yes, you Seafarers will never find her. She hid in a barrel, my clever girl. Can barely walk without me holding her hand but she thought of that. What will she do without her mama?' She leaned back against the wall, her head rocking with the motion of the truck.

'I'm not one of the Seafarers,' Sophia started to say but the woman wasn't listening. What did it matter anyway?

For the longest time Sophia imagined the girl hiding in a barrel. A frightened girl, whose name she didn't know. She picked up the bread and pushed it back into the woman's hand. 'Eat and stay strong,' she said.

Sweat and unwashed skin permeated Sophia's senses. Joel stretched his legs, his eyes half shut. She wanted to shake him, scream at him, how much further before she could get off this bloody truck. The woman shifted awkwardly in one position and then another in an effort to stay seated and Sophia passed a blanket to her. She wished Cassandra were here with her. An inward smile warmed her thoughts before tears choked the back of her throat. *Fancy missing that petty thief.*

Then, from nowhere, a longing to see Grayson swept through her, crippling in its intensity. Already it was difficult to recall his features. She searched for a memory to cut through this sense of amnesia, anything to bring his face back to mind but all she had was blank moments, like chasing vapour, and not a single recollection. Her head hummed with the effort when suddenly through the droning of the truck, she remembered the bees. A picture unfolded in her mind as though the moment was happening again. She had been so careful that day, all wrapped in her protective clothing, netting across her face, holding the smoker in front of a hive that Hannah had set up months before. Beside her Grayson dressed in similar gear, his belt tight around his waist, his shrill voice squealing with excitement. 'Let me, Sophia.' How thrilled he had been when she handed him the smoking can and showed him how to leak the burning wood chips to mesmerise the bees. New at the skill, they both received many stings that day but the sweetness of the honey made up for the swellings on their fingers and arms.

Like a floodgate opened, other memories dredged up from different times engulfed her. The barn at a silvered dusk with Grayson play-fighting with Aiden. Sticks, their weapons of choice, clashing ferociously as they playfully menaced each other. Aiden tripping, tearing his trousers at the knee and then laughingly pleading surrender. 'Stop. Stop,' when Grayson touched the stick to his throat. Then quickly recovering, Aiden turned the tables. 'Now you're the thief. I'll drag you to the gallows, worm!'

'Just try to catch me,' Grayson dropped his stick and ran towards the hedge, as Aiden picked it up and chased him. Memory followed memory as summer after summer, traces of her brothers' untroubled, boyish laughter tripped through her mind and it felt as though she had lost them both. At least the face of Grayson was clear again in her mind, his unruly hair falling in damp curls on his forehead, his dark eyes nothing like her grey ones. He was so opposite to her it was like they didn't belong to the same family and sometimes she thought the only thing they had in common was their allergy to bee stings.

A vicious tearing sound followed by a mechanical rat-a-tat-tat terminated Sophia's reminiscing. The truck stopped abruptly, throwing the woman from her seat.

'That bloody engine,' said Joel and hopped out the back.

A moment later, she heard an angry exchange coming from the front of the truck, accompanied by a number of kicks and iron bangs. Helping the woman back to her seat, Sophia decided to investigate and climbed out of the truck. She nearly bumped into Rudy coming round the back, his hands black with grease, spread out in front of him.

'Out of my way!' he grunted. He jumped into the back of the truck to rummage through a bag of tools he pulled from under the seat.

Callum stood half way between the front and the back of the truck like he was uncertain who to help. Joel had the bonnet up, examining the engine. Clouds of black smoke billowed into the air.

'What's the matter?' she asked.

'The truck's broken down.'

'I *know* that. I'm not a complete fool. Can you fix it?'

'I might manage something.'

The truck had ceased on the brow of a hill, probably too much strain for the old vehicle, Sophia thought, as she wandered away from the stench of smoke pouring from it. Now what? Where did she go from here? The call of gulls squabbling overhead rent the air. *Seabirds*. Maybe the sea was nearer than she thought.

Callum followed her, most likely making sure she

didn't run but Sophia felt there was a tension about him. *Bloody stop imagining stuff,* she scolded herself, and was about to make her way to the back of the truck, when he surreptitiously glanced around before beckoning her over to him. Uncertain of what he could possibly want she walked over cautiously.

'Yes?'

Close up, his face held lines that no young person should have. Small thin creases that ran along his top lip, and straggled up to the side of his nose, which could only be caused by his lips being excessively pinched together. Faint pleats drifted across his cheeks and deeper folds fanned out from the corner of his eyes, his skin like the land in a drought.

He spoke in a thick monotone and, worse yet, he whispered. Sophia could barely understand him. 'What?' He slyly pointed at where the two men worked on the truck's engine. 'Rudy?' Sophia asked. Nodding his assent, the boy continued to point, short jabbing movements that didn't want to call attention to themselves. 'And Joel?' He nodded more vigorously at Joel's name and Sophia felt a sinking inside her. 'What about Joel?'

Callum shook his head. 'He will sell you like the others.'

Sophia stole a glance at Joel. Did she believe that? Was he really capable of such betrayal? The man stared at the engine, although she had a faint misgiving he was really watching her, perhaps because of the limp way he held the spanner that intimated his attention wasn't devoted to whatever was wrong with the truck.

'Why are you telling me this?'

'The Seafarers didn't send us after you. Selling you is just greed. And...' He took her hand. 'I like you.'

Sophia snatched her hand back. There was a danger of being seen. She could take no risks.

'Thank you,' she whispered and turned from the boy and headed to the front of the truck, believing her best way to play the role of the unsuspecting victim was to stay close to the wolf.

'Any luck?' A strange desire to grab the spanner and smack Joel in the face with it seized her. Her voice trembled. Joel glanced up at her and she cleared her throat, hoping her nerves hadn't given her away. She returned his glance with one of her own, the trusting look of a young girl grateful for all his help. Was he fooled, she wondered.

Kasimir

No one has ever offered my mother so much with so little to gain. She looks at her reflection and wonders what he sees. The face is common place enough. The mouth a little wide with ready smiles and quick retorts, hardly the fundamentals to inspire such devotion. And now there is something else. She can no longer deny the connection between herself, and this boy.

His core of steel holds a tender heart and she cannot miss the burning glances he tries to hide beneath his courteous manner. They scorch through her, making her feel she is the only woman for him. Despite the pain that will follow, there is something here that makes her pulse beat a little faster than ever before. Who would not be swayed by such a love as this? The less he asks from her the more she wants to give.

Aiden

The boat out at sea captured Aiden's attention and for a few moments he failed to notice the small quay cut u-shaped into the harbour walls, where a number of boats were anchored. When he finally did realise, instead of feeling better, he became aware of what a mammoth task it would be to find his parents.

'Slow up, Aiden. You can't just charge into town,' said Cassandra.

He wished he was brave enough to do just that. Charge into the Seafarer's port and blow every bastard to smithereens.

'The Seafarers live near the quay, well, mostly,' said Cassandra. 'We'll have to be careful everywhere but the quay holds the most danger.' She hobbled slowly behind him as they passed dwellings nestled into the landscape, small decrepit houses set staggered down the slope of the hill. The trees shook in the wind, echoes of the sea in their whispering. Their leaves scattered down the hillside, russets and golds that captured the sunlight and created resplendent splashes of colour. Hues so bright like they were on fire.

'And the houses further away from the quay?' he asked.

'They belong to regular city folk.'

'Why don't the Seafarers send *them* overseas?'

'They depend upon the city folk for food, clothing, and suchlike. Some build boats down on the quay. But mostly they keep to themselves.'

Aiden had the impression Cassandra didn't think

too highly of city folk. 'Where do you reckon Sophia is?'

'She might be near the quay. There's a garage over that way where the Seafarers park their vehicles. It's a good place to start.'

Aiden wondered where he would go if he were Sophia. 'Is there a good hiding place near the trucks?' he asked.

'There are the warehouses. Some are never used. There's a back way. I'll show you tonight.'

'And there are Seafarers there, too?'

'Right.'

'Then it's too much of a risk for you to come.'

'You need me to show the way. You won't get in on your own, Aiden.'

Aiden felt the strong urge to punch a wall. He did not want to find his parents only to lose Cassandra. 'We'll see.'

At Cassandra's suggestion they turned off from the main road down an untrodden pathway where there was less risk of meeting anyone. She tugged a large shawl from her bag and covered her head, looping a length of it across her face so only her eyes showed. Wide and troubled they stared at Aiden and he found himself putting his arm around her shoulders and pulling her close to him.

'Would many people know you?'

She shook her head. 'Not city folk. They'd neither know nor care about a pregnant nobody. But people down on the quay will know me. The father of my baby lived there.'

Aiden felt his breath hitch. Until that moment he had never really considered the father. If he thought of him at all it was only as aggressor, someone to abhor. But Cassandra had said *father* and *baby* so lovingly.

'*Used* to live?' He latched onto her words, unsure if he had misheard her. 'Where is he now?'

Cassandra's head tilted away from him. 'He died.'

Her voice repeated unbroken in his head. A heavy breath filled his chest. He would have preferred a rival he could fight rather than a dead man's ghost trailing memories across the living and becoming more than he ever was in life. Cassandra shook off his hands and pushed past him. Sighing, Aiden followed her, keeping silent when all the while he wondered if she loved this man as much as her actions said she did and somewhere inside him he prayed she did not.

She led him through the narrow alleyways where the cries of the gulls echoed hauntingly along the cobblestone streets. Their plaintive sounds reverberating around the tall buildings where they perched on broken gutters, before rising and hovering on the air currents. He had never seen so many tower blocks before but like every other man-made structure they were in a perpetual state of disrepair. The sight of scaling paint, shades of ash and oily grime was not unfamiliar to him.

Cassandra watched him, her eyes crinkled in a smile.

'Are you laughing at me?' he asked.

'Mind you don't crick your neck, country boy,' she said. He heard laughter in her voice. He would act the fool ten times over to hear that sound but already it had died away, as a woman wearing a headscarf trundled a wheelbarrow over the cobblestones. A tin bucket carelessly placed inside it sloshed its contents wastefully over the sides. Circles of sweat under the woman's armpits stained her already soiled shirt. A loud crack splintered the air and the wheel broke from its shaft, overturning the wheelbarrow. The bucket rolled onto the road and grey sludgy water spilled everywhere. Water that Aiden wouldn't have washed his feet with, much less drunk. The woman cursed and kicked the wheelbarrow but made no effort to right it.

Aiden came to her and picked up the bucket. 'Can I help?'

She pointed a crooked finger at him. 'Sweet boy.' Then she grabbed the bucket from him and said, 'You want to rob me!' Her voice rose to a wail.

'No granny, we want nothing.' Cassandra pushed Aiden aside. 'Shall we help you home?'

'I can't go home now,' the woman said, her legs wobbling. 'I needed the water for cooking. My children are hungry.'

'Show us where the water is,' said Cassandra. 'We'll fill your bucket for you.'

'I don't know you brats,' said the woman. 'For all I know you want to steal my bucket.'

'We don't care for your bucket,' said Cassandra. 'At least let us help you fix your wheel.'

'Go away,' the woman said. 'I don't need any help.' She got on her knees and tried to force the wheel back into place, but Aiden could see the peg was broken and the woman's efforts were futile.

'Let's go,' said Cassandra, frowning. 'I forgot how distrustful people here can be.'

They skirted round one of the blocks of flats. Aiden tried a door and it pushed open without resistance. Part of him wanted to climb the tall construction just to see the view.

'What do you think? Can we go inside?' he asked Cassandra, willing to be guided by her.

'Yeah, why not.'

Together they climbed the stairs. Saffron coloured dirt caked the torn wallpaper and every corner reeked of urine. Aiden climbed the second and third set of stairs, up, up, up to the top floor. Cassandra panted behind him, doggedly following. This floor was also deserted. They walked through double doors, over what must have once been tiled flooring but was now only a combination of chalky, chipped ceramic. He kicked the loose pieces, which broke further as he trampled on them one after another. The walls creaked, as if the wood, stone and ironwork holding everything together were constantly buckling.

He pushed the nearest door but it held fast, and he tried the next, giving it a rough shove and the catch made a dissatisfied creak before opening. The inside had been ransacked. The disorder of a past life spewed onto the floor, things nobody cared enough to pilfer after rummaging through. Books and magazines with torn, loose pages distorted by previous spillages, an iron table, a rusty radiator, squashed beer cans, a wig, paper bags, and a long faded picture, its glass rim smashed, from which a man and a woman peered out at him, holding hands, their heads touching. They exuded such happiness. Then he found a diary. Aiden flicked to the last page.

"Power kept coming and going yesterday – dead

today. Eight days since Mama left. Papa's not waking up."

He let go of it, not interested in the rest of the contents, and went to the large window that opened onto a balcony. They stepped outside and before them lay the city, an assortment of buildings in various disrepair, a higgledy-piggledy, mish-mash of stone and brick, all the way to the quay. Sea and sky mingled, a grey swirl of cloud and surf, so he was unsure where one ended and the other began. The foamy waves rolled along the shoreline and the boats in the harbour bobbed like playthings with every surge.

Cassandra pointed to a fenced building to the right of the quay. 'The warehouses where your parents might still be,' she said. He thought he made out a machine gun mounted on the roof of one but wasn't sure.

'And you see that house just outside it. That was Edward's place.'

'Edward?'

Cassandra breathed a sigh, thrumming her fingers on the balcony railing. They stole his attention. He watched them, waiting for her to speak, although he knew what she would say. She stopped as suddenly as she started, gripping the balustrade tightly.

'The father of my baby. For a while he was the man in charge of the place. He liked to be in the thick of things.'

The house absorbed Aiden's total concentration. From the distance he could see it was in good repair, no shelled walls, and all the windows intact. His imagination took a leap, and his mind's eye showed a Cassandra of the past, strolling along the path to the front door, freely gaining access to inside the place, greeting her lover, undressing for him...

'Hey, come back. The place was never that interesting.' Cassandra nudged him, dragging him back to the present. Blinded by sudden jealousy, he didn't want to hear about a rival, especially a dead one.

She wandered back into the room, her fingers trailing over things, merely touching them, and an intense desire to *touch her* ratchetted up in him. Her hand caught the strap of her bag and knocked it over. An object fell and chinked on the floor. Light glanced off the small metal case. She picked it up quickly and stuffed it back into her bag.

'What's that?' he asked.

'Nothing.'

'What is it?' He was curious, more by her actions than the object. 'Show me.'

She felt in the pocket of her jacket and retrieved the metal case, which didn't quite close for one of the pins was loose. Reluctantly she opened it further and inside was a lock of light brown hair.

'Edward gave it to me the night before he was killed, like he knew this was his last chance to leave me something of his... well other than the baby, of course.'

Aiden's jaw clenched, his cheeks hardening to granite. How he would have loved to have burned that lock of hair, to watch it smoulder and frizz to nothing.

'Hey, Aiden.' Once more Cassandra pulled him from his thoughts and he looked into her face. She lightly stroked his. 'Hey, I keep it for my baby. That's all. It will be good for him to have something from his father, a sort of link. No?'

He couldn't argue with that. She was so damned earnest. 'Sure,' he said.

She put the case with the lock of hair carefully back into her bag and placed it on the table, then she rested against the sofa, its cushions gone, with her legs dangling off the edge. 'You hungry?' she said. *Hungry for you*, he thought. 'What's that look for?' she asked, and he wondered if desire was scrawled on his face and she had just read it. A flush of shame stretched over him. She had been through so much already. The room closed in on him and he would have turned away except that she called him. 'Hey, come here.' He walked to the sofa as though she was pulling him with invisible ties, a sullen walk that expected only rejection. 'Hey, look at me,' and then he realised she was laughing.

He leaned in over her. It hadn't been his intention to kiss her, not now, at this moment, but her upturned face became irresistible to him. Tentatively, he gave her lips a fleeting touch with his own, then again, all the while waiting for her to push him away and tell him to stop. He held back, struggling not to succumb to the sweet release of crushing her mouth with his, determined this, and all that followed would be of her choosing. Time hung suspended as he waited, his breath mingling with hers, like they were sharing the same portion of air. Then she offered her mouth to him, all softness and open, and it felt like a yielding, something beyond what he had ever known.

Her body possessed a cocktail of odours from the last few days, smells of the mountains, brackish swamp water, even the staleness of the room soaked through her hair, and yet he couldn't help but bury his face in it. 'You fill my head,' he murmured. The curl of his lips melded to wherever he pressed them and he wanted to press them everywhere. 'You're all I see.'

Their kisses deepened and he drew her up to him. Half standing, he pulled down her pants and she kicked them away from her ankles while finding his belt and tugging at the buckle. They shrugged out of their clothes with a kind of desperation, an urgency to feel skin on skin overtook him. Carefully skimming his hands over the domed mound of her stomach, he marvelled at its round perfection, so beautifully part of her, and yet so separate. Absorbed by the awareness of heartbeats, he heard his own, beating fast, intermingled with hers, and the other he could only imagine, the faintest drumming from the darkness of a womb. He almost faltered then, so overcome, but Cassandra placed her hands over his. 'We won't break,' she said, and that nearly broke him.

He followed with his lips the line that stretched along her stomach, neat as a seam and darkened to black due to pregnancy. Small butterfly pecks from her naval, down, down, down, to the tangled triangle of hair, so wiry and womanly. He ran his hands through, parting it, his fingers reaching into her until she clutched his shoulder for support, her legs nearly giving way.

'No, Aiden, not like this.'

He pulled her back onto the sofa, cradling her, kissing tiny nibbles of spine, tasting the salty sourness of her skin. His belly melded across her buttocks, her warmth seeping into him. His hands formed the perfect cup to hold her full breasts. They spilled into his palms, her hardening nipples mirroring his own response. The soft curve of her inner thighs spread for him, invitingly. He pushed them further apart and probed her wetness and then pressed into her, pushing inside, perhaps too roughly, for she dug her head into the dingy fabric of the sofa. He eased back. ‘Sorry,’ he murmured. She lifted her head from the couch, her hair plastered to her forehead and in damp, thick waves along her back. He grabbed a handful and moved it aside to nuzzle into her neck and whisper words of endearment.

Cassandra moaned. Her breath quickened and then paused, only releasing in a sob dragged from her depth. His name.

And then he, too, was lost.

Kasimir

The boy is open in his wanting. He takes my mother like she is a drug for all ills. Maybe she is... for they both feel healed. They are cleansed and regenerated, as though the dust suffused sky holds no contamination.

My mother is the drug that pours into his veins, sweet like fireweed honey, sour like cranberry sauce. The golden elixir swells the river of his soul. A smile slowly dawns.

Sophia

Joel threw down the spanner. 'Fucking damn it,' he shouted at the engine, kicking the front grille until the metal warped and buckled. 'Callum,' he called. 'Get the things together. We'll have to walk.'

For someone hard of hearing, Callum took instructions pretty sharpish and Sophia guessed he must be on a constant lookout for being summoned. 'How far away are we?' she asked him, making sure he could read her lips.

The boy shrugged and cast a glance at Joel, who replied, 'We'll be there by nightfall. Rudy, get the goods.'

Rudy dragged the woman from the truck, scuffing her shins on the metal step as she tripped. He jerked her upright. 'Don't look so dejected,' he said with a malicious smile spreading over his face. 'When I scoop your daughter from the bottom of the barrel, I'll make it my business to deliver her to the Seafarers, too, so *the little thing* won't miss her mama so much.'

How did Rudy know about the daughter? He must have listened through the window of the truck. Such conscientiousness to gain the upper hand smacked of madness to Sophia. The woman's face sagged like wax held close to a flame and Rudy appeared to take a perverse pleasure in twisting her arm. She stumbled weakly against him, as if her legs were made of wood.

The pace was slow. Too leisurely for Joel, who kept chivvying Rudy to hurry up and stop the dawdling. Rudy appeared happy to oblige, seeing an opportunity to goad the woman even more. Cowardly pig, Sophia thought when she noticed Rudy left the captive man alone. The giant of a fellow towered over everyone except Joel. His lumbering walk either speeded up or slackened so as to always keep in step with Sophia and he talked non-stop, taking no notice of any but her. His name was Jim and he lived alone since his mother's death. The area was as familiar to him as his hand and he cursed his misfortune for getting caught. 'A moment's lapse...' He raised his tied hands, 'and I get trapped.' He shook his head as though he still couldn't believe his own stupidity but didn't dwell long on his shortcomings before rambling on, more interested in Sophia. 'Long time since I've seen a woman fresh as you,' he leered. Dammit, he loved to talk. Sophia came to the conclusion he was more gas than substance, and wondered if he were free would he stay to help, or run.

A stream, running alongside them, had broken its bank and tumbled over the pathway, churning it to mud. It seeped through Sophia's boots where they were giving way. Uncomfortable though it was, Sophia was glad to keep moving. All the time they walked meant she was one step nearer to the city where she hoped to find Aiden and her parents.

For a time, Callum walked beside her and offered his own unique conversational skills, communicating with facial expressions. A frown for *not here* when she fiddled with her belt adjusting her knife, an almost imperceptible nod for *hold back* when her voice rose above a whisper, a roll of the eye at Rudy for a warning.

A hint of salty spray crisped the air and nearing the sea brought Sophia a mix of emotions. Relief at reaching her journey's end and the chance of reuniting with Aiden warred with frustration at not solving her imminent problem of escape. They crossed the stream where it was narrow and shallow. First Joel, then the woman, who fell on her knees in the water. She clumsily cupped a palmful, only to have it trickle through her fingers, leaving her licking the drips. Behind her Rudy's boots splashed through the water as he ran forward and clouted her on the head with the butt of his pistol, his actions so quick Sophia had no time to shout a warning. The violent act made her queasy as the woman let out a cry of pain. Blood spilled into her eyes, then dripped, discolouring the water.

'Get a move on, you filthy hag.'

'A hag?' The woman half turned her head to look up at him with the face of a ghoul dredged from a nightmare. 'Well, like a true hag I curse you... with this breath and with my dying one. May you boil in the seething blood of all your victims.'

For a moment Rudy was like a boy chided by his mother for misbehaving, his eyes widening, showing a circle of white around his pale irises. His mouth worked in a wordless cry, spittle gathering in its corners and his breath caught, causing his skin to flush with the suppression of anger. Sophia glanced at Callum who frowned back at her and she realised this rage was not unusual.

Before Rudy struck the woman once more, Joel barrelled into him, knocking him over and landing him in the water with a loud smack. 'Cool off, we need her alive. And woman, I suggest you hold your tongue or I will cut it out and feed it to the birds.'

'She just wanted a drink of water. What the hell's wrong with you?' Sophia hauled the woman upright, repulsed by how light she felt, no more than a sack of feathers.

The woman used her sleeve to dab the blood away. 'Thank you. But I'm as good as dead.'

You're not, Sophia wanted to scream at her. *You must live for your girl. She needs you.* She gave the woman's arm a gentle squeeze, hoping to convey a sense of unity and instil a bit of her own strength and was rewarded with the kindest look the woman had given so far.

'We're wasting time,' said Joel and they resumed walking.

Soon the sea came into view. Wind-swept rockweed strewed the coral sand and had Sophia's heart leaping at the sight, however she wouldn't make her escape here, she'd wait until they reached the city. A drizzly rain began, blurring the horizon and casting a grey wash over land, sea and sky. Sophia looked up eager to see a chink in the cloud but the rain only turned heavier and continuous. She would have pulled her jacket off and offered it to the woman but its pockets housed her gun and knife and she didn't want to call attention to them, convinced that Joel had no inkling of them. She must wait her moment. Already she knew she wouldn't leave the woman and if she freed her she would also cut Jim loose. Each of them would have to take their own chances then. Problem was she was fast running out of opportunities to make an escape.

The woman's curses must have caused a wariness in Rudy for he switched his attention to Sophia and charted her every move as though she was in league with the woman. 'Fucking bitches,' he muttered, casting sideways glances that would have soured milk.

Callum stayed close and so did Jim. Sophia began

to feel hemmed in by them, even the weather, with rain darkening the sky well before dusk, was transpiring against her. These were bad signs, a caution that her intention to escape was common knowledge. Only Joel seemed unperturbed, striding ahead, as if nothing would stop him from completing his task. Definitely not one scrawny girl. Sophia hung onto that to convince herself there was still hope.

At last a diversion presented itself. Joel called Rudy over to him. 'There'll be plenty to do when we get to the port and I want to be home by tomorrow. We'll go straight to the warehouses and dump them off.' He jerked his head towards his captives then proceeded to give a list of instructions. No longer watched by Rudy, Sophia hung back, leaving Callum slightly in front of her, busy watching Joel for any orders that might be barked his way. She pulled out her knife, got behind Jim and sawed through his ropes, throwing a silent thank you to Aiden for keeping it sharpened. Jim held the rope taut and then twisted his hands breaking the last strands. Once free he stood dazed, as though unable to believe his good fortune.

'Don't run,' Sophia hissed. 'Wait your chance.'

Drawing her pistol she pointed it at Callum. 'Untie her,' she said indicating towards the woman. Sophia sent him a quick pleading glance, hoping he'd realise this way he would not be held accountable for her actions. He fumbled with the ropes and Sophia felt sweat drench her as she waited. 'Come on, come on,' she muttered, watching Joel and Rudy.

Glancing back, Joel glowered at Callum. 'What you doing?'

Callum tilted his head at Sophia, and Joel saw the gun. He cursed loudly. 'Forgot you were a fiery one. Just go. No one will chase you. You have my word.'

But Rudy wasn't listening to Joel and moved towards her. Sophia shot at his feet, willing to blast every toe from his foot, then waved the gun between the two men. 'Stay back, I'll aim higher next shot.' Jim lumbered forward with a roar and elbowed Rudy in the throat. He crashed to the ground issuing a rasping noise as his lungs clutched for air. Jim grabbed the woman and they ran. Joel chased after them but Sophia didn't have any expectations he'd catch them. Jim wouldn't allow it to happen twice and Sophia felt a sweeping satisfaction.

'Go,' Callum said in his flat, one-tonal voice. 'Just go.'

Sophia gave a brief nod. 'Thanks,' she said, and ran.

Kasimir

The boy's love is wolfish. The more he tastes her, the more he covets, and the more insatiable his passion. My mother touches her fingers to his neck, his skin is caked with sweat and dirt, and in his grey eyes he waves the white flag of surrender. The colour permeates her mind and she yields herself, sending a shock down to her womb. The boy pronounces his love with solemnity and the ghost of my father awakens in her. He jostles through the doors of my mother's memories, room after room brims with misty darkness. He's restless, but his heart is good. Then suddenly my father is gone and only the boy remains. Only him.

Aiden

Cassandra turned towards him, her face flushed with lovemaking. Slumped beside her, Aiden thought he would never tire of looking at her. If only it could always be this way. The harsh reality closed in on him. He shut his eyes to suppress the feelings surging to the surface.

'What's wrong? Open your eyes.'

He wouldn't. She cupped his face and kissed him, the gentle moistness of her lips was there on his own, the dampness of her breath, warm against his mouth. But only fear coursed through his body. The shaking and creaking of the walls disturbed him, a feeling of hopelessness overpowered him and he sobbed quietly, folding into the crook of her neck. All he wanted was to be far away with her. Somewhere they could grow food where the ground didn't smoke diseased fumes, and fish in rivers that ran clear. Clumsily he wiped his face, but the tears kept flowing. 'I'm sorry,' he murmured, not knowing what else to say. Everything felt too big to be put into words.

'Hey,' she nudged him with her shoulder. 'Hey, look at me.' He did. She gazed at him with a tenderness that had his heart stopping. 'I love you.'

He wanted to tell her not to say that, for somehow it made his apprehension all the more solid and terrifying. 'I love you, too,' he said, and took her into his arms. They made love again, without fuss, not frantically, not greedily grasping one another, but as though they had known each other forever.

Through the window the sky turned into a palate of pinks with the sun setting over the sea. Sweat pooled under his arms and he longed to be clean. If only he could run down to the sea, bathe, and chase the waves. Walk on crumbs of seashell, have them pinch his feet and cram between his toes. Briefly he wondered where the woman with the wheelbarrow had got her water from and thought even that mucky mess would be welcome. Cassandra raised herself to kiss him. She wrinkled her nose and playfully told him he smelt and tasted foul. He longed to set aside his fears and grab her, tickle her, until she begged for mercy but the moment vanished as reality crashed in on them both. Cassandra's smile faltered and they silently stood and dressed.

The day dipped to a twilight, dark enough to wander down to the Seafarer's carpark. Aiden wanted to search the place. He would certainly find the truck. It was etched into his memory, a rusty heap, mud-splattered paintwork and a dirty flap lifting, while his sister disappeared into it. A number plate from a long gone age was still screwed above the bumper. Q174 ABD.

Cassandra wrapped the shawl around her face and cast a glance around the room before squaring her shoulders. 'Ready,' she said.

He longed to tell her they would have other times, good times, but something held him back. He would never tell her anything that wasn't the complete truth. Honesty was the one thing he could give her. And his love, of course.

Outside a lone seagull circled overhead, shrieking to an empty sky. Cassandra grabbed his sleeve and edged in near to him. He loved that she hung on to parts of his clothing rather than held his hand, somehow it was more intimate.

Two people in the distance shuffled towards them, their tattered overcoats hanging loose like rags on a scarecrow. They stood out against the deserted street.

'Just keep going,' whispered Cassandra.

It was only as they neared that Aiden could see the couple were a man and woman, and the woman was clearly struggling. The bag she held bumped heavily against her legs. She shifted it from arm to arm before passing it to the man.

'Don't stare,' Cassandra cautioned but a whimper from the bag had Aiden stopping.

'No more,' came a small voice. The man and the woman looked at each other and then at the bag, as if surprised by the possibility anyone could be inside.

'Please, Papa. There's something sharp in here and I need to pee.'

The man carefully placed the bag on the ground. Two hands surfaced from inside and stretched it open. A small girl appeared through the opening, wearing nothing but a soiled pillowcase with holes cut in for her head and limbs. Her left arm streamed with blood and she waved it at her father as she clambered from the bag. Giving an impatient stamp of her foot, she grumbled. 'There's a nail inside, Papa. Didn't you see it? You said it was safe.'

The man peered into the bag and drew out the sharp metal tack. He flung it into the road in an angry gesture.

The woman showed no interest. 'I'm tired,' she said, as though the mere act of speaking drained her of life.

'You should wrap something around that cut,' Cassandra said. She searched in her bag and found a scarf.

'Here poppet, I don't have any water but I could bind that for you.'

The girl backed away from Cassandra and leaned into her father, like a child well cautioned not to trust strangers. He pushed back her ragged mass of hair and stroked the girl's cheeks before giving her a little nudge towards Cassandra with an encouraging nod.

'What were you doing in that bag anyway?' Cassandra asked as she began wiping the blood from the girl's hand.

'The air is polluted. It makes me sick. It made my brother sick, too. Didn't it made Archie sick, Mama?'

The woman nodded. 'That's right,' she said wearily. 'Made him awfully sick.'

'You can't keep her in a bag.' Cassandra wrapped the wound.

'Thank you,' the girl said. 'But you're wrong. I don't want what happened to Archie to happen to me.'

'I guess I've been wrong before,' Cassandra said with a wry smile. 'But I've never been told so sweetly.'

Down at the carpark, Aiden wandered among cars and trucks. There was no sign of the number Q174 ABD, although a couple of trucks were identical to the one Sophia had got into. Surely the truck would have returned by now, unless it had come and gone again. It would be just their luck to have missed her while waiting for dusk. What a waste of time. He glanced over at Cassandra lurking in the shadow of a black sedan, her shawl pulled over her face, and then couldn't regret the wait after all.

A man strode along the path that led to the quay, heading their way. A dog on a leash walked by his side, occasionally pulling away to sniff the side of the road. Even at a distance Aiden recognised him. 'It's that bastard, Ray, from the swamp. Keep back.' They pulled into the darkest corner and crouched below the level of the cars and watched. Ray opened the door of the largest truck, climbed in and started the engine. He looked like a man with a purpose.

'Evil fucking bastard,' Aiden whispered.

Cassandra whispered back. 'He's my baby's uncle.'

Aiden looked at her. He felt winded, like Cassandra had punched his guts when he had been expecting an embrace. 'He's the uncle? Why didn't you tell me this before?' Aiden didn't like the accusation in his voice but the idea of kinship between Cassandra and that man filled his mind like noxious cloud.

Cassandra spoke low. 'I wanted to. But I felt ashamed and I was right, wasn't I? I've disgusted you.'

Did she? He watched the truck chuck a blast of black from the exhaust before roaring away like it had a prior meeting, a known destination, and Aiden pitied the wretched creature Ray was hunting. Then he looked at Cassandra again. She was about to cry and appeared small, folded in on herself. 'Don't look that,' he said. *She was wrong. It made no difference to him.* Her lips squeezed together, holding back her tears and he gathered her to him. 'It doesn't matter,' he said.

She looked up at him. 'It sort of does, 'cause what the fuck do I say to my child, Aiden, tell me that.'

He pulled her closer and hugged her. 'You tell him he is everything to you, like you are to me.'

It started to rain. Aiden sighed. 'Come on, Sophia's

not here. Point me in the direction of those warehouses, where they keep my parents, and then you go, hide out, back at the...'

He got no further. Cassandra shook her head. 'I'm staying with you,' she said flatly, in a voice that suggested it was not open to discussion.

Aiden still argued. 'But they know you.'

A shot fired that had them both halting.

'It's come from the direction of the warehouses,' Cassandra said. Together they hurried towards the sound cautiously keeping to the shadows, the rain working in their favour for once. A patter of feet on the wet pavement had Aiden dragging Cassandra tight against him as he shrank back into an overgrown shrub hiding from whoever was running towards them. Their combined breath sounded loud to him. The runner was a girl. She hesitated at a junction, her head switching back and forth, as she looked left to right.

'Bloody hell.' Cassandra stood upright, and waved her arms above her head. 'It's Soph.'

Kasimir

So tender he treats us, this unusual man. My mother no longer thinks of him as boyish. The trembling hands placed on my mother's stomach convey his sense of wonder and we are lost in the moment where love encircles all.

He tells her of the rocking horse. All the toys that were his and then his brother's are now untouched but would be good for the baby. Plastic warrior figurines, wooden blocks, spinning tops.

Something interrupts his thoughts. He puckers his brows together. The horse has a broken rocker, he says, but he'll fix it. He'll get to it as soon as they're home.

Sophia

The path led Sophia to the top of the cliffs where she viewed the city below. The quay to her left was stacked with cargo, slowly being unloaded into warehouses by a group of men.

She scanned for somewhere to shelter and hastily descended steps cut into the cliff wall, cursing the uneven slabs for their steepness when they threatened to slow her down. The tide's incessant roar throbbed in her ears and the surge rolled up shells from the seabed. Shades of twilight melted in the swell with the tumble of spume frolicking to the seashore, every wave darker than the one before.

A row of terraced cottages peeked through a dense undergrowth of leaves and vicious twigs that knotted back on themselves in a sempiternal pattern. Sophia slowed, doubling over to catch her breath, her lungs strained for air through her dry throat. A man's face peered out from one of the windows, an old face, wrinkles deepened by irritability as he waved to shoo her away as he would a mangy cat. Worrying he would come out and chase her, Sophia hurried on, constantly checking behind her. The pathway, shiny with rain, forked in three directions. One way was as good as the other, she decided. So many struggles when all she really wanted was peace. A life with her parents and her brothers and later, perhaps, a life with Tucker. Simple things, more precious now they were unlikely to be fulfilled. A loss felt keenly as the rush of adrenaline left her, replaced with a crushing tiredness that had her buckling. To bolster her flagging strength and spirit she reminded herself she was finally in the same city as her parents and, hopefully, Aiden. She was positive he was still alive. Their minds had a special link. Surely there would be some kind of sign if he had died, some breach in her psyche.

Sophia took the nearest fork in the road, attracted by the scattering of houses whose front doors hung open. Maybe she could get a few hours' rest. She pushed her way in, but the door stuck half way and she had to wriggle through the opening. Inside the walls were blighted with mould that flowered like yellowing wallpaper and in the dingy light she saw the dust lifting, disturbed as she walked. The air so powdery every breath clogged her lungs. She wiped her mouth, to rid it of the mucky taste.

A cabinet rested against the longest wall. The doors left open after having been ransacked, one broken at the hinge hung at a jaunty angle. Nothing there to salvage. Sophia tried the kitchen door but the door was jammed shut. She sank to the floor and for a moment was about to give in and sleep where she'd landed, when she saw a bag under the cabinet. Crawling over, Sophia hauled it to her. A memory unravelled, showing scraps of an image. Aiden holding a leather satchel, much like this one, so big in his small hands. He opened it and out fell two dark, paltry pieces of fruit that rolled across the floor. They went after them like cats chasing mice. Aiden, first as usual, picked up the fruits to examine them. 'These are plums,' their father said. 'One for you, Aiden, the other you give to Sophia.' Aiden must have done as he was asked for once, for she remembered the taste. Her mouth moved as her memory conjured up the flavour. If only this one held such treasures. She opened the satchel. No fruit in it, no food, only a photograph. She knew of photographs. Her mother kept one of her grandmother, a willowy woman with a stiff, unsmiling face.

This photograph was of a girl puckering her brows into a frown as she held up her hands in protest, fending off some unseen photographer, although with her sandals held loosely in one hand, fingers casually looped through the back strap, even her protests had a carefree ambience. Sophia wondered at the person on the other side of the camera. Somehow the flirty manner of the girl's stance made Sophia think it was a man. Was he laughing? Begging the girl to look up and smile? Was he a friend? A lover? To have nothing more to worry about than have a picture taken. Sophia couldn't imagine such a life.

The girl, out of this time, exuded wholesomeness, with her face tanned and cheeks plump. Her pleated skirt was off-kilter, stained with grass, her unshod feet wet. A flash of envy stabbed through Sophia and she peered under her own shirt to see her ribs. She had lost so much weight. If a photograph of her was placed alongside that of the girl, her body would shout hunger, whereas this stranger might well have dropped from the moon she was so different. Sophia felt ugly. Hot tears burned behind her eyes. That could have been her in a different time. Life was so unfair. The thought seared as hot as her tears. Reluctant to let go of the photograph, she crushed her hand around it and placed it in her pocket.

A pain came from her abdomen, her bladder was bursting. She stumbled towards the door but then changed her mind, the man might be outside, lurking. She went through to the bathroom, where she could see the basin, toilet, and bath had once matched and been pastel blue. To think such things held enough importance that matching colours were even considered. Now the hand basin had been ripped from the wall and smashed to a pile of chippings. The toilet bowl tilted over on its side, its lid gaping like a smile, and the bath so stained with others' waste the original colour was barely evident. Struggling with her belt, she pulled down her trousers and peed. Her urine, brown and sickly in smell, was one additional bloody thing to worry about. Wearily she stumbled through to another room and found a mattress stacked against the wall. She pulled it free so it thumped onto the floor and then she lay down on it, tucking her hand under her cheek to mask the stench of animal excrement wafting through the spongy surface. She was jolted from her sleep as though prodded with a stick, her gunshot wound radiating flashes of heat and the pain exploded into her consciousness. Groaning, Sophia steeled herself to look at her arm. The wound had swollen through neglect. Frustration at her carelessness threatened to overwhelm her. Dry-eyed and feverish, Sophia was too dehydrated for tears to fall. She shambled from the room and left the house through the backdoor to search for water.

Her mind was tired of being on high alert so when she heard laughter it sounded incongruous after all the tension. Who would be so carefree? She couldn't remember the feeling. With a certain amount of caution she peered around the corner of the street and saw two young boys by a tap set in the middle of a fountain. They each held a bucket. One was filling his while the other slopped water at the first. The boy closest to the tap then placed his finger over the jet causing the pressure to spurt, drenching them both. Their shrieks were loud and uninhibited.

Feeling thirstier now there was a promise of satisfaction, Sophia wished they'd move on. It was only when they were thoroughly soaked did they refill their buckets. It started to rain and she lifted her hot face upwards to try and catch some drops and waited until the place was clear. Then she hurried over to the fountain and drank greedily, spilling the water through her fingers and splashing her face in the unaccustomed luxury of having more than enough. She didn't know where the water was sourced but it tasted fresh. Making use of the opportunity, she took off her boots and held her black feet under the water, rubbing until they were white.

A man with a stubbly chin walked with an easy stride towards her, swinging a bottle. Quickly she pulled her boots on.

'Hey,' the man called, his voice husky. 'Where are you from?'

'I live here,' she said.

'Not seen you before.'

'I never usually leave home.' It took a great deal of effort to stop herself from hurrying as she walked away and only when she rounded the corner did she start to run. Breathless she paused at a junction in the road. A shot rebounded through the air and Sophia skidded off in a different direction nearly screaming when a figure rose from a sidewalk bush close to her. In a flurry of panic she pulled out her gun ready to shoot but then tears sprang into her eyes at the unexpectedness of seeing Cassandra. Then Aiden. He beckoned her over to him. For the first time in hours she had somewhere to go.

Kasimir

My mother dreams. A secret door in the dark opens and she is back through time, to isolated moors from childhood. In the purple-tipped grasses she sits, throws the stone and sees the raven go after it and bring it back. With one wing cut off, he follows her everywhere, or she carries him when he's tired.

Oblivious to all but her bird she raises her hand to throw the stone again, when she is yanked from the grasses and turned around.

'What have you there?' the boy demands.

'Nothing,' she says, staring at his boots and coat.

'Never met anyone with a raven for a friend.' He eyes the bird. 'Has it got a name?'

'No.'

'Well, it should, I reckon. I'm Edward, by the way. Can I ask yours?'

She looks fully into his face for the first time. 'Cassandra.'

'And what are you doing in the middle of nowhere, Cassandra?'

'Nothing.'

'I bet you're hungry. We have food in our camp. Care to join us?'

She hesitates but is too hungry to refuse. She nods and the boy smiles and takes her by the hand.

Grayson

On the morning of the hanging Grayson loitered in the kitchen watching William ready himself for the event. He was scrubbed clean of any painted daubs, dressed in freshly laundered socks, a clean shirt that bagged over his trousers and a flat brimmed hat perched on his spiky hair. He swallowed hard, his pronounced Adam's apple protruding through his skinny beard.

'I'm going to represent you, Grayson. It's not the place for you.' He gripped Grayson's shoulder in a sturdy hold and Grayson took it as a gesture of support. Then William was gone. His gangly gait almost dancing through the door, no longer as ridiculous to Grayson as it had once been. He liked William now and appreciated the effort he was making on his behalf but also knew he would have to go and see the hanging for himself. It would take place behind the old barn that held the meagre crop from last summer and Grayson was determined to be there.

Jake. The name burned in his mind like a fiery brand. Jake had changed him. Grayson had become like the white candles Sophia used to immerse in oils, and on retrieving them, were the colour of olives. That's how he was now. The same, but different somehow. Jake had done that to him by showing another, bigger, more terrifying world, unlike the one he knew. And Jake's kind had hold of Grayson's parents and for that Grayson would watch him die, even if he vomited every day for the rest of his life.

Helen sat on the bottom step of the stairs. 'I've never seen a man hanged before.'

'And you're not going to now.'

'Really? And who'll stop me? You?'

For all her feyness there was a core of steel through Helen, and Grayson didn't have the strength to argue with her. 'You promise to do as I say?'

'Okay.' She spat in her palm and the action made him smile. Had he really taught her that? He felt that boy no longer existed.

Outside a gale was rolling in from the countryside. The grasses ruffled, undulating like waves. Helen stared at the racing dark clouds as though rapt in meditation. The wind bit into Grayson's cheeks and tore at his clothes. 'You cold?'

'No. You?'

'A bit.'

She looked at him as if ready to share a secret but all she said was, 'Let's go,' which he could hardly hear above the swirling wind.

The autumn coloured vines crept along the windy knolls, their leaves, the red of spilt blood, trickled down the valley all the way to where the brook ran into a rushing stream. Racing together, they ran alongside the churning water, the sound drowning the stamp of their feet. Veering away from the stream, they crossed the barren field where clumps of earth bowled over themselves with the force of the storm. With the wind behind him urging him forward, Grayson wished he could run forever and was almost surprised when the old barn came into sight.

The hanging tree was a sturdy horse chestnut that looked almost magical with its leaves a spillage of golds on the ground and woody fingers of root stretching from the earth. The prickly cases that had fallen lay split open, revealing a shiny brown conker within. Normally Grayson would gather them and thread string through a hole punched in the centre to use in conker fights with Aiden. Or store them in a jar until they had shrivelled and lost their sheen. Today he barely noticed them.

Thrown over one of the higher boughs the rope hung. It looked like a set up for a game, except for the noose, waiting for Jake's neck to fill it. Could something so simple really end his life this morning?

Climbing up the hillside, Grayson and Helen stayed close to the surrounding line of trees. He shivered but the movement was lost in the increasing gale-force winds that rippled through his clothing. Helen's hand crept into his own, offering comfort. They crouched by the roadside not to be seen when they noted a few townspeople walking over, William among them, looking uncomfortable but nudging his way to the front. This was not going to be a huge public display and Grayson was glad they were not that kind of people.

Miranda and Oliver led Jake to the chestnut tree, holding his tied arms as he climbed onto the stool. Josiah stepped forward and spoke but Grayson didn't hear anything, only saw Jake shaking his head and then spitting at the priest. The sight of Miranda looping the noose around Jake's neck and tightening the rope mesmerised Grayson. Only the soft sigh from Helen made him look away. He thought her face a reflection of his own, her eyes huge as an owl's in her thin face. Both their hands were clammy and he didn't know who was giving comfort to whom anymore.

Oliver pulled away the stool.

Kicking in the air and at the tree bark, Jake brought his hands to the noose, straining at the rope, securing no relief. The bough shook with the struggle and the cold, heaving wind. At the end Jake didn't kick anymore and only the fierce wind jolted his body.

Nausea rolled through Grayson. The townspeople quietly bowed their heads. Nobody looked like they had wanted this. Then they slowly dispersed but Grayson and Helen remained where they were. They watched Oliver cut Jake down and load him onto a handcart. There was no leaving him for the birds to pick clean. He had paid the price with his life and that was enough for the townsfolk. Grayson wondered if it was enough for him. He made no attempt to follow the cart, feeling relieved he didn't know where the dead man would be buried.

Scrambling down the slope of the bank he went over to the noose. He reached out to touch the rope but changed his mind, curiosity and revulsion warring within him, and he put his hand in his pocket, trapping his fingers in the material to prevent them escaping.

The ground was soft underfoot and he placed his feet in the imprint made by the dead man's weight. Jake had stood here, alive and then dead, yet the indentation only looked like crushed earth now that the cart had gone over it. It had no story to tell.

A few conkers lay beside the dip. A couple were real beauties and Grayson picked them up. Maybe he could teach Helen the conker game, she might like that. He knew he would.

Tears started. He brushed them aside. It didn't feel right to shed them. He was not a little boy anymore.

'Come. Let's go home,' Helen said. *Home*. The word tore at his heart. Then, as though reading his mind, she said, 'They'll be back soon, Grayson. Your family. Not much longer to wait. Come, now. You'll catch a cold.

Kasimir

The fast beat of my heart strums along the cord that ties me to my mother, and fuses with her pulse. She nourishes me in many ways but floods me with her love.

Glimpses of future journeys, real or imagined, stream before me. Moonlight, hoar-white, along the land. Powdery frost of midnight clings to my mother's clothes and hair.

'I'm cold,' says a voice I recognise as my own.

Struggling to survive, still she listens. 'Almost there,' she whispers.

She keels over and lays panting. All I see is the gloomy sky. Then her eyes. 'Let's sleep, little one,' she says, 'just for a while.'

Aiden

Cassandra whistled shrilly and waved both arms in the air. Sophia stopped abruptly and looked like she might take flight in a different direction but then she let out a cry of recognition and clattered over the wet pavement towards them. She ran awkwardly, clasping her arm, but before Aiden could ask if she was injured, she was on him, her drenched body crashed into his embrace, saturating the front of his shirt through his open jacket. 'There's a man coming after me,' she gabbled.

Aiden pulled her into the bushes with him and Cassandra, and they all ducked down and waited. 'I can't see anyone,' he said, scouring the wild growth for any traces of movement. 'Come on, let's go somewhere safe.'

'Somewhere safe?' Sophia echoed the words as if she'd misheard. 'Is there such a place?'

Cassandra tugged Aiden's sleeve. 'Let's go back to where we stayed,' she suggested. 'We can take stock and decide what to do.'

He nodded and felt his face flush at his sister being privy to their intimacy but she must have been poorly for she didn't react. All the while they walked she kept reaching out to touch him, as though to reassure herself he was really there. 'Can't believe I've found you,' she said.

Cassandra gave a low cough. 'Well, to be perfectly accurate, Soph, we found you.'

Sophia smiled at her. 'So glad you did.'

The block of flats were still deserted and they let themselves back to the room they had stayed in. Strange, it had a feel of coming home to Aiden, as though the walls held memories of their previous occupancy.

Sophia visibly relaxed. She sat down on the sofa, leaned her head back and closed her eyes.

Cassandra unwrapped the remains of the goose from her backpack and plumped it onto Sophia's lap. 'You must be starving, Soph.'

Sophia opened her eyes and groaned. The smell of meat, strong in the room, must have hit her starving senses for she reeled back before tearing off a lump and stuffing it into her mouth. 'Thanks,' she mumbled.

Long moments passed with only the sound of Sophia chewing. Her face still remained pinched and gaunt, though some colour returned to her cheeks but not enough for Aiden to stop worrying. He paced the room while she ate, not wanting to question her before she had finished her meal but casting pointed glances at her hand, which curled limply across her lap. She had barely pushed the remnants of her meal aside and swallowed her last mouthful before he asked, 'You hurt?'

'A bit.'

It was such a barefaced lie, Aiden puffed out an exasperated breath and his fringe rippled in the breeze of it. 'Best show me.'

Sophia nodded, slowly easing out of her jacket. The covering over her hand had a yellowish stain where the wound had oozed onto it. She lifted the edge and Aiden could see the livid red leaching across her hand. 'Damn. How did you get that?' He sounded annoyed, even to his own ears.

'A bullet. Don't think it hit the bone but it's infected.'

Cassandra grimaced and opened her mouth to speak. Aiden saw Sophia give her an imperceptible headshake and whatever Cassandra was about to say remained unspoken. What was it with these girls and their coded communications? Did they think he was blind? 'At least wrap it in something cleaner,' he said.

Cassandra sat herself on the sofa next to Sophia. 'We need to discuss how to get to your mum and dad. It's tricky but can be done.'

Sophia's eyes lit up. 'Journey's end?'

Aiden watched the two girls he loved most in the world calmly discussing the perilous mission as though it was just some every day task without any serious consequences, and he knew he wanted them nowhere near the danger. 'Maybe you should stay here,' he said to Sophia. His attempt was half-hearted for he already knew the answer.

'No. I'm coming with you.' Her teeth chattered and she pulled her jacket back on.

'Your wound is infected,' he said bluntly.

'You're not going without me,' she answered, equally blunt.

There was no point in arguing with her. He wondered if Cassandra would be more biddable than his sister. Unlikely. 'We'll need you to give us directions,' he said to Cassandra.

'Don't be daft, directions won't do, you'd get lost. You need me to show you the way.'

'I can't allow that.'

'*Can't allow*?' Cassandra tilted her head and sent him an amused, enquiring glance.

'It's too dangerous.' Why couldn't she see that? Frustration swelled inside him.

'More dangerous than being chased by dogs and armed men, you mean?'

'Well, no... or maybe *yes*... more dangerous than that. There's a fence. If we're caught, we're caught, there's no escape. Besides, you can't really *steal* inside, can you, with you being this pregnant?'

Sophia nodded. 'He's right. It'd be easier to find mum and dad with you, but it's too risky. We can't ask that.'

Cassandra patted Sophia's knee. 'But Soph, you're not asking. It's my choice. Look, the dock is a very big place, you'd only get lost if you go by yourselves. Make one wrong turn and that will be it.'

Aiden sighed wondering whether she was just being difficult. Oh, hell. Why was he surrounded by obstinate women? He pinched the bridge of his nose, same as his mum would do when remonstrating with his dad and knew she was about to lose an argument. She would also pour herself some gin, but unfortunately for him, Aiden didn't have any to hand. 'Would it really be too hard for us to find our way there?'

'*Yes.*'

'Care to explain?'

'First, you need to find the key to the building where they keep your parents, that is if they still keep all the keys in the same place. Then you need to find that building.'

'Sounds like a lot of running about,' Sophia said. 'She's right. We do need her.'

Aiden knew when he was beaten, there was no way around this.

They waited in the dying daylight, each wrapped in their own thoughts. Sophia fidgeted, moving back and forth from the door to the balcony, while Cassandra sat by Aiden's feet, leaning against his legs. He stroked her hair, loving the freedom she was his to touch.

Sophia gave him a quizzical look. 'You and Cass?'

Her question caused him a prickle of embarrassment. 'Yeah. Do you mind?'

Sophia smiled. 'Yeah.'

He grinned back at her, momentarily enjoying the brief interlude. It was soon over. The rain began to fall heavier and water dribbled through the cracks in the ceiling. Aiden stood and began to pace.

Cassandra groaned. 'Bloody hell, you two will have walked miles before we've even left the building.' She hauled herself back onto the sofa while Aiden pulled his gun from his jacket pocket, sat down at the table and methodically disassembled and reassembled his gun, inspecting the parts. Counting bullets, he checked them twice, recounting as though the figure could change at any given moment. Thirteen in his gun, and another full clip. 'How many bullets do you have left?' he asked Sophia.

'Eight in the gun. And that's about it.'

He wandered over to the balcony. Swathed in misty rain, a ship sailed into the harbour. The bobbing shaft of light loomed from the darkness and the bell's slow knelling reminded him of a funeral he had once attended. He looked to see if Sophia had heard, wondering what disasters she would read in the signs. The only good sign he could see was he had no stomach ache. No premonitions of imminent deaths? Perhaps they would get through this.

'Okay. Let's go.' He opened the door and together the three of them slowly descended the stairwell in the dark. Moonlight pricked through cracks and crevices, guiding their way.

Cassandra peered through the rain. 'Down there is where we want to go,' she said, pointing to a cluster of firelights. Aiden struggled to hear her, the wind snatching her words, and cupped his hand to his ear. She pushed in close to his face. 'We can't go this way. They'll see us coming and their machine guns will rake the ground before we're thirty feet from the fence. We'll go to a place they hardly ever guard.' Aiden nodded. 'We'll get through a hole under the fence. It's the way I used to sneak in and out of the compound.' She glanced at him and he felt in awe of her. The rain pelted them and the salty wind bit into their faces.

Obeying Cassandra's every instruction, he stopped when she told him, and moved at her nod. Right now he would have stood on his head if she asked. She slid down a muddy bank and disappeared. 'Careful,' she said. 'There's a ditch here.'

Down in the ditch he soon heard the sound of slamming waves and knew they were getting closer to the docks. The rain eased and the clouds shifted, revealing a sheen of moonlight rippling on the water he walked in. They clambered from the ditch. Prickly seaweed scattered the shore and before them a wooden fence ran from the docks to the city. High warehouses towered above them, looming over the fence like sentries, the roofs covered with earth and thatch.

'Ready?' said Cassandra.

'Okay.' Aiden's nerves tingled with suppressed

energy. When they reached the fence, Cassandra got on her knees and began to dig until a hole appeared. 'The good old way,' she said.

'Let me go first,' said Aiden but she didn't even look back to tell him no. He refrained from grabbing her by the shoulder and silently followed her lead. Wriggling through the gap, the gritty sand sprayed his face, sticking to the dampness on his skin. He cuffed his mouth with his hand and spat as more sand leaked through his lips into his mouth. Cassandra already standing, stooped to help him from the hole. The cool grasp of her hand surprised him with its strength as she pulled him free. He gave her palm a fleeting kiss, before helping Sophia.

They walked along a tangled, damp trail between two warehouses, stooping below the windows so they wouldn't be seen. Under a hole boarded up sloppily and laced through with barbed wire, he stopped as he heard a long drawn moan. Someone was pressed against the boards, straining to peer out. The gaunt, corpselike pallor of a ravaged face, sunk around a pair of protuberant eyes, made Aiden jump. Blinded, the woman's eyes were marble white. Cassandra tapped him. 'Okay?' He nodded a yes, while thinking how everything was far from okay.

They moved on, going the length of the wall. A low fire burned in an empty patch of soil, its flame eating through the pile of leaves that had collected in a hollow of mud. A couple of dogs slumbered beside it and a man poked the flames with a stick, humming to himself. Cassandra pointed at a stone building some distance behind the man. 'The keys are in there.' Aiden wondered how they would get inside as he watched the dogs move in their sleep, their legs kicking toward the fire.

Cassandra left the protection of the overhanging roof of the warehouse and they followed her, prowling across the courtyard and behind the building. Cassandra's speed showed a knowledge of the place, a sense of being there before. She approached one of the windows, hit the wooden frame with her hand and gave it a nudge but it didn't open.

'Let me try,' said Aiden. He pulled his knife from his belt and wriggled it between the wood and the frame, jiggling the blade and forcing it. The window opened with the sound of splintering wood. They waited a moment to make sure no one had been alerted by the noise.

'Help me inside,' said Cassandra.

Aiden squatted down and patted his thigh. 'Put your foot here.' She stepped up onto his leg and grasped hold of one of the shutters. 'Mind your belly,' he warned, as he pushed her bottom to raise her to the window. He heard a muffled laugh before she clambered inside and an inward smile warmed him. Sophia awkwardly followed, and finally he scrambled through.

Cassandra opened the door into a hallway. A lantern flickered on a bureau in the room across the corridor. Inside the room a man slept on a mattress, his pistol beside him. They tiptoed up the stairwell to the second floor, stopping before an iron door. 'The keys should be in here,' whispered Cassandra, as they entered the room.

Frigid sea air from some unattainable, distant shore gusted over them through an open window. 'Who's there?' came a man's voice from the dark corner. Without hesitating, Aiden dashed forward and headbutted his stomach. The man was knocked to the floor more by surprise than force, and the adrenalin shooting through Aiden had him up, pointing his gun almost before the man had hit the ground.

'Not a fucking word,' Aiden breathed heavily.

The man glanced at the girls, skimming disinterestedly over Sophia but Cassandra had him faltering in his reserve, recognition flared across his features.

Aiden caught the look. 'Give me something to tie him with,' he said. 'Might have something in my backpack. *Shit*... I left it where we came in, by the window.'

'On it,' said Cassandra.

'You're making a mistake,' the man said as soon as Cassandra had left the room. 'Trusting that Cassie cow. She'll double-cross you.'

'Don't listen to him,' said Sophia.

'Of course I'm not listening,' Aiden said, madder at her for suggesting such a thing. Did she really believe him so fickle? Besides, fate would really have jeered at him if the girl he loved so thoroughly had set up so intricate a betrayal.

'Dumb kids.' The man's spittle sprayed the air in heavy droplets. 'The only reason Cassie's here is to be rewarded. You, boy, will make a fine slave. And you, pretty thing,' he glanced at Sophia, licking his top lip. 'You'll make many a man happy.'

Aiden smacked him in the mouth with the butt of his gun.

Cassandra returned with his backpack. If she overheard the man, she gave no sign of it, just pulled out the rope and began tying his hands and legs.

'Been telling them about you,' he mumbled through his swelling lips.

'Really?' Cassandra said before she gagged him.

The large storage cupboard in the corner was so well oiled it didn't make a sound when they opened it. Inside was a small tin box with numbered keys. Riffling through, Cassandra fetched number 508 from the pile. She crossed her fingers. 'This was the number they always used before.' A tiny frown of uncertainty wrinkled her forehead.

Aiden took the key from her, then took the whole box and stuffed it in his backpack. 'Aw, fuck it. Let's not take any chances.'

They skulked stealthily downstairs bypassing the man who still slept, and through the open window. When they rounded the corner they followed Cassandra to three warehouses where someone with a surfeit of ostentatious blue paint had daubed each of the doors. How ironic that the colour used as a barrier to curtail others' liberty was the same colour as the sky and the sea, the very things symbolising freedom. The number 508 was written in a black scrawl across the top middle section of the door, as though someone had thought carefully where to place it. Aiden's hand shook as he turned the key scratchily in the lock but it was Sophia who pushed forward as soon as the door opened, as if she could no longer wait a moment more.

Kasimir

I sense a change. I dominate my mother's thoughts as we journey nearer to the birthing time. Do I live? Any movement I make brings relief momentarily, and she prods her dome of stomach whenever I sleep. Complications rise within her, a canker's growth gorging into her peace of mind. Would she cope? How to protect me? I know and trust she will. My mother is resourceful. She could bargain with the devil and win.

Sophia

The stench of humanity, sweet and cloying with undertones of futility and anguish, held Sophia in the doorway as a sense of foreboding assaulted her spirit. Shuffling forward, she moved further into the room, not stumbling due to the moonlight flickering sporadically through the window, revealing a place seething with people. If Death was looking for somewhere to stay this would be it. Bodies lined the walls, hunched or leaning against the brick panelling, some barely distinguishable as people, exhausted from their struggle to survive they were wasting to mere shadows.

Now as she hunted through the jaded faces, staring at each one before dismissing them, she wondered if she would even recognise her parents. These people were reduced to less than animals, shipments of goods. How did anyone retain their sense of self? Surely if her parents were here they would call to her, but only apathetic faces stared back at her.

Aiden pushed her further into the room, peering over her shoulder in an attempt to see things for himself and Cassandra closed the door quietly behind them. A tiny fanlight in the window was the only ventilation for the people crowding the room.

Sophia felt a limb underfoot. 'Mind, there's a child,' someone said, pushing her leg and nearly toppling her. *Shit.* Just when she thought she had seen everything now she was scared to move for fear of treading on a child.

'Mum? Dad?' Aiden called. His voice sounded husky, as though he was holding back tears and didn't sound confident of gaining an answer. This hellhole must be full of misplaced parents, probably half a dozen could answer to mum or dad.

Cassandra had the right idea. 'Seb? Amelia? You here?'

A small girl sitting on a woman's lap looked up at Sophia. The woman had her eyes shut and could have been dead she was so still, but the girl watched Sophia's every move, her eyes lit with an intelligence this forsaken place failed to tear from her. Wearing only a pair of soiled underpants, the girl's skin had a covering of grey, scaly dirt creating the illusion her emaciated body was fully clothed. Opposite her, lying in excrement, was a giant of a man with irons riveted to his legs. Sophia shuddered, fighting to curb the feelings of revulsion that threatened to empty her stomach, the stench so overpowering.

Whispers in the air grew louder and gained momentum, as more people realised something out of the ordinary was taking place. Much as she would have loved to have thrown back the doors and freed everyone, it was impossible. Surrounded by so many obstacles, the main task kept slipping from her and she had to remind herself it was her parents she was searching for. Sophia scanned the people near her, skimming over faces in an attempt to discover their whereabouts. Stopping beside a woman huddled on the floor, Sophia knelt by her side, lightly stroking her arm in an attempt to see her face hiding under the long, matted hair. 'Mum?' The woman only snarled, wordlessly, as a feral animal.

Sophia backed away and felt a gentle tugging at the edge of her jacket. The little girl had found Sophia through the scrum of people. 'Yes, sweetheart? You want something?'

'Who's your mummy?' the girl asked.

'Amelia,' said Sophia. 'You know her?' The girl nodded and took her hand, her fingers bony as a chicken carcass. A rush of expectation washed through Sophia and she looked round to call to Aiden. Were they really at the end of their journey? The girl moved to the other side of the room, pushing her way through the tangle of half-naked men and women that closed around them.

Tendrils of fire curled from the corner by the door. Aiden was attempting to light a torch. 'No,' Sophia called to him. Light would give them away to the guards outside. Determined to get to him she pushed back against the crowd. 'Aiden, no,' she called again.

'What's going on?' A murmur of voices rose. 'Who are you?' Snatches of conversation, confused questions and querulous demands burbled around her. A woman implored that they leave. 'The Seafarers will kill us all,' she wailed, and from the desperation in her voice Sophia saw no reason to doubt her.

A flame sparked and a dim sheen reddened the faces in the cramped space not half as big as the darkness had led Sophia to believe. Six children were crammed together on the iron bed clamped to the wall. Tallow-faced and shivering, they blended into one another like modelling clay, the youngest kissing the crook of her arm, cuddling an imaginary doll.

A man nudged Sophia's shoulder roughly. 'Who are you? What are you doing here?'

'I came for Amelia and Seb. My parents. Do you know them?'

'Sophia? Is that you?'

A woman she barely recognised came forward and a sob wrenched from Sophia's throat. 'Mum?' How disfigured she looked. Her face, riddled with welts, had wilted and sunk in on itself and her dark swollen lips were an obscene distortion of her once pretty mouth. The thick hair her mother took such a pride in was unkempt and showed a bald patch where it had been torn from the root.

Sophia put her arms around this strange yet familiar woman, rubbing her cheek against her roughened skin. She leaned into Sophia with scarcely enough strength to stand.

A sallow faced man in a tattered brown shirt emerged from the crowd, hitching up his trousers, and Sophia felt like someone had punched her in the stomach when she realised he was her father. An air of bewilderment clouded his expression as he searched over her face. 'My Sophia? Here?' he whispered. He lifted a hand and traced through the air in front of her, as if committing her face to memory. 'My Sophia,' he said again and embraced her fiercely. His bristled beard scratched her cheek and his touch made her sob. She mustered her will not to but failed. Her father tentatively kissed her forehead, dry pecks from grizzled lips, as he entreated her not to cry. But how could she not, he might as well have asked her to leap to the moon.

Her father put his hands on her shoulders. 'What are you doing here?'

'We've come to take you home, Dad.'

'Take us home?'

'Yes, Aiden and me, and a friend of ours.'

'Aiden's here?' her mother said. Sophia heard the need in her mother's voice and turned and glanced in her brother's direction. He stood tall, holding Cassandra's hand. Her mother passed through the crowd towards Aiden and almost fell upon him. She pushed the fringe of hair from his eyes and squeezed him. Even in here he was her favourite. No matter what the circumstances were, their mother would always love him the most. The cold, sobering realisation ran deeper than the frigid air, all the way to Sophia's heart. No doubt their mother saw in him a certain something that was lacking in Sophia. She wished she understood what it was. Moonlight fell around Aiden and their mother like a waterfall of light, as though even the heavens blessed them. 'Why would you come here?'

'To bring you home,' said Aiden.

'What were you thinking?'

'It's okay, Mum. We're here. We can go now.'

'Is Grayson safe?'

'Grayson's safe, Mum,' he said and then looked at Cassandra. 'You remember Cassandra, don't you? We wouldn't have made it here without her.'

Their mother pulled Cassandra into her embrace. 'Of course I remember. To think fate made you cross paths with my son.'

'Where's Annabelle and Emmet?' said Aiden.

'They... were killed... when the truck was ambushed.'

For no other reason than the mention of his name, Sophia thought of Emmet's shiny buttons and realised she had known he was dead from the moment Cassandra had first offered her one, back in the mountains, all those days ago. She pushed back the sadness that threatened to rise in her throat.

A man pushed forward. 'What about the rest of us? Are you just going to leave us here?'

'We have to be smart, Kyle,' Sophia's father said. 'There are many of us and we can't just stampede outside.'

'We're not staying behind.'

This wasn't how Sophia had envisioned the rescue. All the days she had been making her way here she had never considered the others. Just the three of them had barely slipped past the guards and the dogs, what chance would so many people have?

Cassandra came close to Sophia and whispered to her and her father. 'We can't sneak so many people past the dogs. It won't work.'

'Can't we go out four at a time?' her father said. Sophia felt so proud of him, even now he considered the others.

'Every time we go past the dogs we run the risk of making ourselves known, especially now it's stopped raining,' said Cassandra.

'We'll have to be very quiet when we go out and split into groups of fours, maybe fives. We'll go out a group at a time and every hundred feet or so, each group will stop and signal the one behind it to advance,' her father said. Kyle nodded then joined the crowd behind him and the people in the room began to organise themselves. Sophia peeked outside through the cracks in the walls to check they hadn't been discovered. No movement, only the reflection of firelight in the puddles.

'Everyone's ready.' Aiden tapped her on the back.

Every person in the room had split into clusters with most having one or two children. The man in irons held the chain to prevent the links chinking. Already he appeared a different person to the dispirited heap she had tried to avoid earlier and the tenacity of the human spirit filled her with hope. Maybe there were things the Seafarers couldn't vanquish.

'Make sure the children understand they must keep absolute silence,' said Kyle. How could they stop five-year-olds from crying? This could go disastrously wrong. Cassandra opened the door a crack and after a moment motioned Aiden to come to her and they stepped outside together, the others following. The mud squelched under Sophia's boots and the cold clung to her body. She saw the children treading as lightly as feathers for fear of waking the dogs, their breath puffing wisps of cloud. They crept closer toward the fire that had smouldered to embers. The guard rose and carefully poured a can of kerosene over the ashes, resurrecting an immense blaze. The fire hissed and spattered and lit the area.

When they were about to round the corner of a wooden house, Cassandra turned to the group behind, Kyle, a woman, and two children, and signalled them to keep low and take the turn ahead to the left. Sophia's father gently pulled her closer to him. The dogs whimpered in their sleep.

Two men appeared on the path coming from the sea, sinister outlines in long trench coats. Behind them, galloping waves broke on the shore, their spray glittering like specks of pewter. The taller man led the way, his profile showing a pointed goatee.

'Aw, shit. That's the man from the swamp, Ray,'

Sophia heard Aiden. 'Evil fucker.' She waved for the people behind to halt. At first, Kyle appeared puzzled by her intentions but then he observed the approaching men and grabbed the children and he and the woman dropped down and lay on the ground among the tangle weed, covering the children with their bodies.

The men in the trench coats strode straight to the fire, stretched out their hands to warm them and exchanged a few words with the other guard. Then the smallest of the three shouted. *Had he spotted anyone?* Then, in horror, she watched the man run toward Kyle and the children, pointing his shotgun to the shrubs. Towering over Kyle, he smacked him in the face with the butt of the gun. The children scrambled from under him, wailing, and the dogs sprang from their slumber and ran barking, toward the children, grabbing hold of them. They rattled them in their mouths and tossed them in the air like ragdolls. Aiden fired in the direction of the two men by the fire and they ducked. At the same time, the men and women outside the warehouse managed to overpower the guard assaulting Kyle, and fighting the dogs they quickly scared them away.

Sophia ran toward the children. Their trousers were ripped and their legs bled, but they were alive and managed to stand. 'We have to go,' she shouted.

The desperate men and women poured from the brick building, trampling over one another. Instead of small groups, they were now a loud, disorganised mess of people, swarming like incensed bees, and they ran after Sophia toward Aiden and Cassandra. From all around came the shouts of guards and barking dogs. Sophia ducked when she heard gunshots. She aimed her gun but didn't see who was shooting at her. People around her were hit and fell. Warm blood sprayed on her face, moistening her lips and the rusty, sickly smell made her gag. Dogs, frenzied by the commotion, snapped and bit whoever they fell upon. People cried out in pain and begged for mercy, which the guards were none too willing to grant. A man behind Sophia collapsed on her, crushing her beneath his weight. She crawled from underneath him and felt her wounded hand could hardly accommodate the pain pulsating all the way to her elbow. Disoriented, she searched for her parents in the crowd, but couldn't see them, the night sky so dark, with the exception of a distant arch of stars, a nacreous cascade spilling into a black pool.

Kasimir

The smell of the womb has gone. Fumes of kerosene fill my motherly chamber and seep into the amniotic fluid. The heavy tread of boots surround us and I curl up, making myself small. The umbilical cord loops around me and I reach out to hold it close. Even as the dark shadows pour into the womb, my mother's tenderness enfolds me. 'Don't be afraid, little one,' she whispers.

Aiden

In the wild scrimmage of people, Aiden grabbed Cassandra's hand and held it tightly. He had already lost sight of Sophia. He wasn't going to lose them both. Using a parked truck as cover he attempted to discover a way out from this hellhole. Shots rang around them, bullets ricocheted off the warehouses, followed by groans and cries from people hit. In his hurry to steer Cassandra to safety he stumbled, sending them both rolling in the sodden dirt.

'For fuck's sake,' he hissed at his own carelessness. He groped through the muck to find Cassandra but she was already on her feet, facing one of the Seafarers who had his gun pointed at her.

'Don't shoot,' she said and crouched beside Aiden, slipping a hand under his armpit. 'Get up,' she said, struggling to haul him to his feet.

'Step away from the gun,' the man said. Cassandra kicked it toward him. 'This is your doing, bitch. Ray should have smothered the life out of you when he had the chance.'

'Go get him. He'd want to see me,' Cassandra said.

Aiden felt his insides folding in on themselves. He had seen what Ray had done to Martha in the woods. The thought of such an evil, depraved man anywhere near Cassandra sickened him.

'Get in there.' The man shoved them inside a small storeroom and shut the door behind them.

'I'll get you out of this,' Cassandra said.

'How?' Aiden wondered what she was on about.

Cassandra grabbed his sleeve. 'Listen Aiden, Ray wants me. He's always wanted me...' she gave an embarrassed grimace, 'to love him...'

'Huh? What's that? Love him? The man kills for pleasure. You could never love him.'

'Listen to me. You're not listening. This is the only way out.'

She looked up at him, her face wretched. 'It's no good. You won't stop me. I'll make myself love him, what little I can, if anything at all. I'll learn to be sweet to him.'

'I don't believe that. You only came back here to help us. To help me,' he said softly. 'You came back for my sake.'

'Look, just go with me on this.'

'I can't.'

She turned away from him. The silent pause separated them like a chasm. How he longed for a safe crossing over it but the chances of that were receding with the inevitable route Cassandra was determined to take. 'It's the only way I know to free you all. Soph... your parents... Let me do it for them if not for you.'

Aiden groaned, gathered her to him and buried his face in her. 'Please, Cassandra, don't do this. I'm begging you...' How could she not see her love was stripping him of his manhood? Somehow he knew this girl would be his undoing.

Kasimir

Desire and passion war with common sense. My mother is both the adult and the child. She berates herself for the wanting but cannot turn her face from his. How will it end she asks herself repeatedly. Badly. But not for *me,* her child. On that she is determined.

Sophia

The shooting stopped and in the quiet the only sound was the rush of the waves with its infinite variation. The Seafarers moved among the living, a discreet, deadly force, sifting the wounded and providing their own particular form of retribution. They scooped up a girl huddled behind the body of a dead woman and threw her against a stack of kindling that dispersed in a clatter. She shrieked and then stayed motionless, sprawled on the soot-black mud. Someone roughly grabbed Sophia and pulled her to her feet and she braced herself for the end, only to discover her rescuer was her father. She stood wobbling and her mother moved alongside her to steady her. All the fight had left them and any aspirations for a success deserted her when she saw their crushed faces.

One of the Seafarers came up to them. He carried a torch and sweated profusely with the heat it threw onto his cheeks. Cocking his gun, he snapped Sophia's away, picked it up and tucked it into his belt. She made no attempt to stop him as he jabbed the muzzle into her chest. 'In there,' he said and pointed to the warehouse behind her. 'Get in there.'

Amid rough-hewn timbers, racks of pelts and sable tipped furs, sat Cassandra and Aiden, their backs against the wall. Aiden, hardly recognisable with dirt on his skin and his hair plastered to his face, wet with perspiration. The man stood at the doorway for a moment, glancing at Cassandra, hard-eyed, before leaving, shutting the door behind him and turning the key. The cabin smelled powerfully of naphthalene and tar, markedly intensified with the door closed.

Her mother crumpled and held her arms out to Aiden. His face mirrored the same relief and Sophia thought whatever happened next at least they were together.

They sat there for a while, until the door was thrown open. In the doorway stood the man with the goatee. He carried himself differently to the others and Sophia recognised him as the man Aiden had called Ray. With him was a heavily built man with a meaty neck and a solid stance. Both held guns and had their attention solely on Cassandra.

'Wait outside,' Ray said, and his companion stepped backward and left, closing the door behind him. Ray tapped his gun against his leg. 'When they told me you were here, I couldn't believe it.' Cassandra stared at him but said nothing. 'You know, I have every right to hang you.' His voice dropped to a whisper. 'But I'd much rather nail you up a nice little coffin and bury you alive in the dirt.' He demonstrated with his hands the small dimensions of the coffin he had in mind. 'I'll sit and listen to your screams.'

Cassandra lifted her chin up a notch. 'Threatening to murder the girl who carries your late brother's baby? You can't mean it, Ray.' She stood up. Aiden stood too but she pushed him away and faced Ray. 'Only blood matters. Isn't that what your brother said? He'd kill and die for you, because you are blood.' She stepped closer to Ray, pushed his gun aside, took hold of his free hand, and placed it on her stomach. 'I carry your bloodline in my belly, Ray.' She pressed her own hand over his. 'Feel him. He calls out to you. Sings for you, begs for your protection. Kill me and you spill your brother's blood.'

For a moment Ray was quiet, then he pulled her close against him. 'You came to hurt my trade. No one steals from me, girl, don't you know that?' He brushed the back of his hand along her cheek, then let it fall to her breast where it lingered.

Sophia thought she saw a softening in Ray as he gazed at Cassandra, though his hungry expression was that of a red kite.

'Hear me out, Ray. I would have died if it weren't for them.' She indicated to Aiden by her side and Sophia sitting with her parents. 'You have to let them go.'

Ray stepped closer to Sophia. 'These are the people you came here with?'

'Yes.'

'Why would I let this girl go? I'd much rather strangle her with my bare hands for costing me heads.'

'They saved me from a flogging, Ray. Helped me escape from a town in the mountains. That's when I realised I was foolish to leave and decided to come home. I missed you, Ray. Didn't think I would, but I can't be without you. You make me feel safe.'

As much as Sophia hated the idea of Cassandra giving herself to this man, she couldn't help but believe they might yet escape with their lives. The untruths slipped from Cassandra's tongue with conviction and Sophia had to hand it to her, she didn't falter and was a compassionate liar, her lips telling the tale her listener wanted to hear.

Ray's eyes narrowed as though he was judging the authenticity of what she was saying before nodding for her to continue. 'As a thanks for saving my life, I promised to help them free their parents. It meant hurting your trade, but I had to do this, Ray, before I could be yours again. It was only fair.'

'And what of him?' Ray jerked his head at Aiden, who stood beside her. 'Is there anything between you?'

'Of course not. He's a boy. He means nothing to me. There's no reason for you to be jealous, Ray, he just wanted freedom for his parents. It is a small price for you to pay, no?'

Ray pulled her to him with an air of possession, casually waved the hand holding the gun in the air and said to no one in particular, but Sophia took it to mean them all, 'Leave. Go.' They were free. Then he pressed Cassandra hard against him, taking no more notice of them as if they were flies, with only eyes for her. 'Oh, Cassie, Cassie, Cassie, I was afraid you'd lose the baby. You dumb girl. What mother risks her own child like that?'

'I've been so stupid, I know that now. Please forgive me.'

'Now that you're back there'll be no more running away again. You'll give birth to a baby boy, and then you'll make children with me. We'll be family.'

'Perfect, Ray. That's all I want.'

Sophia was aware of a minute movement from her brother at the same time Cassandra was saying *perfect,* and freedom just a breath space away, when Ray raised his arm and fired. Cassandra gave a small, surprised yelp, and for a moment Sophia thought he had fired at the ceiling as everyone stayed as before. But then slowly, so slowly, Aiden tumbled in on himself, like a tower demolished, a perfect neat hole through his temple.

A scream stuck in Sophia's throat. Some instinct propelled her towards Aiden. He looked so lonely there on the floor. His eyes, wide open, stared at her accusingly and she wanted to beg him to forgive her for not seeing this coming, for not protecting him. Her parents knelt beside him and her mother tucked an arm under his head and pulled him to her, rocking back and forth.

'You're free to go,' said Ray.

Free to go? Ray's voice came from a fog. His words made no sense, just a jumble of sounds, only her mother's keening resonated with her. Gently her father looped his arms over her mother's shoulder, raising her up, allowing Sophia time with her twin. She kissed Aiden's lips, skimming her fingers across his forehead and cheekbone, and then closed his eyelids, so he looked no different than if he were sleeping. The tip of a green rock peeked from his pocket and she reached for it and held it, hot tears coursing down her cheeks as she thought of what Lila's gift had meant for him. Then she replaced it back in his pocket. Much as she wanted to hold onto it, Lila had given it *to him* as keepsake, and Aiden hated when Sophia took his stuff without permission.

'I said, go.' Ray interrupted her and Cassandra made eyes at her to move and for the first time Sophia realised the high price the girl was paying for their liberty.

Kasimir

My mother is lost to me. Her pain overrides everything. She is in torment but there is no sign, no flicker to show her loved one lies dead by her feet. Her grief cuts our time short. It stifles the life force that feeds me. But already my mother is determined that although my uncle rules the hour, he shall not own the day. I am caught in a riptide of pulsating torrents, compressing and stretching and twisting. Fluids slip over me, a tidal wave of strength. My mother's body no longer provides a safe haven. She screams as each contraction propels me forward along a designated path from which neither of us can escape. It is time to lose the restraints of my mother's womb, her loving sanctuary.

My uncle dangles me like a landed fish and I feel a stinging blow as he slaps me. I scream at the shock and take my first gasp of a different life.

Sophia

They carried Aiden's body to a place just outside the fence and dug in the cold grey light, spadesful of peat-scented earth, until her father put his hand on Sophia's shoulder and said, 'That will do.' Then they lowered his body into the ground.

Sophia looked at the sky not wanting to see her brother laying in the gloom of a grave, but then torn, she feasted her eyes on him knowing this would be the last time she could gaze at him. She wished she had a photograph like the one of the girl in her pocket. But what would it show? His dead face? And would some girl in the future find it and think he slept? All she had now were memories. Sharp and bright but how long would they remain that way? When would their crispness blur? Desperately she sifted through her thoughts and snatches of his facial expressions ran like a story. His smile, his scowl, the pensive stare he wore when he didn't know he was watched.

She remembered a time they went into the hills and cooled their feet in a sun dappled river. The riverbed, pebbled and rust-coloured, was strewn with prickly weeds. Still they found a spot where they could sink their toes into sand. They climbed to the precipice where they caught their breath. Aiden paused to wait for her to catch up and never missed an opportunity to tease and banter for she wasn't as fast as he. Up on the peak, the distant glens appeared like creases in the land. Shaded and unapproachable. They called to Aiden's spirit of adventure and he spoke of how they would journey together to explore them and promised they would always be there for one another and she thought *always* meant many years to come.

No one wanted to throw the first scoop of soil to cover his face. Her father visibly steadied himself to perform this last duty but it was her mother who threw herself into the open grave. She clutched at Aiden as if by doing so he would awake. They didn't stop her and let her sit there and weep, as seawater seeped inside the grave and mingled with her tears.

Later they climbed from the sea front through trails of mist, burning in the morning sun. Leaving Aiden behind on foreign soil wrenched at her innards as though a clenched fist ripped them from her body. Two seagulls fought midair, their long swoops and rises so graceful they could have been dancing. They drew her gaze upward. One day she would wander the desolate mountains her brother had spoken of. Up where the sun's golden hues tinted the clouds Aiden might still be alive. On those heights that had gripped his imagination she might see through his eyes and then, perhaps, meet him again.

www.jclinden.com

Printed in Poland
by Amazon Fulfillment
Poland Sp. z o.o., Wrocław